INCREDIBLY ALICE

BOOKS BY PHYLLIS REYNOLDS NAYLOR

Shiloh Books
Shiloh
Shiloh Season
Saving Shiloh

The Alice Books
Starting with Alice
Alice in Blunderland
Lovingly Alice
The Agony of Alice
Alice in Rapture, Sort Of
Reluctantly Alice
All But Alice
Alice in April
Alice In-Between
Alice the Brave
Alice in Lace
Outrageously Alice
Achingly Alice
Alice on the Outside
The Grooming of Alice
Alice Alone
Simply Alice
Patiently Alice
Including Alice
Alice on Her Way
Alice in the Know
Dangerously Alice
Almost Alice
Intensely Alice
Alice in Charge
Incredibly Alice
Alice on Board

Alice Collections
I Like Him, He Likes Her
It's Not Like I Planned It
    This Way
Please Don't Be True

The Bernie Magruder Books
Bernie Magruder and the Case
    of the Big Stink
Bernie Magruder and the
    Disappearing Bodies
Bernie Magruder and the
    Haunted Hotel
Bernie Magruder and the
    Drive-thru Funeral Parlor
Bernie Magruder and the Bus
    Station Blowup
Bernie Magruder and the
    Pirate's Treasure
Bernie Magruder and the
    Parachute Peril
Bernie Magruder and the Bats
    in the Belfry

The Cat Pack Books
The Grand Escape
The Healing of Texas Jake
Carlotta's Kittens
Polo's Mother

The York Trilogy
Shadows on the Wall
Faces in the Water
Footprints at the Window

The Witch Books
Witch's Sister
Witch Water
The Witch Herself
The Witch's Eye
Witch Weed
The Witch Returns

Picture Books

King of the Playground
The Boy with the Helium Head
*Old Sadie and the Christmas
    Bear*
Keeping a Christmas Secret
Ducks Disappearing
I Can't Take You Anywhere
Sweet Strawberries
Please DO Feed the Bears

Books for Young Readers

Josie's Troubles
How Lazy Can You Get?
All Because I'm Older
Maudie in the Middle
*One of the Third-Grade
    Thonkers*
Roxie and the Hooligans

Books for Middle Readers

Walking Through the Dark
How I Came to Be a Writer
Eddie, Incorporated
The Solomon System
The Keeper
Beetles, Lightly Toasted
The Fear Place
Being Danny's Dog
Danny's Desert Rats
Walker's Crossing

Books for Older Readers

A String of Chances
Night Cry
The Dark of the Tunnel
The Year of the Gopher
Send No Blessings
Ice
Sang Spell
Jade Green
Blizzard's Wake
Cricket Man

INCREDIBLY
ALICE·

PHYLLIS REYNOLDS NAYLOR

Atheneum Books for Young Readers
New York • London • Toronto • Sydney • New Delhi

With special thanks to the Minneapolis Naylors
for their help throughout this book

ATHENEUM BOOKS FOR YOUNG READERS
An imprint of Simon & Schuster Children's Publishing Division
1230 Avenue of the Americas, New York, New York 10020
This book is a work of fiction. Any references to historical events, real people, or real locales are used
fictitiously. Other names, characters, places, and incidents are products of the author's imagination,
and any resemblance to actual events or locales or persons, living or dead, is entirely coincidental.
Copyright © 2011 by Phyllis Reynolds Naylor
All rights reserved, including the right of reproduction in whole or in part in any form.
ATHENEUM BOOKS FOR YOUNG READERS is a registered trademark of Simon & Schuster, Inc.
For information about special discounts for bulk purchases, please contact Simon & Schuster
Special Sales at 1-866-506-1949 or business@simonandschuster.com.
The Simon & Schuster Speakers Bureau can bring authors to your live event.
For more information or to book an event, contact the Simon & Schuster Speakers Bureau
at 1-866-248-3049 or visit our website at www.simonspeakers.com.
Also available in an Atheneum Books for Young Readers hardcover edition
Book design by Jessica Handelman
The text for this book is set in Berkeley Oldstyle Book.
Manufactured in the United States of America
First Atheneum Books for Young Readers paperback edition May 2012
2 4 6 8 10 9 7 5 3 1
The Library of Congress has cataloged the hardcover edition as follows:
Naylor, Phyllis Reynolds.
Incredibly Alice / Phyllis Reynolds Naylor. — 1st ed.
p. cm. — (Alice)
Summary: Maryland teenager Alice McKinley spends her last semester of high school performing in
the school play, working on the student paper, worrying about being away from her boyfriend,
who will be studying in Spain, and anticipating her future in college.
ISBN 978-1-4169-7553-3 (hc)
[1. High schools—Fiction. 2. Schools—Fiction. 3. Theater—Fiction. 4. Dating (Social customs)—
Fiction. 5. Family life—Maryland—Fiction. 6. Maryland—Fiction.] I. Title.
PZ7.N24Io 2011
[Fic]—dc22
2010036982
ISBN 978-1-4169-7556-4 (pbk)
ISBN 978-1-4424-6248-9 (eBook)

To Hannah, Becca, and Melissa,

who love the Alice books

Contents

1
PLANS

If I could characterize my last semester of high school, I think I'd say it was full of "might have known," "should have thought," and "wouldn't have guessed in a million years." Surprises, that was it, and decisions like you wouldn't believe.

When I woke on New Year's Day, I thought it must be ten in the morning, it was so light out. But when I got up, it was only five after six. A fresh blanket of snow had fallen after the ice storm of the evening before, and everything looked untouched, untested. Like it was up to me what to make of it.

I used the bathroom and jumped back into bed, pulled the comforter up under my chin, glad there was nowhere I had to go, no special ritual connected to this particular holiday. And though I don't much believe in New Year's resolutions because

I so seldom keep them, I wondered if there was anything I really wanted to do before I graduated. Come June, I didn't want to look back and wonder why I'd missed the chance for something big.

Yeah, right. As though I weren't overscheduled enough as it was. But I went through the exercise anyway. Sports? I'd never been especially good at them, so I didn't crave to be on the girls' soccer team or anything. Student government? I'd served on Student Jury last semester, and that was all the student government I needed. Journalism? I was already features editor of *The Edge*. I had no regrets.

I opened my eyes again and stared at the light reflected on the ceiling. Maybe I was comparing myself with my friends and what they had done—Gwen on Student Council, Pamela an understudy in *Guys and Dolls* last year, Liz in a folk dance group. I suddenly realized I had never really competed for anything. *Anything*. I didn't try out for girls' track team—I did my solitary running a few mornings a week before school. Stage crew? You didn't have to try out to be on the props committee. Student Jury? I was appointed. Features editor? I'd started out as a lowly roving reporter, no experience necessary, and worked my way up.

It's weird when you discover a new fact about yourself. Like a birthmark you never knew you had on the back of your thigh. Was it unnatural somehow not to be competitive? My grades were reasonably good, but I was only competing with what I'd done before. Was I *afraid* to compete, or was I just genuinely not interested?

Who knows? I concluded finally. It was too late in the year for any kind of team I could think of, and I wasn't going to join something just to be joining. I decided to hunker down under the covers and wait for the impulse to pass, and after a while it did.

Sitting in the hallway outside the cafeteria on Monday, our legs sprawled out in front of us, lunches on our laps, Gwen said, "I've got an idea for this summer."

I lowered the sandwich I was eating and stared at her—at the short brown fingers with magenta polish that were confidently peeling an orange without her even looking. Here was someone ready to sail through the next few months of assignments without a care in the world, already planning her summer.

"You're going to intern for a brilliant scientist in Switzerland?" Pamela guessed.

"Nope. This time it's something fun," said Gwen. "I'm going to apply for a job as a waitress/housekeeper on a new cruise line, the Chesapeake. Why don't we all do it?"

Now she really had our attention.

Liz had the look of a puppy who thinks someone just said the word *walk*. Her head jerked up, blue-violet eyes fixed on Gwen. "We can sign up just for the summer? We could still make the first day of college?"

"Depends on the college, I guess, but I've got the dates already. I think they rely on college help, because the summer cruises end in mid-August and the fall cruises begin with a new crew."

"Where does it go?" I asked.

"Mostly the Bay. A sister ship will be ready in a few months, but for now, this is the maiden voyage of the Chesapeake *Seascape*. A hundred and forty passengers."

I tried to jump forward to summer. Patrick's folks had moved to Wisconsin, so there wouldn't be any house here in Silver Spring for him to come back to. If he was there, and I was here, and there were 750 miles in between . . . Why *not* work on a cruise ship?

"Sounds *great!*" I said. "Providing it doesn't interfere with the prom."

"It doesn't. Training starts the day after graduation," Gwen told us. "I tried to get Yolanda to come too, but she doesn't want to leave her boyfriend. They're going at it hot and heavy."

"You make it sound like a wrestling match," said Liz.

"You might call it that," said Gwen. "Anyway, we could have a blast, just the four of us."

Pamela was leaning forward, elbows resting on her thighs— *shapely* thighs, I might add, because everything about Pamela is shapely. "Will there be guys?"

"Of *course* there will be guys," Gwen said. "There are deck-hands, you know, plus the regular crew. Bare-chested, sun-glazed, bronze-colored, muscle-molded, heat-seeking—"

"Stop! Stop! I'm burning up already!" Pamela cried, clutching her heart. And then, singing, "I'm in the moooood for love."

Gwen laughed. "Puh-lease! Not a summer romance."

"Why not? That's how you and Austin met, isn't it?"

"Austin's here! We can see each other as much as we want."

"Well, remember what happened to Liz and Ross," I said, thinking about the great guy she had met when we were camp counselors, the summer after our freshman year.

"I still miss him," Liz said in a small voice. How any guy could keep his distance from Liz, with her long dark hair and creamy complexion, was beyond my understanding.

"You never hear from him?" Gwen asked.

"We text now and then. But he's got his life to live there in Pennsylvania. We just decided it wouldn't work."

"But you have Keeno!" Pamela chirped, hoping to get us back in a happier mood. Liz and Keeno really had seemed to be hitting it off in recent months.

But Liz gave a little shrug. "I like him. He makes me laugh. But I don't *like* like him, know what I mean?"

"Aha! Somebody else is looking for love!" Pamela crooned. "Go ahead and get the applications, Gwen. I'm in."

"Me too," I said. "Sounds like a great summer. At least Patrick's coming for the prom."

"You've got the best of all possible worlds, Alice," Liz said, breaking a huge cookie in half and holding up one piece. Gwen and I grabbed for it at once. Gwen won. "He's in Chicago, you're here, he comes back for the big stuff. Meanwhile, you're free to date other guys. . . . *There's* a long-distance romance that's working."

"He's only been gone for six months," I reminded her. "And now that his parents have moved to Wisconsin . . . Well, I don't even want to think about it. No, I *do* want to think about it. We've got this understanding that we're special to each other, but . . ."

This time nobody jumped in with assurances. No one made a joke.

"It's rough," said Gwen. She broke off one bite of the cookie half and handed the rest to me, like a sympathy card, and I accepted. "This is make-each-moment-count time, everybody, because who knows where we'll be a year from now?"

That was to be our motto, I guess. Make each moment count. I remembered that a long time ago, when my brother and I were quarreling a lot, I'd decided to live each day as though it were the last time I'd ever see him, and it worked. It stopped the quarreling, but it got so real that I was always imagining Les choking on a chicken bone or something. There had to be some kind of balance here, but I wasn't sure what it was.

And I wondered why, just as in physics, for every action, there's an equal and opposite reaction; for every new thing I looked forward to after high school, there seemed to be some opposite feeling I could hardly describe. Anxiety? Sadness? *Don't be a basket case,* I told myself, and meant it.

It was Phil's idea. Phil—as in editor in chief of our school paper, *The Edge.* Phil—as in tall, once-gangly, now-square-shouldered head honcho.

"Let me handle the neo-Nazi stuff if it keeps kicking around," he told me that afternoon. "With all that's happened at our school, we—and you in particular—need some R and R."

He was talking about the death of two students last summer, the white supremacy stuff, the prejudice against our Sudanese student, Daniel Bul Dau, and Amy Sheldon's molestation by a substitute teacher. That was a lot for any of us to handle, but I wasn't sure what Phil was getting at.

"You want me to do R and R as in . . . writing about spring fashions? Healthier food in the cafeteria? The summer plans of graduating seniors? Serious fluff?"

"Get off it, Alice," Phil said, giving me that you-know-what-I-mean look. "Write anything at all, something people can sink their teeth into, but different from all the Sturm und Drang of last semester."

I did know what he meant, and I did need a break. I'd think of something, I figured. In the meantime, I checked the school calendar for coming events. Last year we did a girls' choice dance. This year we were going to put on a 1950s-style sock hop, and when I got all the details, I wrote it up:

February 11—Save the Date!
Ask Gram for those poodle skirts, those Elvis wigs, those 45s, those glow bracelets, 'cause this school is gonna rock!

Last year we did Sadie Hawkins, but this year it's Sock Hop.
We're going to go back sixty years and have a dance marathon.
We're gonna have root beer floats at a drive-in. There will be inflatable instruments, a jukebox, a balloon drop, pizza, pom-poms, pastel pearls, and bouffant hairdos galore.

Get a photo of you and your friends in a '57 Chevy. Leave your
shoes at the door and buy a pair of bobby socks for charity.
Watch *The Edge* for more details.

"This fluffy enough for you?" I asked Phil, handing him my
copy.

"Perfect!" He grinned. "Now go find a poodle skirt to show
your heart is in it."

I did better than that. I assigned one of our senior reporters to write up instructions for making your own circle skirt
out of a piece of felt. I asked another to research places where
people could buy an Elvis wig, rent a guitar, learn to jitterbug,
make their own pom-poms, and we had all our girl reporters
do up their hair beehive-style so that Sam could take a picture
of it for the paper.

"You guys are *rockin'*!" Miss Ames told us. "Good show!"

Patrick called me that evening.

"So how was your first week back?" he asked.

I lay on a heap of pillows, cell phone to my ear. "Interesting," I told him. "Remember the white supremacist guy I told
you about, Curtis Butler? The one who was writing those letters
to *The Edge* last semester? He transferred to another school."

"Well, that should make life easier for you," Patrick said.

"And worse for the school that got him, probably," I said.
"But . . . in other news . . . Jill says she and Justin 'have big
plans'—I'm betting they'll elope; Gwen wants us to get jobs on

a cruise ship this summer; and the school's having a sock hop."

"Whoa," said Patrick. "What cruise ship? To where?"

"The Chesapeake *Seascape*, cruising the Bay. A new line. Gwen thinks it would be fun."

I was about to ask if he wanted to apply too when he said, "So you'll be on the Bay and I'll be in Barcelona."

It took a moment to sink in. "Spain?" I gasped.

"Yeah. This professor I'm working for—he wants to go get settled before the fall class he'll be teaching there, and he's offered to take me with him. He wants to finish his book this summer—that's mostly what I'm researching for him. And . . . here's the really big news . . . only you won't like it . . ."

"Oh, Patrick!"

"He's going to see if he can arrange for me to do my study abroad in my sophomore year instead of my junior, so I can stay on in Spain when the fall quarter begins. I'll be living with a bunch of students all the while."

Why was I not surprised? Why didn't I know I couldn't fence Patrick in? And why did I realize that even if I could, I shouldn't? Patrick had the whole world ahead of him.

"I . . . I guess I didn't know you *wanted* to do a year abroad."

"I have to. Part of my major. But here's another way to look at it: The sooner I put in that year abroad, the sooner I'll be back."

That was comforting in a strange sort of way. It seemed to mean that Patrick was looking ahead. Way ahead. That the two of us had plans.

"I want the best for you, Patrick—you know that," I said. "But I'm not sure I can stand it."

He chuckled. "I think you'll stand it very well on a cruise ship with a lot of hunks around."

"You won't be jealous?"

"Of course I'll be jealous. You could fall for the first mate and get married on Smith Island and be raising a little deckhand by the time I get back."

"I'm not laughing," I said.

"It's not like I'm leaving tomorrow," he told me. "There's still your prom."

"You *will* be here for that?"

"I'll be there."

That was reassuring, but . . . Spain? For a whole year? Still, after we'd talked and I put my cell phone back on my nightstand, I wondered why I didn't feel worse. Maybe I felt safer with Patrick in Spain for a year than on the University of Chicago campus, surrounded by all those free-thinking college girls. Now that there was no home here to come back to, I had wondered how he'd spend his summer. And since I'd be on a cruise ship . . .

Okay, I told myself. *Make the most of it. Quit worrying.* When I made new friends at college and they asked, I'd be able to say, *Oh, yeah. I have a boyfriend in Spain.*

2
THE UNEXPECTED

I rode in with Dad when we went to the Melody Inn on Saturday.

"Are you going to hire a part-time clerk after I go to college, or do you want me to drive back to Silver Spring once a week?" I asked.

I could tell by Dad's expression that the question took him by surprise.

"If you go to the University of Maryland, you mean? I don't know," he answered. "But I doubt you'd want to get up every Saturday morning and drive all the way over here."

"I'll need to work somewhere if I want some spending money," I said.

Dad slowed as we approached the small parking lot behind the Melody Inn. "Won't be the same without you in the Gift Shoppe."

"Should I take that as a 'yes'—that you'd still want me to drive over?"

He pulled into the space marked MANAGER. "That's nine months from now, Al," he said. "Let's see how it all plays out."

Kay Yen, our new full-time clerk, was hanging up her coat as we walked in. Marilyn Roberts had already opened the store and would be turning the key over to Kay after her baby came. It was due February 17, but Marilyn looked as though she could deliver any day.

"Kay and I are working up a special display for Valentine's Day," she told Dad. "DVDs and CDs of all the great songs, operas, ballets—anything that has to do with love."

"I'm all for that," Dad said. In retail, the minute one holiday is over, you start marketing the next one.

"I've already ordered some valentine stuff for the Gift Shoppe," I told them. "Heart-shaped music boxes, red coffee mugs—I wanted to include a lacy red thong with sixteenth notes on it, but I figured that was going a little too far."

"Correct," said Dad, and gave me a look.

"We could even have a drawing for a strolling violinist," Marilyn said. "Kay and I were talking about it yesterday. Like, from February first to the twelfth, all cash register receipts would go into a box, and on the twelfth, you draw one and the lucky winner gets a dinner for two on Valentine's Day, with a strolling violinist."

"It would be a big hit, Mr. M.," Kay said.

"Yes! Do it, Dad!" I chimed in.

"I *would* have offered Jack to play and sing his love songs for free," said Marilyn, "but with my due date so close, we'd better not chance it."

"Well, I think the Melody Inn can spring for both a dinner and a violinist," Dad said. "Great idea! Keep 'em coming."

I set about opening up the Gift Shoppe—a cubbyhole beneath the stairs to the second floor. Up there, instructors give lessons in soundproof cubicles, and on Saturdays kids troop up and down the stairs with their trumpets and saxophone cases. But here, I slide a drawer into the cash register, open up the little cylinders of nickels and dimes, recount and record the bills. Then I wipe off the glass countertop and turn on the light in the revolving case where we keep the music-themed jewelry. On the shelf behind me, I straighten the Beethoven sweatshirts, the keyboard scarves, the Bach notebooks, and the dancing bears, and I keep an eye on the sheet music department so I can help out there if I have no customers.

This particular Saturday, Kay seemed distracted. I caught her standing with palms resting on a counter across the store, shoulders hunched, staring at nothing. She answered the phone, then flipped through a box of index cards, paused, stared into space some more, and started all over again.

Around eleven, when Dad brought by a box of heart decorations, Kay saw us together and came over.

"Mr. M., your family was so nice to invite me to your house at Thanksgiving, I'd love to take you two and Sylvia out to dinner.

Or I could even bring food over if that's more convenient. Would you be free tonight?"

"Why, Kay, you don't have to do that," said Dad. "We were glad to have you. You're part of the Melody Inn family."

"I know, but I'd really like to do it. How about tonight?" she insisted.

"Actually, Sylvia has me programmed all weekend," Dad said. "We're eating with some of the faculty from her school tonight, then joining another couple at a concert tomorrow."

Kay looked not only disappointed, but somewhat desperate. "Well, another time, then?"

"Of course!" said Dad.

After he moved on, though, she turned to me. "What about you? Are *you* free tonight? I'd really like to make it tonight."

"I don't have any plans yet," I said. "Sure."

She looked a little embarrassed. "Alice, would it be all right if I got some takeout food and brought it over?" As though I were doing *her* a favor.

"Whatever you want. Sounds great!" I said.

Dad and Sylvia went out around six, and Kay arrived at six thirty with a bag of little cartons of Chinese food from a restaurant I'd never heard of. I put place mats and silverware on the table while she heated water for the tea. The whole thing seemed sort of weird, but I figured this night must be special somehow. Maybe she had an announcement to make or something.

I was half right.

We'd just started eating—Peking duck, cashew chicken—when her cell phone rang. I heard the music coming from her bag in the living room.

At first I thought she wasn't going to answer. Then she suddenly excused herself and leaped from her chair. I saw her check the caller ID before she answered in Chinese. The conversation was short and, as far as I could tell, polite.

When she returned to the table, she gave a big sigh and leaned back in her chair. "Yi, yi, yi, yi, yi," she said, and looked across at me. "I'm going a little bit crazy. My parents are back from China. . . ."

"They just got in?" I asked.

"No. They got home yesterday. They apologized all over the place for interrupting our dinner just now. They thought it was for later this evening."

I didn't understand, so I waited.

"But . . . you know that man they wanted me to meet? The reason they wanted me to go to China with them last November?"

"Yeah," I said, remembering how she had refused, how she'd told them Dad needed her at the store over the holidays.

"Well, they brought him back with them. They want me to have dinner with him."

"Now?" I said.

"No. They *wanted* me to have dinner with them tonight, and I . . . told them I had to eat with my boss. So they invited me to dinner tomorrow night. I made up another excuse. I don't *want* an arranged marriage."

"Oh, wow," I said. "Have you . . . even seen this man?"

"Only photos. But once we meet, and *then* I say no . . . His parents and my parents have been friends for decades, they tell me. Before I was born. They say we'll learn to love each other once we're married."

"What about your boyfriend here? Can't he do something about this?" I asked.

Kay buried her head in her hands. "We broke up after Christmas. He could see that—with all the pressure from my parents—I come with too much baggage. He wasn't even thinking of marriage, and neither, really, am I. I've got grad school coming up next year, and I'm saving for that."

I smiled as I helped myself to more rice. "So you're having dinner with your boss's family tonight, right?"

She smiled a little. "Yeah."

"An invitation you couldn't refuse."

"I hate to lie to my parents."

"Well, this takes care of one evening, anyway. How long is this man going to stay?"

"A few months. He's supposedly here on a consulting job. The whole thing is just so phony. I know why he's here and he knows why he's here and he probably knows I know why he's here and—"

"Do you even know his name?"

"James. James Huang. My dad thinks he's perfect for me, but I want to choose my *own* husband. I want a man who chooses me; I don't want his parents to do it."

It was sort of exciting being in the middle of all this intrigue, but it didn't ruin my appetite. I took another bite of duck. "What did you tell your parents just now?"

"I said we were right in the middle of dinner and I'd let them know later. They apologized, by the way, and begged you to forgive them for interrupting our meal. My friends are arranging all sorts of things to keep me busy, but I can't put this off forever."

"You've got my sympathy," I told her.

Over the weekend Sylvia was in her "nesting mode," as Dad calls it—making soup and meat loaf and spaghetti sauce for the freezer. Dad says if we got snowed in from now till May, we wouldn't have to buy groceries once.

Sunday afternoon she asked if I'd take some over to Lester. When I called to see if he was home, he said that he and his roommate had been advertising for a third person, now that George had married and moved out, and that someone named Andy was coming by to see the place that afternoon. So he'd be home all day.

I like to play "rescuer" to my brother, even though he doesn't need it. When he was still in school, he sponged meals off us a lot. But now that he's got his MA and is working in the admissions office at the university, he takes *us* to dinner sometimes. Sylvia still can't resist the impulse to send him home-cooked food, though, and he doesn't exactly refuse it.

I parked outside the large old house in Takoma Park, its

yellow paint beginning to peel a bit on the porch railing, and took the side staircase up to the apartment on the second floor.

Les has a good thing going and he knows it. He and the other two roomies got the apartment as grad students, rent-free. Elderly Otto Watts, who owns the place and lives downstairs, has a caregiver during the day. But he lets Les and his buddies have the upstairs on the condition that one of them is always there during the evening and all night, should he have an emergency, and that the men help maintain the house and do minor repair work about the place.

I knocked and heard Les yell, "It's open," so I went inside.

"Care package for Les McKinley," I called, taking the bag to the kitchen down the hall.

"Sylvia send any of her chili?" Les called from the living room.

"A little of everything, I think," I told him, and began arranging the stuff in his freezer compartment to fit it all in. "That guy come by yet?"

"No. He said he'd be here before five."

"Hope he's hot," I said. "I'll bring you more stuff if he is."

Les was reading the sports section with one leg thrown over the arm of the lounge chair. Even when he doesn't shave, he's handsome. Dark brown hair (with receding hairline), dark eyes, square face, square chin. He was dressed in sweats and a tee and socks so old, they had holes on the bottom.

"I thought there would be a line halfway down the block," I said. "Nobody wants a rent-free apartment?"

"We have to pay for our phone and utilities," Les said. "The real drawback is taking turns being here in the evenings and caring for Mr. Watts when he needs it. Most grad students don't want to commit to staying home two or three nights a week, and at least half of them have never picked up a hammer, much less helped an old man in the bathroom."

"This guy okay with that?"

"Says he worked in a nursing home one summer—can handle anything. I said great, if he likes the place, he's—"

The doorbell rang just then, and since I was leaving anyway, I answered. There stood a woman in her late twenties, I'd guess, with a purple streak in her long copper-colored hair, red-framed glasses, wearing a fake-fur parka, jeans, and ankle boots.

"Hi," she said, and I knew from her voice how Les got the wrong impression. Tenor. Not alto: tenor. Baritone, even. "I'm Andy," she said. "Came to see the apartment."

"Oh, yeah!" I said cheerfully. "I'm just a relative. Come on in."

I led her down the hallway, trying hard not to smile too broadly. I'd been thinking of going to the mall, but now I decided to stay and watch the show. "Les," I called. "Andy's here."

Lester put down the paper as we came in, and his mouth froze in an unspoken exclamation, his leg sliding off the arm of the chair. "You're . . . Andy?" he asked.

"Yes. Andy Boyce." She had a wide face—somewhere between plain and pretty—and she smiled as she shook his hand. "Nice," she said, looking around.

I took off my jacket and plopped down on the couch,

wishing I had some popcorn. I locked my face into a friendly smile to keep from laughing out loud.

"Which room is mine?" Andy asked. I'd only heard one or two women in my life with a voice as low as hers, but Andy's was more sultry. Maybe she was a nightclub singer or something. There were three piercings in each of her earlobes.

"Uh . . ." Les let the newspaper fall to the floor, and his feet fished around for his loafers. "Mr. Watts has the final say," he said quickly. "A caregiver's a pretty personal choice, so you'd need to meet him." Then he added, "The room to the right of the entrance."

"Thanks. I'll look it over," Andy said, and started back up the hall.

Les stared at me with wide eyes, and I covered my mouth. He lifted his hands helplessly, palms up, his mouth in the shape of *Wh . . . ?*

"You're in for it now, bub." I giggled.

Les went out in the hall. We could hear a closet door opening and closing.

"Cross circulation. That's good." Andy's voice, checking out the windows.

"Bathroom?" she asked, coming back.

"End of the hall," said Les, following after her. "But, you know, you might want to see Mr. Watts first before we go any further. . . ."

"And this is the kitchen?" Andy stopped at the makeshift kitchen, with appliances along one wall, the sink on another. "Well," she said, "I've seen better, but it'll do."

In the bathroom she checked out the medicine cabinet and the space under the sink. "This Mr. Watts—he have any specific issues?"

"Quite a lot of them," Les replied. "Takes a ton of medicines."

"Is he ambulatory?"

"In a matter of speaking, I suppose, yes. But he's old and frail. And he also has male problems—you know, urinary incontinence. Needs assistance in that area, so I don't know how he'd feel about a woman—"

"No sweat, I can handle it," said Andy. "Who's the other renter here? What's he like?"

"Paul Sorenson?" I could almost see the wheels spinning in Lester's brain. "Eccentric. Very eccentric. An odd duck, actually. Hard to get to know at first."

"I think we'll get along fine," said Andy. She thrust her hands in the pockets of her parka and looked straight into Lester's eyes. "Well, I can move in anytime. Let's go meet Mr. Watts."

I waited while Les took Andy down the outside staircase and heard the doorbell ring far below. Les was back in a matter of minutes and leaned against the door once he got inside.

"What's happening?" I asked.

"I'm probably having a heart attack or something," he said. He walked slowly into the living room and sprawled on the couch. "He's interviewing her now. He said he'd give me a call."

"He wasn't surprised she was a woman?"

"I don't know. How the hell will I explain this to Paul?"

I pressed my lips tightly together to hold in the laughter. "You didn't specify you wanted a guy?"

"I guess not. Just said we wanted a nonsmoking grad student and gave the conditions. Oh, man, I'm dead."

"Yeah," I said. "What if Paul bolts and it's just you and Andy?"

"Don't *say* that!" he yelped. "Can't you see I'm suffering here?"

"Where *is* Paul?" I asked.

"Ten-day ski trip. Which means I can't go out at all in the evenings until he comes back. He said to go ahead and get a roommate—he'd trust my judgment. Oh, brother, am I fried!"

"Well, let's try to look on the bright side. What's her major?"

"History . . . English lit . . . I forget."

"Smoker?"

"No."

"Drinker? Did you say you didn't want wild parties?"

"Why would I say that? What am I going to do if I want to invite someone to stay overnight?"

"Oh, the two girls will probably get along famously. They'll spend the whole evening in the kitchen talking," I said breezily.

Les jumped to his feet and ran one hand through his hair, then paced back and forth, taking deep breaths. "*Why* didn't I tell her the room was taken? I hadn't even met her before! I must have been out of my mind to let her see the place."

"Relax," I told him. "Watts won't want a woman in the bathroom with him."

Lester stopped suddenly and peered out the window. "Hey! There's hope! It's Andy, heading for her car."

I leaned forward.

"Hold it," Les said. "She's opening the passenger-side door. Taking something out."

"A suitcase?" I jumped up and joined him at the window, but it wasn't a suitcase. Something Andy held in both hands. She disappeared again under the roof of the porch.

Les and I sat down opposite each other. He looked so miserable, I almost wanted to give him a hug. We waited two minutes. Five.

The phone rang and Les picked it up. Mr. Watts was yelling. He's stone-deaf without his hearing aid, but always takes them off when he's on the phone.

"Lester?" I heard him yell. "She brought me some apricot strudel! She's in!"

Two days later Les was sitting at our kitchen table with the news that Andy had moved in, books and all.

"So? How goes it?" Sylvia asked.

"I don't know. We don't have much to say to each other, which is probably good," Les said. "She doesn't ask, she announces: 'I'm taking a shower now,' not, 'Need the bathroom before I shower?' Or she'll say, 'I used the last of the milk.'"

"You should be able to work that through. Set some ground rules," Dad said.

"It's just weird having her around, Dad. I walked in the bathroom yesterday and knocked over a shampoo bottle turned upside down on top of another, draining out every last drop of shampoo."

"That's called being frugal, Les. And it's not a crime," Dad said.

Les looked helplessly around the table. "Look. She washes her underwear in the tub with her feet."

I burst out laughing. *"What?"*

"How would you know that?" asked Sylvia, amused.

"Because I found sopping wet pants and a bra in the tub that she forgot to wring out after she showered. I could hear her stomping around in there. I figure she saves on detergent by letting her soap and shampoo rain down on her underwear while she washes her hair."

"Marry the girl, Les! She'll save you a ton of money!" Dad chortled. "Look, Les, every person has idiosyncrasies, you included."

"She's loco, and Paul's going to hate her."

"Mr. Watts likes her?" Dad asked.

"He's crazy about her. Her strudel, anyway, which I happen to know came from the Giant."

"Oh, boy, you're in it for the long haul, Les," said Sylvia.

Scary, I thought. Kay Yen would be starting grad school next year, and Les had already received his master's. The first four years of college were behind them, but problems just kept coming, no matter how much education you had.

There ought to be a recess. A time-out. Some plateau you could count on where absolutely nothing happened, good or bad, and you could catch your breath. When did that happen? After you married? Had your children? Retired? Never?

3
BODILY PERCEPTIONS

Gwen invited Liz and Pam and me for a sleepover and included her friend Yolanda from church.

We propped ourselves up on pillows around the living room floor with a bowl of dip and Fritos and traded catalogs from many of the colleges we had applied to—Frostburg, William & Mary, Clemson. . . . Gwen's parents and brothers were out for the evening, and her grandmother was asleep in a back bedroom.

With rings on every finger, some with two, and her finely arched eyebrows rising and falling with every word, Yolanda read aloud the names of courses that sounded interesting.

"Here's one for you, Pamela: Theater of Revolt," she said.

"I like it! I like it!" said Pamela. "No, wait a minute. I'll take Sensory Exploration Lab. Woo! Hope it's coed."

"What about Witchcraft and Magic in Premodern Europe?" said Liz, reading from her Bennington College catalog.

"Hand Percussion and Dance Accompaniment. That's for you, Pamela," I said. "And this is for Gwen: The Nature of Moral Judgment."

"Naw, I'm taking judo or scuba diving," Gwen told us, checking the catalog in her lap.

It was amazing. The depth and variety of college courses made high school look like kindergarten. It was almost embarrassing to think about going back to physics and economics on Monday. We, here on the floor, were a huddled mass, yearning to breathe freely of the intoxicating air of adult discussions and debates: Advanced Logic; American Humor, 1940–1965; The Psychology of Sexual Response; Storytelling and Film. . . .

I saw Gwen nudge Yolanda and point to a course. "Reading the Body," she read. "'Our bodies and our perceptions about them constitute an important part of our sociocultural heritage . . .'"

Yolanda only shrugged.

"I've *got* to get into Bennington!" said Liz. "I've practically memorized the map of the campus. You know how sometimes a place just seems like home?"

"That's sort of the way I felt about William & Mary," I said. "But . . . I feel the same about the University of Maryland. I applied for early admission at Maryland, but I've got until April first to make a decision."

"I'll take anything as long as it's in New York," Pamela told us. "I've applied to four schools in Manhattan."

"How are we going to stand waiting until April to find out?" said Liz. "This is absolutely the worst part of senior year."

"What's the best part?" asked Yolanda.

"Prom," said Pamela.

"Graduating," said Gwen.

"I think it's being together, like this," I said. "We've only got four more months."

"Seven," said Gwen, "if we work on that cruise ship together this summer. Speaking of which . . ." She reached around behind her for a manila envelope and waved it in the air. "Applications, everybody. They have to be in by March first."

"What's Lester doing this summer?" Pamela asked. "You should talk him into coming, Alice. Really! He'd make a great deckhand. Now that he's got his master's, he can do something different for a change. Can you imagine how wild it would be if he was on board?"

"He's got his hands full," I said. "He's sending out résumés for a new job. And he's also dealing with a new roommate he thought was male, because she had such a low voice over the phone."

"Is she hot?" asked Pamela.

"I wouldn't call her that, no. But her low voice certainly doesn't seem to bother her; she's obviously lived with it all her life."

"I don't know how you could change your voice even if you

wanted," Liz said. "If I could change one thing about myself, though, I'd have curvier legs. My calves are too straight."

Gwen shook her head. "It always amazes me how some of the most beautiful girls don't even know they're gorgeous enough."

"You've got to be kidding," said Liz, frowning down at one leg.

"See? I rest my case," said Gwen.

"If I could change one thing about *me*, I'd take a pound off each of my thighs and put them on my breasts," I said, dipping another Frito in the sour cream dip.

"A whole pound? Like a pound of butter?" said Pamela, laughing. "Alice, you'd be falling out of your bra."

"I wish my fingers were longer," said Gwen, placing both hands on one of the cushions and studying them. "Mine are too short and stubby. I've always wanted long, elegant fingers with tapered nails."

"Well, I wish I could tan more easily," said Pamela. "If we get that job on the cruise ship, I'm going to look freakishly white in shorts. I hope we get hired, though. I'm getting psyched for it."

"Me too," I said, and looked around the group. "Are we all in?"

Gwen glanced at Yolanda.

Yolanda hugged her knees and rested her chin on top of them, a black coil of beaded hair on one side of her face dangling down her leg. "I don't know," she said.

"She doesn't want to leave her boyfriend," Pamela teased.

"It's not just that. I'm probably earning more waiting tables than I would on a cruise ship. Summers I work full-time, and those tips really add up."

"Oh, come on, Yolanda. It would be fun! Money's not everything," I coaxed.

"I really need it, though," Yolanda said.

It was the way Gwen was looking at her sideways that cued us there was more to the story.

"College fund?" I asked.

Gwen raised her eyebrows, still looking at Yolanda, waiting.

"A little surgical procedure," Yolanda said finally, and sat back against the couch, her eyes on the floor.

Okay, so we were probably all wondering the same thing—abortion? Why else wouldn't she discuss it? My mind went through a simple calculation I'd been through before: Of me and my original two best friends, Elizabeth and Pamela, only Pam had had sex. Intercourse, I mean. Two virgins, one non. Once we added Gwen, that was two virgins, two non. Add Yolanda from another school, two virgins, three non. Add Jill from our school, two virgins, four non. Add Karen and Penny . . . I had no idea.

When the silence got heavy, Liz asked, "What's wrong, Yolanda? Tell us."

"*Nothing's* wrong," Gwen said emphatically, continuing to frown at Yolanda. "She only *thinks* something's wrong, and I'm about to beat bumps on her head if she goes through with it."

Yolanda gave her a defiant look. "Everybody has something

they'd like to change, including you. You said so yourself. Well, I want to change something else." She glanced around at us. "It's just a girl thing."

"Boobs?" Pamela prodded. "Are you serious?"

Yolanda sighed, knowing we wouldn't give up. "It's personal. . . . I sort of stick out down there, and there's a surgery you can have . . ."

I think each of us cringed, wondering exactly what she was talking about but too embarrassed to guess. Not Gwen, though. It had gotten this far, and Gwen wasn't about to give up.

"Her labia. It's got a name, Yolanda," she said, and then, to us, "I keep trying to tell her that this is a normal sexual characteristic, and every girl's different, but she won't listen."

I finally thought of something to say. "Yolanda, have you read Maya Angelou's *I Know Why the Caged Bird Sings*? She was worried about the very same thing until her mother persuaded her it was natural."

"Well, some doctor advertises that he does this kind of surgery, and Yolanda's borrowing four thousand dollars from a cousin to have it done," said Gwen.

"Four thousand!" we spluttered in unison, and Liz choked on her Sprite.

Gwen turned to Yolanda again, and her voice was more gentle, almost pleading. "Listen, Yolanda. Some girls have labia all tucked up inside them like . . . like petals on a carnation. Other girls' are more like rose petals, half in, half out; and some are like . . . the open petals of a tulip."

We laughed, and that helped relieve the awkwardness, if not the embarrassment.

"Gwen, you should write for Hallmark," I said. "'Ode to the Labia' . . . a rose is a rose is a labia."

"I guess I'm a tulip too," said Pamela thoughtfully, making us laugh again. "I never thought much about it. But Tim sure liked the way I looked. In fact, I heard a guy say once that girls with big ones are supposed to be more sexually responsive than girls with small ones—like pouty lips, I guess. Next, girls will be getting collagen injections in their labia to make them pouty."

I was all for changing the subject at that point, but I realized we had Yolanda's attention.

"Where did you get the idea that something was wrong with you?" Liz asked her.

Yolanda hugged her knees again. "My boyfriend said I didn't look like the girl in a movie we watched."

"Must have been some movie!" said Pamela.

"Okay, so it was porn, but we got a good look, and he's right. I *don't* look like the girl down there."

"So you're going to have surgery? Lop them off just for your boyfriend?" said Gwen. "To look like a *porn* star?"

"It's a regular surgery, not a back-alley kind of thing," Yolanda said. "This doctor's done hundreds of them."

"*Listen* to yourself!" said Gwen. "If hundreds of women think they 'stick out down there,' as you put it, it only proves it's normal! Somebody's feeding them a bunch of crap. And it's risky. What if you went through with it and found you didn't feel as much as you did before? That there was nerve damage. What would your boyfriend think about that?"

Liz was trying to comprehend it. "How . . . I mean . . . does your boyfriend . . . like . . . *examine* you all over? 'I like this part' and 'I don't like that'?"

More embarrassed laughter, but a little louder.

"Well, he sees what I look like down there. Any guy would when you've been having sex."

I shrank back against the cushions. "Arrrrggghhh! I want a guy who loves all of me, not just a part. 'It's a package deal,' I'd tell him. Yolanda, what if you go through with this and he decides he doesn't like something else? What if he says your belly button should poke in instead of out? Would you fix that, too?"

"Then he'll want a boob enhancement," said Pamela. "I think it's a control issue."

"Yeah. What if you go to all the trouble to make your labia smaller and the next guy who comes along wants them larger? You going to have them stretched?" I said. "I've got a better idea. The next time your boyfriend wants to do a clinical exam, tell him you'll trade places. Put *him* on the table."

"Yay!" the others cheered.

"Yeah, stretch him out buck naked and tell him all that body hair has to go," said Liz.

"And *that* thing could be a little . . . uh . . . thicker," said Gwen.

We shrieked.

"And *those* could be a little tighter," said Gwen. "'How about doing a testicle tuck just for me?'" she suggested.

We howled.

Yolanda was laughing so hard, she had tears in her eyes. In fact, I wasn't sure if she was laughing or crying. Relief, maybe.

"Now tell me something good about yourself," Gwen urged her.

Yolanda just wiped her eyes and gave a half smile.

"Well, I may not like my fingers, but I like my hair," Gwen continued. "If I want to press it out and get it straightened, I can do that. If I want to go natural, I can. I can dread it and twist it. I've got great hair."

"I like my arms," I said, holding one out. I don't know that they're different from anyone else's, but they're pretty arms. "I've always liked my arms and elbows."

Pamela jumped up and paraded around. "I like my butt!" she said, and gave herself a slap on the behind, and we applauded.

We all looked at Yolanda. "I like my feet," she said finally, wiggling her toes with their bright red polish.

"The only part of you that's got any sense," said Gwen.

4

AN UNTIMELY OFFER

After AP English on Monday, Mrs. Rosen asked if I could stay for a few minutes after class. I figured there was something she wanted me to cover for *The Edge*, so I had my pen in hand when I went up to her desk.

She waited until the other students had left the room, then said, "Thanks for staying, Alice. I wonder if you're familiar with the Ivy Day Ceremony here at school?"

"A little," I said, remembering that a few days before graduation each year, I'd seen the seniors, in their caps and gowns, gathering in the hallways and going outside for a procession around the block—around our ivy-covered building—for some kind of ceremony in the courtyard.

Mrs. Rosen motioned for me to sit down and sat in the

chair opposite me. In her white turtleneck and black pants, she looked more like an usher than a teacher, but I liked her shoes—really great purple and black shoes with a little curved heel.

"Each year the teachers choose an Ivy Bearer—usually a girl who is deemed to be one of the most focused, well-rounded seniors. This is a seventy-year-old tradition in our school. Each class plants a little pot of ivy in the courtyard, symbolic of the senior class having planted its roots in this school. Walking along with the Ivy Bearer is the senior class president on one side and the Ivy Day Poet on the other. The president gives a short dedication as the ivy is presented, the principal accepts it, and then the poet reads an original poem. I'd like you to try out for the poet."

My eyes moved from her shoes to her face, a small face, deep-set eyes. I'd had the vague hope as she talked that perhaps I was going to be the designated Ivy Bearer—that focused, well-rounded girl. Had she really said "poet"? Had she said "try out for"?

"Here's the way it works," Mrs. Rosen explained. "The English teachers invite four or five students to write an Ivy Day poem—about our school, their class, the meaning of Ivy Day to them—and each of the students reads his or her poem aloud at a faculty luncheon in early April. That week the faculty votes on which of the poems should be read at the Ivy Day Ceremony, and the author is appointed the Ivy Day Poet. I'd very much like you to be one of the contestants."

I was still staring at her. "I . . . I don't really write poetry," I said, stupefied.

"Well, many of our previous poets hadn't either, until they were asked. You write some very fine articles for the school paper, and poetry is an excellent way to learn to distill your writing down to its essence. Whether you win or not, you'll have a chance to perform before the faculty, and that's both an honor and good experience for college."

My pulse was going ninety miles an hour and my throat was dry, but not, I think, from excitement.

"I just . . . I don't know," I said. "I've never thought about it."

She reached out and touched my arm. "Well, will you think about it for a few days, then? You don't have to decide this minute. Take a week if you need to. But I know several teachers who would be very happy if you agreed."

I ended up in Mrs. Bailey's office the next day. The minute I saw a free space on her sign-up sheet for after school, I wrote in my name.

"I've never written much poetry, nothing I really liked," I lamented. "I don't do abstract very well. I mostly enjoy writing about people. What am I going to tell Mrs. Rosen?"

My guidance counselor had made each of us a cup of chai tea, and she nodded as she listened, letting the steam warm her face. She was a sixty-something woman with gray hair, still brown in places, gently curled. Soft skin. Laugh lines at the corners of her eyes.

"I've already got loads of stuff to do—things I *want* to do—

and I feel sure that there are other people who write poetry better than I could," I continued.

"Is it possible you might surprise yourself?" Mrs. Bailey asked.

"It's possible I'd surprise myself; it's possible I'd spend the next three months writing and rewriting a poem that isn't very good, and I'd stand up at the faculty luncheon and humiliate myself," I said.

"Well, you've given some reasons why you feel you shouldn't accept. Can you think of any reasons you should?"

"I really tried to do that," I told her. "The only reasons I could think of were that Dad would be proud of me and Sylvia would be pleased, simply because she loves poetry."

Mrs. Bailey was quiet for a few moments. "And you?" she asked finally.

"I don't want to do it, Mrs. Bailey. I wouldn't enjoy it, I'd obsess over it, and I'd rather be doing other things."

"So . . . ? Where's the problem?"

"Mrs. Rosen really wants me to try out for it, and evidently, some other teachers do too. I feel I'd be letting them down. I just . . . what if I'm saying no because I'm afraid I'll fail? Actually, in this case, I'm sure I would. But how do I know if I might be refusing for the wrong reasons?"

"Ah! A question for the ages, Alice."

"For the aged?"

"No, my dear, I mean, this is a question we all wrestle with each time we make a decision."

"But how do we ever *know*?"

"We don't. Each time you make a decision, you have to factor in everything you know at that moment. And later, if you see you chose wrong, you remind yourself how it seemed the best choice at the time. Some decisions are reversible, while others aren't."

"I keep telling myself that if I say no, I'm closing a door. They'll ask someone else and I will have lost the chance to be class poet, to have that honor."

"And if you say yes?"

"If I say yes, I will probably be miserable for the next three months and fool around over and over again with verses I don't even like. There's just no *joy* here, except to think how proud Dad would be."

"Did it ever occur to you that by saying no, you could also be opening a door? That there are other ways to win the praise of your dad?" And when I didn't answer, she asked, "Isn't he proud enough of you as you are?"

I slouched down a little and smiled at her. "I think you just talked me into saying no."

"My job isn't to talk you into anything—just to help clear up the picture a bit," Mrs. Bailey said.

"Well, it really helps," I said, but made no move to leave.

Mrs. Bailey sipped her tea again. "How are other things going in your life right now?"

"Mostly good," I said. "I'm excited. Happy. But, well . . . a lot of the time I also feel sort of . . . lost."

"Lost? As in . . . ? Can you put your finger on it more specifically?"

"Well, sad in a way. Scared in a way. Like . . . all along I've had a good idea of what was coming next. When I was a freshman, I'd watch the sophomores, and so on. Suddenly I'm a senior, and stuff like this starts coming at me. *Be the class poet.* My last chance to do something big in high school. Graduating's like . . . like jumping out of a plane, doing something I've never done. I don't know what to expect after high school, not really."

"You said you'd decided on the University of Maryland?"

"Well, not exactly. I'd like to see if I'm accepted at William & Mary. It would be great if I could go there. But Maryland would be good too. It's not just school, though."

I let out my breath, then inhaled again and blew on my tea. She waited.

"It's like I'm leaving one whole life, almost, and starting another. Leaving one part of me behind," I said. "I guess that's the sad part, and yet . . . I mean, it sounds crazy . . . ,"—she smiled at that—"but for as long as I can remember, I've had this beanbag chair. Even after we moved from Chicago to Maryland, even after I redecorated my bedroom, I kept that beanbag chair in one corner because I was so comfortable in it. I curled up in it when I was sad, when I was happy, when I was scared. I always wondered if it was a substitute for my mom's lap. I never wanted to give it away even when it looked out of place, which it does.

"And the other night . . . I don't know why . . . I just got the urge to go sink down in it, and . . ."—my voice actually quavered a little—"I didn't feel comforted, I felt ridiculous. And I'd always believed I'd take it to college with me and keep it in my dorm. All it's good for now is a footstool, and I . . . I . . . m-miss it."

I tried to laugh through my tears, and Mrs. Bailey nodded and smiled.

"Alice, if you only knew how common this feeling is. Not everyone expresses it as easily as you have," she said, "but I've almost come to expect this of seniors the closer they get to graduation."

"Expect what? Everyone missing a beanbag chair?"

"The blues. The uneasiness." She put down her cup and folded her hands in her lap. "It's a kind of mourning, actually, the way I see it, because you really are experiencing a loss. Loss of your childhood, even though you're glad to be growing up. A certain loss of security, a familiar routine. The pattern of high school life."

"But I've always looked forward to college! I thought I *wanted* to be on my own."

"And you do. But right now, as you put it, you're preparing to jump into your future, and you don't know exactly what you'll find when you land. You've never been there before, only heard about it. And sometimes you just want to fly back to home base, where you feel safe and loved."

"Everyone else seems so excited about college, about graduating."

She laughed. "They'd probably say the same thing about you."

"Really?"

She nodded. "You guys are good at hiding feelings from each other."

I took a minute or so to think about that and sip the tea.

"So . . . how do I deal with it? When I get this . . . sadness?"

"Acknowledge it. Take time to say to yourself, 'I'm feeling really sad'—or nervous or scared, you supply the words—'and I'm wondering how I'll get along in college.' This much I can promise you: It's a lot less scary when you recognize what you're feeling instead of trying to hide it from yourself."

"I'm not sure that will be enough."

"It may not be. You also need to talk about it with whomever will listen, and you know I'm always ready to listen. Remind yourself of the things you've faced in the past and how you managed to get through them."

"Not exactly like this, though."

"No?" She waited.

"Well . . . losing my mom, maybe. That was worse."

"Really major."

"And moving a couple of times."

"Uh-huh."

"And Mark dying." Somehow the things I'd had to deal with before seemed a lot scarier than just going off to college. "I guess you sort of have to take a deep breath and tell yourself to get over it," I said.

"No. Not get over it. Get through it. Go into it staying up front with yourself and remind yourself of all the ways you have of coping. When you get to college, make friends with your counselor early on. Tell her what we've talked about here, so that when you come to a bump in the road, you're already friends."

I could feel my panic, like a gas bubble in my chest, slowly evaporating.

"In the meantime," Mrs. Bailey said, "why don't you write about this?"

"Write it?"

"A feature article for the paper. You'd be helping a lot of people who, like you, think they're the only ones who feel this way."

"Wow!" I said. "I'm not sure I'm the one to do it."

"If not you, who?" Mrs. Bailey asked.

She was right. It couldn't be someone from outside the pain and panic, looking in. It had to be someone inside, looking out. And better this than a poem about ivy.

"Okay," I said. "I'll think about it."

5
NEW LIFE

Sylvia and I went to a baby shower for Marilyn after work on Saturday. I'd known Marilyn since I was in sixth grade. Of all Lester's old girlfriends, she was probably the one I liked most.

I'd always thought of Marilyn as the original "flower child," like the ones we read about back in the sixties. She was earthy and natural and sweet—as close as I could get to an older sister—and I'd always hoped she and Les would marry. But it never worked out, and she and Jack were happily married, playing their guitars, composing folk songs, and playing at weddings and anniversaries and stuff.

The shower was supposed to have been at the home of one of her friends, but Marilyn had been having back trouble, so they were bringing the shower to her. I had her address, and Sylvia was doing the driving.

It's sort of fun to be invited to an adult thing with your mom—stepmom or otherwise. Like you're accepted now as a woman. An acknowledgment that this would be happening to you—love, marriage, sex, a baby, not necessarily in that order.

I was wondering how Sylvia felt, going to baby showers when she'd never had a child herself. It was something I didn't feel I could ever ask. And then Sylvia answered it herself.

"I used to dread going to baby showers," she said, steering with one hand as she turned the radio down with the other. "It was the way the women looked at me, or I imagined they were looking at me—their side glances—when little sweaters and booties were held up to be admired. As though I might cry or something. They even said things like, 'Well, it's not all baby powder and cooing, you know. There are diapers.' To make me feel as though I wasn't missing much."

I couldn't believe Sylvia was telling me all this, things she'd probably never told her friends.

"So that . . . wasn't the way you felt—that you were missing something?" I said hesitantly.

"Of course I'm missing something. But I've never seen the Taj Mahal either. I never played the violin. I never wrote a novel or learned to fly or met a president. When people infer I'm incomplete somehow because I haven't given birth, I think, 'We're all incomplete in some way.' I don't know anyone who has done *every*thing she wanted to do in life."

"Well, I guess I'd like to have children if it works out," I told her. "I'm just not sure I'd like the birthing part."

She laughed. "That wouldn't have held me back, but I wanted any children of mine to have a dad they loved as much as I did, and until I met Ben, that just hadn't happened."

I didn't say, *And now you've had a hysterectomy, so it's too late.* I didn't know what to say, but finally I managed, "Well, if you *did* have children, I think you would have made a good mom."

She didn't laugh out loud, but even without looking at her, I knew she was smiling.

"And now that I *am* a mom?" she asked.

"I think you're doing pretty good, considering what you inherited," I said.

Sylvia glanced my way and gave me a grin. "I think I was pretty lucky with what I got."

"I'm not out of the nest yet," I told her. "Eight more months before college. But there's a possibility I'll be out of your hair this summer. A bunch of us are applying for jobs on a new Chesapeake Bay cruise line—waitressing and making beds."

"Really!" she said. "Now, *that* would be fun. See? That's another thing I always wanted to do and never did."

The Robertses' rental house was a little Cape Cod off Route 28 out in Rockville. It was on a dark winding road, set back from the street, the trees much larger and older than the houses.

We saw Kay Yen's Toyota parked in front, and it was Kay who answered the door. We could hear the chatter of women's voices as we came up the steps.

"They put me in charge of the door," Kay said, grinning, and held it wide open. "I don't know—is there some symbolism in this?"

"Like catching a bride's bouquet?" Sylvia said, and laughed. "I doubt it."

I gave Kay a hug as I stepped inside, conscious of how slim she felt, in contrast to how Marilyn looked, sitting on a straight-backed chair, her abdomen huge and resting, it seemed, on her thighs. At the store she was mostly standing or perched on a high stool behind a counter. Now, sitting down, her knees apart, she looked as though she could deliver any minute, and she still had a month to go. I guess on smaller people, an eighth-month pregnancy resembles a basketball under the clothes, but every time I tried to imagine that baby pushing its way out, I had to remind myself that everything stretches.

"I know," Marilyn said when I hugged her, as though she could read my thoughts. "I look huge."

"You look mama-ish," I said. "It's exactly how you're supposed to look."

"Well, I'm ready," she said, and patted her tummy. "But I guess this little person still has some finishing to do yet."

I sat down on the floor beside her chair as the other women gathered around, each of them with a photo of herself as a baby pinned to her shirt, as requested on the invitation. Sylvia's photo was of a newborn, lying on her back, fists clenched, legs in the frog-kick position, a little red-faced, hairless wonder. It was impossible to see in that baby the beautiful woman she was now.

For my photo I'd chosen a picture of me in a sundress at around fifteen months, sitting on the curb with an ice-cream cone. It was fun to look at each other's baby photos and try to see something of the woman-to-be in them, even women I didn't know.

Along with the stroller and bottle warmer, the diaper pail and mattress cover, Marilyn received some novel gifts as well. The Melody Inn gave her a crib and a fancy mobile to hang above it. There were five different sound tracks a parent could choose to put her baby to sleep—Bach, Mozart, Beethoven, Brahms, and Liszt—while colorful little birds, with tiny lights in their wings, swirled around and around with the music. Kay's gift for the baby was a tiny hand-embroidered robe from China, with little silk slippers to match.

"This is fun," I said to Marilyn as she held up each outfit for inspection. "Aren't you excited?"

"Excited, scared, impatient, eager . . . ," she confirmed, and the other women laughed.

"Don't forget tired," someone reminded her, one of Marilyn's friends with a platter of little frosted cakes that looked like baby blocks.

Another friend, who had been working in the kitchen, pulled a chair into the circle next to Sylvia. "Hi, I'm Julia," she said.

Sylvia smiled and shook her hand. "Hello, I'm Sylvia," and, nodding toward me, she said, "and this is my daughter, Alice."

"Hi," Julia said, smiling at me. "Yes, I see the resemblance," she added, looking back at Sylvia again. Then, "I'm glad we moved the shower here. When your back hurts, you just seem to hurt all over," and she made room for still another woman to join the circle.

I sat flushed with . . . what? Surprise? Astonishment? Was I offended that Sylvia had claimed me as her daughter? As much as I'd always wanted her to marry Dad, there was a part of me that held back, that told me I belonged to Mom. I tried hard to concentrate not on how I thought I *should* feel at that moment, but on how I truly did feel. And I was pleased.

Did we have to go on saying *stepdaughter* and *stepmother* forever? I could never deny my true mother, never remove her picture from my dresser or forget the few years I had with her, but if Sylvia wanted me to be the daughter she never had, then whenever I was with Sylvia, she could call me her daughter. And I found I was smiling.

I handed Marilyn each gift and helped unwrap them if they were large, stacking them all behind her when she was ready for the next one. When the last present had been opened and I was gathering up wrapping paper, Marilyn asked, "Alice, would you mind going up to our bedroom and bringing me a little green pillow to go behind my back? You may have to hunt—I use it during the night, and it could be under the covers or even under the bed—a small flat pillow. Top of the landing to your left."

"Sure," I said, getting up and stepping over boxes. I went up the short flight of stairs and into the bedroom on the left.

It felt sort of strange walking into a couple's bedroom. I turned on a lamp on their nightstand. The bed was unmade, the covers awry. The usual bedroom scene—a T-shirt hung over the closet's doorknob, a pajama bottom and shoe on the rug. I looked around for the pillow but didn't see it, so I crouched down and found it poking out from under the bed, just as Marilyn had guessed.

As I stood up again to turn off the lamp, I hesitated. The drawer of the nightstand was slightly ajar, and it occurred to me that if I just took a peek, no one would ever know. It wasn't as though I had come into Marilyn and Jack's bedroom as a spy. But people often kept their most intimate stuff in their nightstands, and it was normal to be curious, wasn't it? It would only take a second to peek.

But I didn't. Marilyn had trusted me to go into her bedroom as an adult, and I wanted to come out the same way. As my fingers groped for the light switch once more, I took one last look at the bed. Both pillows were there in the middle, touching, sort of turned toward each other, as though Jack and Marilyn were used to talking together in the night. It gave me a happy feeling, and I was still smiling a little as I went downstairs and tucked the pillow behind Marilyn's back.

There was an empty chair beside Sylvia, and she was holding a little dessert plate of cream puffs.

"I know you like these, so I saved some while I could," she said, handing it to me.

"Thanks, Mom," I said, and sat down beside her. We grinned at each other, and she patted my knee.

Jack came in a little later, a light dusting of snow on his cap and sprinkled in the dark stubble of his face. He went around the room greeting the women, hugging the ones he knew. Someone begged him to take a plate and join in, but Jack said he had a present first for his wife. Then he brought out his guitar and sang a song he had composed for their baby. He said he was performing it for the first time here at the shower, the first time Marilyn had heard it too:

"Been waitin' for you, baby child,
Wonderin' when you'd come.
Mama gettin' bigger,
Pacing to and from.

Bedroom's been all painted,
Car seat's set to go;
Daddy's growing restless,
Mama gettin' slow.

Once you're here, we'll hold you,
Kiss your downy head,
Count each chubby finger,
Keep you dry and fed.

Breathe upon my shoulder,
Sleep upon my chest.
You're the little sweetheart
Gonna make us blest."

When he had finished and strummed the final soft chords, we all had tears in our eyes, and Marilyn reached over to hug him.

"It's so beautiful, Jack. So beautiful!" she kept saying, and the woman named Julia made us laugh by passing around a box of tissues.

Jack broke into a lively song next, as the women gradually started straightening up the living room, gathering coffee cups and plates to wash, collecting the gift bows. Sylvia and I worked side by side, and it felt incredibly good.

I couldn't put it off any longer. I had to give Mrs. Rosen an answer. For a week my mind had toyed with the same dull phrases, and then, like a balky horse, it just stopped working. *The ivy grows / it climbs ever upward, / reaching higher.* So what? Nothing profound about that. *The ivy in the early spring / is colored like the evergreen . . .* A thousand yucks.

I delayed gathering up my stuff at the end of class on Monday and waited till everyone else had gone.

"Mrs. Rosen," I said, "I've been thinking it over, and I just don't feel I'm the right person to compete for Ivy Day Poet."

"I know others have felt the same way, Alice. Are you sure you don't want to try for it?"

"I'm sure," I said. "I really don't. But I appreciate your thinking of me. And I hope you get a great poem."

I called Les that weekend to see how things were going. His voice sounded tired and pained.

"Paul says it's either him or Andy—one of them has to go," he replied.

"Paul would leave? He actually said that?"

"Not in so many words. He says with her around, everything's changed. No more breakfasts in his shorts. No more gratifying belches with our beers. She tutors, she tells us, but as far as we're concerned, Andy's about as social as a mole. Shuts herself up in that bedroom and even takes her meals in there from what we can tell. Students come in and out occasionally, but even then, her door's closed. Food appears and disappears from the fridge, bathwater turns on and off. Once in a while we get a fleeting glimpse of her in the hallway."

"So what does it matter if you belch or not, if you never see her?" I asked.

"It doesn't feel like home to either of us. She's like a spook when she's around, and all we do is plot to get rid of her."

"But at least you and Paul can go out on the same night."

"Yeah, and don't think we don't take advantage of it. We told her Paul and I each stay home two evenings a week and she stays home for three. She asked why she got the short end of the stick, and Paul said because she was the shortest."

I laughed. "What did she say?"

"I quote: 'You're so full of human kindness, it's coming out your ass.' I think it was meant to be funny."

"Whew!" I said. "The temperature's rising already. Why don't you and Paul just tell her it isn't working out?"

"Because we need to have at least one person here who

knows how to care for Otto in case we get jobs somewhere else. We've both got résumés circulating, and we'd still have to find two other people to take care of Mr. Watts if both of us moved out."

"Of course, the next two people could not only have purple streaks in their hair and hide in their rooms, but they could be making counterfeit money," I said, enjoying myself.

"Not to worry. Nobody else gets a room up here without a shakedown, fingerprints, and an FBI check," Les said.

6

CALL FROM AUNT SALLY

Gwen drove us to school on Monday because her brother was buying another car and she was negotiating the sale of his old one to her.

"I just want to see how this really drives before I commit all my earnings," she said, testing the brakes. Liz and I were glad to give our opinion, which was that any car that ran was a good car.

After we picked up Pamela, Gwen said, "You'll be glad to know that Yolanda's filled out an application to work on the cruise ship. And I think we've talked her out of her little procedure. That's the good news."

"Yay!" we said. "What's the bad?"

"She's trying to talk her boyfriend into applying too."

"Boo!" we hissed.

I went to the newspaper office when we got to school and had barely walked in when Phil said, "There's some protest going on outside the library, Alice. Would you check it out for a story? When Sam gets here, I'll send him down for a photo, if it's worth it."

I had a half hour before first period and had planned to proof a couple of stories, but Phil said he'd do it for me, so I headed for the library. I could see a line of protesters as soon as I turned the corner.

A few of the students were carrying homemade signs: FREE THE CAGED BIRD, read one. BAN BONEHEADS, NOT BOOKS, another. And DON'T CENSOR THE INDIAN'S DIARY.

Now what? I wondered.

The protesters seemed to be mostly juniors, a few sophomores, their faces serious and defiant. The library itself was empty.

"What's up?" I asked a guy, falling in step beside him as he picketed back and forth. "Is the library closed?"

"Close-minded," he said, and pointed to a large sheet of paper they had stuck to the door: NOW RESTRICTED READING. MAKE YOUR VOICES HEARD.

I got out my notebook and wrote down the titles that were listed below: *The Color Purple*; *The Absolutely True Diary of a Part-Time Indian*; *Catcher in the Rye*; *I Know Why the Caged Bird Sings*; *The Kite Runner*; and *The Diary of Anne Frank (Definitive Edition.)*

Through the window of the library, I could see Miss Cummings back in the workroom, peering tentatively out at the gathering crowd. I stopped another girl who was handing printouts to anyone who passed by. "When did this happen? These can't be checked out?" I asked.

"Not without a note from mama," she said. "Some parent wants them removed from the library, so Miss Cummings put them on a restricted shelf. Mrs. Garson would never do something like this. I don't even remember a restricted shelf."

Mrs. Garson, I knew, was on medical leave for a month.

Someone started a chant: "We want books! We want books!"

Sam appeared with his camera. "Any idea what's going on?" he asked me.

I motioned toward the sign on the door. "All those authors are restricted reading. Parent's signature required."

"Are you kidding? Alice Walker? Maya Angelou? What did Maya do to deserve this?"

"Got raped," I said. "Probably some mother doesn't want her daughter to read about it."

"Is this high school or grade school?" Sam murmured, taking a picture, then another of the protesters.

"It's sure not college," I said.

Someone tried the door of the library and found it locked. He rapped on the glass. Miss Cummings was on the phone.

Then Mr. Gephardt was coming down the hall, a puzzled, bemused expression on his face. When the protesters saw him, they began chanting in earnest. "We want books! We want books!"

"Whenever we want," added a loud voice.

"Whenever we want." The crowd took up the chant.

Miss Cummings came to the door of the library, now that she saw the vice principal. She unlocked it.

"What's going on out here?" Gephardt asked her.

Miss Cummings tried to put on a brave front. "I think this must be about the books I've placed on the restricted shelf, waiting a final decision," she said.

"Just because a parent wants them removed from the library doesn't mean that *no* one can read them!" a girl said, speaking above the chants.

Mr. Gephardt looked at the sign. "You took all these out of circulation?" he asked the librarian.

"Only until a decision is reached. I promised the parent," Miss Cummings said hesitantly.

"Let's go inside," he said, and followed her back to her office.

While Sam took a few more photos and I made some notes, the students milled around, making up new chants, and Mr. Gephardt came back in five minutes. "A simple misunderstanding," he said. "We have a procedure in place for anyone making a complaint, and the parent will have to come back and put it in writing. Then it goes before a faculty committee. But for now, I think you'll find those books back where they were."

I figured the answer would be something like that, but everyone cheered. Actually, I think they would have preferred a larger battle. The leaders looked a little crestfallen, reminding me a bit of myself in earlier semesters.

"It just goes to show that we keep fighting the same battles," said Phil when Sam and I got back to the newsroom.

"Yeah, but maybe it's a good thing that each class learns something from the one before," I said. "Last year it was us having a protest march because a parent complained about Mrs. Cary. Remember?"

"Yeah. Wonder what we'll protest when we get to college," said Sam.

"The food," said Phil. "What else? Start with food and work your way up to Wall Street."

Wouldn't you know, Aunt Sally called that very night? She likes to make sure we're all living and breathing and eating our vegetables. When she promised my mom she'd take care of us, she'd meant what she said. Never mind that Dad married again and Les lives in an apartment and I'll be going away to college soon; Aunt Sally keeps her word.

"Hi, Aunt Sally," I said. "How much snow did you get in Chicago so far?"

"Oh, it's not as bad as last year," she said. "How are things in Maryland, dear? I haven't heard from anyone since Christmas."

"We're doing fine," I told her. And added, "Lester's living with a woman now, you know."

Why do I do these things? Aunt Sally cared for us for a long time. She washed our clothes and cooked our meals and braided my hair, and I still can't resist the urge to set her off.

I started counting the seconds of silence. Finally Aunt

Sally said, "Just tell me this, Alice. Has she reached the age of consent?"

"Oh, she's beyond that," I said. "I think she's in grad school."

"Did he choose her for her looks?"

"Not likely," I said.

"Her body?"

"Doubtful."

"Is she wealthy?"

"Not at all."

"Are we talking about the same person—your brother Lester?" she asked.

"One and the same."

"Then she must be quite a catch," Aunt Sally said.

"Oh, he's not chasing her," I said. "They're not even sleeping in the same room." And then I stopped tormenting her. "They're just roommates. She's moved into George's room."

Aunt Sally gave a long, loud sigh of relief. "Well, tell me what's going on in your world, Alice," she said.

"For one thing, I covered a protest today," I said.

"Good heavens, what was that all about?"

I told her about book censorship and the restricted shelf, the people with signs and chants.

Aunt Sally listened quietly, and then she said, "Alice, you have pierced ears, don't you?"

I wondered if I'd heard right. *"What?"*

"In the future take off your earrings before you go to a protest. It's important!" Her voice was grave.

"Why?" I croaked. "No one's against earrings."

"Earlobes can get torn in protest marches. I read that women should always remove their pierced earrings if they take part in riots."

"It wasn't a riot, Aunt Sally," I told her. "I guarantee there isn't a person in school who wants books banned from the library. We're all on the same page."

"Oh." There was another sigh from Aunt Sally. "Alice," she said finally, "did you ever feel that you were out of step with all the women who came before you, the women who were the same age, and the women who came after?"

I thought about that a minute. "I'm only seventeen, Aunt Sally. I guess I haven't."

"Well, I have, and I do. When my mother used to tell us about the twenties, I could never understand why women would want to bob their beautiful hair. When I became a woman, I couldn't understand how some of us wanted to burn our bras. And now I can't understand why girls who are crazy enough to punch holes in their ears would risk having their earlobes torn off by taking part in a riot."

I sort of ached for my aunt just then. I guess I always do when she gets personal and lets me in on her world a bit.

"Aunt Sally," I said, "I probably won't ever understand the world that you and Mom grew up in, but I love you for it just the same. How's Uncle Milt?"

"Not so good, Alice," she said. "He takes so many medications he hardly has room for lunch. And he's slower than he used to be. He says that everyone walks too fast, talks too fast, eats too fast, and he can't keep up."

"Well, give him an extra hug from me," I told her.

"We need all the hugs we can get," Aunt Sally said.

The next day I was coming out of a restroom stall just before first bell when I heard someone vomiting in the handicapped stall at the end of the row.

As I washed my hands at the sink, I studied the stall in the mirror and realized there were two people in it. I was drying my hands when the stall door opened partway and Karen came out for a paper towel. She moistened it at a faucet and, with a secretive glance at me, took it back inside. A moment later Jill came out and rinsed her mouth at the sink.

When she stood up at last and wiped her mouth, I saw her eyes fasten on me in the mirror.

"You guessed it," Jill said. "I'm pregnant."

I stared. "Oh . . . wow! I—I'm—"

"She's happy!" Karen explained. "Don't be sorry."

"Well, I . . ." I didn't know what to say.

But Jill had a satisfied look on her face. "It's all part of the plan," she said.

7
A PIVOTAL MOMENT

I couldn't believe what I was hearing. All I could manage to say was, "Well . . . when is it due?"

"September, I figure," Jill said, cupping her hand under the faucet again, then splashing water into her mouth.

I don't know how anyone can look gorgeous right after she's barfed, but Jill did. Cheekbones, hair, figure, everything done up neatly in a package of denim and rose-colored wool.

Karen was grinning. "Nine months from the night of the Snow Ball. The way she looked in that dress, Justin couldn't help himself."

It could have been nine months from almost any time at all, because Jill and Justin had been having sex for years. I started to ask about college, but I knew how ridiculous that was now.

The first bell rang, but I didn't make any move to leave, and neither did they. Jill fished a little bottle of mouthwash from her bag, took a sip, and rolled it around in her mouth before spitting it out.

"Well . . . I guess congratulations are in order, then," I said, sounding too nerdy for words. Nothing I ever say to Jill and Karen sounds smart and sophisticated. But I was still too curious to leave. They hung out with my crowd occasionally—often came to the Stedmeisters' pool with the gang when we'd gathered over the summer. But Jill and Karen had their own inner circle of friends here at school, and I never had felt welcome in that. Yet here they were, letting me in on a secret.

"Justin knows?" I asked. Stupid comment number two.

"Duh!" said Jill. "My mom said once that she didn't really start to show till the sixth month, so I can probably hide it till May. If Justin's folks agree to a church wedding, fine. If they won't, we'll go to a justice of the peace. One way or another, we're getting married right after graduation. We'll both be eighteen by this summer, and then Justin will have access to the trust fund his grandfather left him."

"But . . ." I winced. "From all you've told us, won't his parents be furious?"

Jill gave a little laugh. "Of course! But Mr. Collier has always wanted a grandchild. A boy, preferably, to take over the business. Justin's their only child, and this baby may be the only grandchild he's going to get. Justin thinks they'll come around." She glanced at her watch. "Jeez. Lab day. All those chemicals.

See ya." And she headed for the stairs and the science labs below, arm in arm with Karen.

Gwen and Liz and Pamela and I sat at a corner table at lunch-time. It was sleeting out, and the halls still had muddy traces of boots tramping, bringing in the damp. All we wanted to talk about, of course, was Jill and Justin. It was obviously not a secret any longer, because Pamela had already heard, and I think the reason Jill told me was so I would spread it around. I figured that Jill wouldn't mind if the word reached the Colliers, if Justin didn't get up the nerve to tell them first. The sooner Jill could start planning her wedding, the better.

"I just can't understand it," I said. "I believe in planned parenthood, but *this* . . . !"

"Desperate people do desperate things," said Liz. "I think they were simply sick of all the fighting with Justin's parents and decided that having a baby would settle the whole thing."

"But to put a *baby* in the middle of that mess?" I said. "It's only going to add more tension."

"And a mother-in-law who hates you like poison," said Gwen. "Who wants to start a marriage with all that baggage?"

"I didn't even know that Jill wanted a baby," said Pamela.

"She wants Justin," said Liz. "Who wouldn't?"

We pondered that for a while over our grilled cheese. "Isn't it weird that you can't drive a car until you've taken lessons and passed a test, but you can have a baby without any preparation at all?" Gwen said. "Even murderers and child abusers can have babies, and nobody stops them until something happens."

"But how do you ever know you're ready to be a mother?" I asked. "I still feel sometimes like I need to be taken care of myself, and if I'm a mom, *I'm* supposed to be in charge. What if my baby got really sick or something? I'd be a basket case. I'm not the least bit brave."

"But sometimes we find out we're a lot braver than we think," said Gwen.

I wondered what Pamela was thinking during our conversation. About her own miscarriage. About Tim. About the two of them miraculously dodging the bullet. About how a baby is a blessing for some couples, but for others, it's a bullet.

On Saturday, Kay hung up her down jacket in the storeroom and let out a prolonged sigh. Then she realized I was back at the mailing table and gave me a wan smile. "Sorry."

"For what? Sounded like something that needed to come out," I said.

"It was the sigh of a half-deranged daughter who has upset her parents and, according to them, shown them the greatest disrespect."

"They still want you to meet this guy, huh?"

"I did! I went home for dinner." Kay sat down on a folding chair and tucked her hands beneath her thighs, shoulders stooped.

"How did it go?"

"Awkward. Very, very awkward. I'm convinced James could tell I didn't want to be there. My parents certainly could."

"What's he like?"

"Mr. Great Stone Face, that was him. I'm sure he's got the same mind-set as my dad, that I'm supposed to be the dutiful daughter and marry whomever Dad says. Oh, the room was full of artificial smiles, mine included. Frozen smiles. I tried not to look at him and let my dad do most of the talking. I asked James once how long he planned to be in the States, and he said he didn't know. Then Dad asked if I was going to have a free weekend soon so we could show our guest around the capital, and I said *I* didn't know. All Mom did was sip her tea and stare right through me for not helping out more with the conversation."

"Is he staying at your parents' place?"

"No. Some hotel. He's supposedly here as a consultant for some networking firm. That's the story, anyway."

"Interesting," I said. "There's a girl at school who's going all out to marry her longtime boyfriend, but his parents are against it; and you're giving it all you've got *not* to marry someone your folks like."

"So what all has she tried?" Kay asked.

"She just got pregnant. That's the latest."

"Great. I'll find some guy to impregnate me, and then neither my parents nor James will want me," said Kay.

Wouldn't it be wonderful if we could shift problems around? I was thinking. I'll take yours for a day, you take mine? On the other hand, the biggest problem I had faced in the last few weeks was saying no to Mrs. Rosen, so I wouldn't want to trade places with Lester or Kay. And I certainly wouldn't choose to trade places with Jill.

On the first Monday in February, Drama Club had its first meeting of the semester. Everyone comes to this one—both backstage and onstage members—because it's the first announcement of the spring production. Last year it was a musical, so this time it would be a play. That's how our school does it—we alternate. I hoped it would be something exciting or racy or funny or wild. *Noises Off*, maybe, or *A Streetcar Named Desire*.

Mr. Ellis smiled as he held up a manila envelope, like this was the Academy Awards or something. "As you know," he said, "we strive for variety in our spring productions, and every so often we do a period piece—always popular with the community."

Our faces dropped. We knew we needed ticket sales to keep the productions going, and we needed to have the community behind us. But period pieces didn't raise the heartbeat much.

"Last year," Mr. Ellis continued, "we did *Guys and Dolls*, with a lot of scene changes. This year we'll have only one set to worry about—the living room of a Victorian house. It has a lot of features, though: a stairway with a landing, two doors, a window, wallpaper, the works. It's a family story."

"What's the name?" someone asked.

Ellis reached into the envelope and pulled out a green script book. "*Cheaper by the Dozen*," he said. "An old favorite."

Most of us had heard of it, but some hadn't, so Mr. Ellis explained that it was the story of Frank Gilbreth, a motion study engineer back in the twenties, who believed that the same time-saving methods he devised for factories in World War I could be used in the home with his twelve children. A comedy. Well, at least it wasn't *Our Town*.

Ellis passed out scripts so we'd be familiar with the play. Mrs. Cary, the speech teacher, would be designing the set.

I figured I'd be on props again, but I didn't want to be in charge and was glad when a guy named Joel volunteered. Those of us on stage crew read off the list of things we had to find for this play—stopwatch, umbrella, large floppy hat—and when we came across *flimsy underwear*, Joel said, "I'll get that one," and we laughed.

I'd tucked my copy of the script in my backpack and was preparing to leave when Mrs. Cary came over. "You've worked on props before, Alice. How would you like to be on my set design committee? Love to have you."

"Sure," I said. Why not? It would be something new. I didn't have to say no to *everything*.

Seniors began forming themselves into separate crews—props, lighting, set, sound—our last chance to strut our stuff; and the lower classmen waited around to be chosen for a crew. If we went into theater in college, we'd be at the bottom of the totem pole again.

The play was officially announced the next day during morning announcements, and a list of the characters, with a brief description of each, went up on the door of the dramatic arts room, along with the dates for tryouts. Other students could sign out a script overnight, and that afternoon there was a swarm of students waiting outside the classroom.

Pamela called me that evening and said she was going to audition for the part of Ernestine, the second-oldest daughter.

"Is she the one who wears the flimsy underwear?" I asked.

"What? Oh, man, I hope so!" Pamela said excitedly. "Where did you hear that?"

I laughed. "Someone mentioned it at the meeting yesterday."

"I'll read the whole script tonight," Pamela said. "But I noticed that Ernestine and Frank Jr. open the show. Don't you love it? The curtain opens and there I am! I want to talk Liz into trying out for one of the other five daughters."

"Who's trying out for the part of Frank Jr.?" I asked.

"Somebody hot, I hope," Pamela said.

"He's supposed to be your brother, Pamela."

"So?" she said. And laughed.

I'd scanned the script a few times, trying to picture the stage set in my mind, the way it was described, but I was feeling strangely unsettled. When I detected the scent of cinnamon in the air, I knew that Sylvia was making Dad's favorite snack. She takes a piece of thinly sliced bread, butters both sides, sprinkles them with cinnamon and sugar, and then browns each side in the toaster oven, just enough to melt the butter and caramelize the sugar a little. I didn't know if I was more hungry for cinnamon toast or for company, but I went downstairs and joined them in the kitchen.

"Somehow I knew you'd be down, so I made some extra pieces," Sylvia said, pushing the plate toward me.

I poured a glass of milk and sat down across from her.

"Homework all done, or are you taking a break?" Dad asked.

"I'm actually done for a change." I bit into the warm toast and savored the buttery taste. "Sylvia," I said, "when you think about your senior year, what was your favorite time? The most exciting thing you did?"

She thought about that a minute. "I guess I'd have to say it was the solo I sang in the choir concert. It's the first thing that comes to mind, anyway. I worried I'd get a cold or something, but after I sang the first couple of notes, I knew I was going to be fine." She shrugged. "I don't know where it came from, but I really sang beautifully." I was surprised to see her blush a little. "Now, didn't *that* sound conceited."

"Not at all," Dad told her. "I don't know why people who do things well can't just say so."

"Was it the singing itself or the applause that made it special?" I asked.

"Both. Obviously, if I'd been singing in the shower and nobody heard it, it wouldn't have been nearly as exciting. But . . . well, it wasn't quite a standing ovation, but I could tell by the applause afterward that I'd done well."

I smiled and looked at Dad. "What about *your* best moment?"

"Next to kissing Joanna Lindstrom, you mean?" We laughed.

"Probably the game against North High. I was a second-stringer on the basketball team, and one of our players fouled out, so I was put in for the last six minutes or so. I wasn't anything great—not like Ed Torino, who got the three-pointers. But it was the next-to-last game of the season and we were tied—the usual story. Ed missed a jump shot, we had about thirteen seconds left, and I retrieved the ball. I jumped and put it in."

"Wow!" I said.

"The crowd went nuts. Of course, North High could have made another shot in those last seconds, but they didn't. Everyone was pounding me on the back and yelling my name and crowding around me, and it was like . . . I don't know. It wasn't that my shot won the game, because everyone's basket counted. Just that mine was the last shot, so I got the glory. Silly, but that was my big moment, something I'll always remember."

They both turned to me. "What about you?" they asked.

"Well, I still have a semester to go," I said. "It's not any one thing. I like it when people comment on my feature articles."

"And well they should! They're excellent!" Sylvia said.

"And they have depth. You always have something to say," Dad told me.

I half sat, half lay on my bed, surrounded by pillows, swathed in a fleece blanket, with the script of *Cheaper by the Dozen* in my hands. It wasn't racy, like *Guys and Dolls*. It wasn't heartrending, like *Fiddler on the Roof*. But it was funny, had its poignant moments, was based on a real family, and I certainly knew about family.

I opened the green script again, and this time I felt my mouth drying up, my pulse racing. I read each page hurriedly, then found myself going back and reading them again. I leaned back against the pillows and closed my eyes.

I started to reach for my cell phone, then stopped. Reached for it again and put it in my lap, breathing out of my mouth, my heart thumping.

Finally I punched in Pamela's number, and when she answered, I said, a quaver in my voice, "Pamela, tell me if I'm crazy, but I'm going to try out for the part of Anne."

8
GETTING READY

A long squeal came through my cell phone.

"Alice! That would be so cool! If Liz got the part of Martha, we could all be the older sisters and—"

I laughed. "I didn't say I was getting the part. I said *maybe* I'd try out for it."

"No, you didn't!" Pamela said fiercely. "You didn't say 'maybe.' You *are* going to try out for it. This will be great. We could all go to rehearsals together, the cast party . . ."

I got that sinking feeling. Wasn't this just like our old dream of going to the same college, getting married the same summer, helping raise each other's kids?

"To tell the truth, I'm scared half out of my wits," I told her.

"Alice, this might be our last chance to do something like

this ever again," came the determined voice over the phone.

"Did you see the crowd waiting for scripts this afternoon?" I asked.

"So? Not all of them want to be Anne."

"What if I bomb? I've never done acting, even in grade school."

"What do you mean? You were in the sixth-grade play with me."

"I was a bush, Pamela. A bramble bush, and you were Rosebud, tripping around the stage in a long dress, singing."

"Well, nobody has to sing in this play, and if you don't try out, I'll kick your butt," said Pamela. "Hard! How's that for motivation? And besides," she added, and I could hear the change in her voice, "if you try out for Anne, *you* get the flimsy underwear."

That made me laugh. "She doesn't *wear* it, though."

"I know. If she did, *I'd* be trying out for the part."

I lay staring into the darkness long after I'd turned out the light. I shouldn't have told Pamela. Now I'd really committed myself. How would my audition go? What would Ellis ask me to do? Was I really going to audition in front of other people or could it be private? Omigod. I'd already told Mrs. Cary I'd work on set design with her. How was I going to get through the next week when I was so miserable already?

Most of the talk at school was about the sock hop that coming Friday, but among seniors, the buzz was about who was trying out for the play and predictions on who would be chosen for each part. Seniors always got priority. A few people, like Pamela, were candid about the roles they wanted, but most of us held back and said, "Oh, I don't know. I'm just going to tryouts and see what happens."

Wednesday evening, when Dad and Sylvia were out to dinner with friends, I took over Dad's big armchair in the family room, wrapped in a robe and a blanket, and carefully reread all of Anne's lines.

It was the story of a teenage girl's relationship with her father. In some ways I was like Anne, and in some ways I wasn't at all. She was the oldest child in her large family; I was the youngest in my small one. She was from a wealthy background, her father famous in his field. Mine wasn't rich at all, and except for musicians in the Washington area and our friends at church and in the neighborhood, no one except relatives knew of Dad outside of Silver Spring.

We were alike, though, in that Anne had to be the trendsetter, the scout, the pathfinder for her siblings. She had to pave the way for wearing lacy underthings and silk stockings and for having a boyfriend. I didn't have any sisters, but I had to fight my own battles. And while both Anne and I loved our fathers and knew they loved us, they could be so stubbornly old-fashioned at times.

I remembered how, after Dad saw Patrick kissing me once on the front porch in the dark, he always had the porch light on after that when I was out with Patrick during junior high school. I remember how I had to argue and argue with him to go to a coed sleepover. Strange how life turns out sometimes. We ended up having the coed sleepover here at our house. And that was the night of the fake kiss between Patrick and Penny.

The more I thought about it, Anne's disobedience in buying underwear her dad disapproved of wasn't much compared to my riding on the back of a motorcycle with a guy I didn't know, and even that was mild. So yes, I knew how desperately Anne felt about the rules in her household, the way her father interfered in what she wanted to do and where she wanted to go, even though her story took place in the 1920s.

I was breathing through my mouth again, and I felt the strange thumping in my chest. I realized that I wanted to play the part of Anne in this play in my senior year almost more than anything I'd ever wanted.

Being on the props committee, standing behind the curtain and waiting for a scene to end so I could replace breakfast dishes with a book and reading glasses, didn't make my heart race. Coming onstage with the rest of the crew for a curtain call, all of us dressed in black, wasn't something people would remember me for.

I didn't want to be the girl behind the curtain helping Pamela change costumes, or the girl in the gym cheering Liz on as she played Stupefyin' Jones, or the friend in the auditorium clapping for Gwen getting her scholarship award—proud as I was of all of them. For once in my life, *I* wanted to be center stage, the spotlight on *me*. *I* wanted to be the one the audience was applauding.

But my chances! Charlene Verona could probably get the part of any character she tried out for. I'd seen a couple of cheerleaders waiting in line for a script. *Face it, Alice!* I told myself. *The odds are against you. Understand that!* I did. I think. It was just that I was burning bridges behind me. I'd said no to Mrs. Rosen about trying out for class poet. I was about to say no to Mrs. Cary for set design.

I closed my eyes and took another deep breath. *Just do it!* I told myself. *Get up there and take a chance.* If my only big accomplishment in high school was features editor of the paper, that wasn't so bad. I was doing this for me. I'd made a decision and, right or wrong, it was mine.

Beside the tryout schedule posted on the door of the dramatic arts classroom, there was a sign-up sheet. Auditions would start the following Monday.

I wished I could just concentrate on Anne's lines over the weekend, but Phil had assigned me to cover the dance Friday night. Seniors seemed divided between those who wanted to squeeze in every possible activity they could to remember always and those who were losing interest in high school stuff. Some who had already been accepted for admission had even sent away for college sweatshirts! Gwen was going somewhere with Austin but said they might drop in later. So Pamela and Liz and I went together in the matching poodle skirts Mrs. Price had sewn for us. Poodle skirts and saddle shoes, our hair in the strange pompadour style of the fifties that Sylvia helped us with.

The junior class had done the decorating this time, and Sam was taking pictures, of course. The school had rented a jukebox with a Plexiglas window so you could watch vinyl records drop onto a turntable for the next song.

The cheerleaders were there in their own poodle skirts, demonstrating the jitterbug and getting people to try it. There was even an Elvis Presley impersonator sitting at the wheel of a '57 Chevy, waving to people, then getting out and strolling around the gym, signing autographs as though he were really Elvis.

Amy Sheldon arrived with two other girls, and though her "Hi, Alice!" could be heard halfway around the gym, I waved and laughed along with her when Elvis gave her a hug as he made another tour of the gym.

"Do you know what I feel like?" Liz asked as we circled the dance floor for the third time, looking for people we knew. "I feel like somebody's mother, here to chaperone. I used to be wild for things like this. And it *looks* like fun, but . . . What's the matter with us, Alice? Have we suddenly grown too old for this?"

"Speak for yourself," said Pamela.

"Maybe it's just overload, everything piling up on us at once. Are you trying out for the play?" I asked Liz.

She shrugged. "I might. But it's no big deal if I don't get a part."

I guess that was a major difference between us. For me, it was. I wanted to be tested. I didn't want to go on dreading things like this forever.

There were little tables off to the side of the gym where people could sit down, and a couple of girls on roller skates with rubber wheels came out of a shed, taking orders for root beer floats.

Penny was at a side table with one of the cheerleaders and waved us over to join them, so we ordered floats too.

"Isn't this fun?" the cheerleader said. "The decorations committee did a great job. But it was one of the sophomore dads who got the Chevy for us."

Penny, as always, looked great. She probably wears size two jeans, and she paired them with a short-sleeved sweater with a Peter Pan collar, fifties-style. I wondered if I would ever get to the place where I could look at Penny without feeling even an ounce of jealousy. Sometimes I felt I was *almost* there, but not quite.

The fact that Patrick had once—for a while, anyway—liked her best . . . liked her, held her, kissed her . . . would always keep us a little distance apart, like two polarized magnets, I suppose. If it weren't for that, we might be close friends.

"Do you ever wish you lived back in the fifties, when they had drive-in root beer places and drive-in movies?" Liz asked.

"My grandmother says life was a lot simpler," Penny told us. "Girls were either 'good girls' or 'bad girls,' and basically they had four career choices—secretary, housewife, nurse, or teacher—though if you were really adventurous or talented, you could become an airline stewardess or an actress."

"Yeah, but you got to wear these cute poodle skirts and dance to Frank Sinatra and Bobby Darin," I joked.

"Or be one of the girls who marched with the ROTC and carried a flag," said Liz.

"Hey, you can still be the lucky girl who gets to be the Ivy Bearer on Ivy Day," said the cheerleader, rolling her eyes. "Or even the Ivy Day Poet! Whoopee! Mom says they had that ceremony when *she* went to our school. Somebody left an annuity or something, and we have to do it."

I took a deep breath. Close call.

About an hour into the evening, the jukebox stopped playing and the junior class president made a short announcement. He said that "The Shack" would be selling hot dogs for the next twenty minutes and that the dance committee had worked up a special combo to play during that time.

"Combo?" said Liz.

"A band," the cheerleader explained. "Oh, here they come."

We watched some guys cross the floor with their instruments—saxophone, clarinet, the same instruments people played in the fifties—but there, walking along with them, was Daniel Bul Dau, our Sudanese student who's been in the United States for only eight months or so.

"Hey, Daniel!" Liz and I yelled.

The tall, thin guy with the high cheekbones looked our way, smiling, and when his eyes found us, he grinned.

He took his place with the others on a glittering makeshift bandstand, and for the first two numbers he didn't do much, mostly sat with the school drummer, his own drum between his knees, and accompanied a little. But when they started a third number—I didn't know what kind of dance it was, a Latin beat, I guess—he began drumming out his own rhythm as an accompaniment.

As the music went on, his fingers began to fly on the drumhead, a complicated beat that none of us could identify. We couldn't even copy it. The other musicians just grinned and shook their heads. Daniel grinned too and went on playing, his rhythm intricately bound up with the music. At one point the other guys stopped entirely and let him have the spotlight. Students gathered around to watch. It was a rhythm all his own, and Daniel played with his eyes closed now, his head tilted back in concentration, his fingers just a blur over the drum.

It was as though his hands were playing two different rhythms at the same time. Sweat broke out on his forehead, and his head began to nod in time with the beat. Daniel was off in Sudan somewhere far away, and we could hear, through his drumming, his missing of home.

9
READING FOR MR. ELLIS

I did want to hear how things were going with Lester, though, so on Sunday morning, after I'd done my homework, read over Anne's lines again, and plucked my eyebrows, I finally called him. Too late, I discovered I'd punched in his apartment phone instead of his cell.

"Hello," said a low voice, and it wasn't Lester's or Paul's.

"This is Alice. Is Les in?" I asked.

"Hold on," said Andy.

I could tell Les was grumpy the moment he said hello.

"How are things?" I said.

"Don't ask," he told me. "I'll call you back on my cell," and he hung up.

A few minutes later he called.

"Where are you? Barricaded in your room with your dresser against the door?" I asked.

"One of the worst mistakes I ever made, not checking Andy out before she got here," he said. "She's not only a recluse, but when she *does* come out, she's got to be the pushiest female I ever met. She never says, 'Would you mind turning the TV down?' She waits till you go get a beer, then turns it down for you. Throws out any food over the sell-by date. Suddenly the corned beef you were saving for those last two pieces of rye bread is gone. And she'll make a grilled cheese for herself with the bread. You don't take your clothes out of the washing machine, you'll find them in a bucket. She wouldn't think of tossing them in the dryer for you. Whatever Andy wants, it seems, Andy gets, including a rent-free apartment with the jackass who let her in."

"That would be me," I said. "I opened the door."

"You know what I mean. The advertisement I wrote without mentioning gender and letting her go meet Mr. Watts. I refer to her as Nurse Ratched because she thinks she knows what's best for us, but Paul calls her Mother Superior because of the mystical way she eats our corned beef or throws our clothes in a bucket without our ever seeing her do it."

"Well, maybe you'll be moving yourself one of these days," I said to console him. "Any interviews yet?"

"Only one, and you wonder why they bothered. I've got a major in philosophy, a minor in psychology, and I'm looking for a job working with people, I tell them. So I get there, and what do they want me to do? Digitalize all their records."

"Well, it's a job," I say.

"I'll stick with the university till I get something more my line," he said.

"Meanwhile," I told him, "what you need is some fun in your life."

"Yeah, all the babes are in hiding," he said. "Seems like all the girls I used to know have moved away."

"Well, I'm doing something sort of fun," I told him. "I'm going to audition for a part in the spring play."

"No kidding? It's not a musical, is it?"

"No, Les. I don't torture anybody by trying to sing. But there are dozens of other people trying out."

"So you give it your best shot, that's all," he said.

Tryouts for the female roles were scheduled for Monday and Tuesday, male roles Wednesday and Thursday, and the cast would be posted on the door of the dramatic arts classroom Friday morning at eight o'clock. Charlene Verona, the perpetual diva, let it be known that she'd be there "with bells on," as she put it. Petite Penny said she was going to try out for the part of Lillian, the youngest daughter being cast.

As it grew closer and closer to the last bell on Monday, and other names came floating by of people who were trying out, I could feel an uproar in my insides and panicked when I had an attack of diarrhea in the restroom. Never mind expression and diction and whether or not I could memorize the lines. If I couldn't even control my bowels, what business did I have getting onstage at all?

At last I got myself in shape and went out in the hall, where Pamela and Liz were waiting.

"You okay?" Pamela asked.

"No, but let's get it over with," I said.

She grabbed one arm, Liz grabbed the other, and we set out for the dramatic arts room.

"What's the worst that can happen?" Liz asked me. "We don't get parts, that's all. Life goes on. The prom's coming up. College . . ."

Pamela was in her wiseacre mood, though. "No, the worst is that we could all get parts and throw up together onstage."

"Pamela!" Liz scolded.

We passed the water fountain and turned the corner. Just as I suspected, a dozen or more girls were moving through the doorway of the classroom, scripts in hand. From the noise inside, we knew there were even more already there. I heard an audible gasp from Pamela on one side of me, from Liz on the other.

"Oh, Pamela, I don't have a chance," I said, feeling weak in the knees.

She squeezed my arm. "You have as much of a chance as anyone else. Just be yourself."

Why do people always say that? As though anyone's self is everything good, just naturally funny and clever? What if *my* self was mousey, silly, plain, ordinary, and boring?

Only the people actually trying out were permitted inside, so some of the girls had to leave. There were nineteen left. Nineteen girls wanting the same female roles, and there were two days of tryouts. Thirty-eight girls, maybe, wanting parts? The best parts?

We went up to the blackboard, where sheets of paper were taped in a row—one sheet for each of the seven roles: Mother; Miss Brill, a teacher; Mrs. Fitzgerald, the housekeeper; and four of the daughters—Anne, Ernestine, Martha, and Lillian. We were to sign our names under the character we most wanted to play.

The longest lists were for Ernestine and Anne.

I picked up one of the pencils in the chalk tray and signed my name under *Anne*, my eyes roaming the page for the other names on the list. And then my stomach churned in earnest when I saw Jill's name near the top.

I turned, and there she was in the second row, beautiful and demure-looking in a white cashmere sweater.

How could this be? Maybe she wasn't pregnant after all. Maybe she'd had a miscarriage. Maybe the whole rumor was just a big joke, and now that I'd gotten my nerve up to do one of the most difficult things I'd ever done, Jill would do it for me, ten times better.

I wondered if this was how it felt to enter a beauty contest—all the girls smiling at everyone, secretly sizing them up. I wished the auditions could take place in private, just a solitary room where Mr. Ellis could ask me to read a page and then tell me, *Sorry, Alice. I don't think so,* and I could leave without a gaggle of smirking girls watching me go.

We were all sitting in chairs scattered about the room, and there was a lot of nervous chatter. Liz leaned over to whisper, "Is she *serious*? Jill, I mean?"

"Maybe she'll play the mother," said Pamela. "If she's already had a dozen children, what's one more?"

Yeah, right, I thought—as though Jill looked like she'd had a dozen children. And if she wasn't due till September, she'd hardly even be showing by the time of the performances in April.

The door opened and Mr. Ellis came in with Mrs. Cary. *Oh, great!* I thought. Mrs. Cary was going to be in on the casting, and I still hadn't told her I was trying out for a part and wouldn't do set design if I got it. What were my chances now?

Mr. Ellis was carrying a clipboard and the script, and he smiled at all of us.

"Good to see so many of you here," he said, and walked along pulling the sheets of paper off the board, attaching them to his clipboard. "Here's how it works, girls. I'll have two of you reading at a time, maybe even three or four, switching parts around. Don't try to figure out what I'm up to." He grinned. "You'll definitely have a chance to try out for the part you want, but Mrs. Cary and I will be listening and watching for a number of things. The best advice I can give you is to play each part we assign you with as much honesty and feeling as you can."

Charlene read first for Ernestine, the role Pamela wanted, and, as usual, Charlene was good. Very good. I could feel my stomach tightening up for Pamela. Charlene had been taking acting lessons since she was nine, she'd told us once. Pamela gave me a helpless look, but I mouthed *Go, Pam, go!* when it was her turn, and she took the high stool that Charlene had vacated.

"Take it from the top, Pamela," Mr. Ellis said. "I'll read for Frank Jr. Go ahead."

Charlene had cupped one hand to her ear on the first line, but Pamela read it straight, with a touch of nostalgia: "Can you hear the music, Frank? I think it's coming from down the street."

"I thought I heard something else," Mr. Ellis read.

Pamela smiled faintly. "Songs like that make you remember ..."

Mr. Ellis had her read another page, and then he chose a third girl to come up and try out for the same part. Every time a new girl auditioned, we tried to read Mr. Ellis's expression. We watched Mrs. Cary's face. Mrs. Cary smiled encouragingly at everyone, and Mr. Ellis looked pleasant enough. Now and then I detected a smile on his face. Sometimes he dropped his eyes to his lap. But he'd just say, "Good, thank you," after someone read a part, and then he'd call on someone else.

"Alice?" he said at last. "You signed up for the part of Anne."

I got up and took my place at the front of the room, my palms wet, mouth dry.

"Let's try . . . um . . . start at the top of page twenty-five," Mr. Ellis said. "Pamela, read Ernestine's part for now, will you?"

We didn't even exchange looks, afraid it would spook one

of us. In this scene the sisters were arguing with their dad about silk stockings.

Holding the playbook in one hand, Pamela said, "But that's the way everybody dresses today."

And I read, "Boys don't notice when everyone dresses that way."

Ellis, reading the father's part, said gruffly, "Don't tell me about boys. I know all about what boys notice." The rest of the girls laughed.

"You don't want us to be wallflowers?" I read.

"I'd rather raise wallflowers than clinging vines," Mr. Ellis retorted.

I studied the script. It said that I clutched my package with determination. The flimsy underwear package. "I'm *going* to wear these," I said, hugging my script to my chest for moment. "I'll not be a wallflower anymore!"

And Pamela read, "And I'm going to buy silk stockings too!"

"And me!" Mr. Ellis read in a high voice, imitating a younger sister, Martha. Everyone laughed but Pamela and me. We knew enough to stay in character.

"I won't let you out of the house with them!" Mr. Ellis boomed.

He skipped a few lines after that, looking at me and pointing to the bottom of the page: "Listen to me, Anne. When a man picks a wife, he wants someone he can respect."

This was so weird, acting out a scene with a teacher. I was supposed to brush past him then and start up the stairs. But I just read my lines with passion: "They certainly respect me," I said, and my voice quavered a little. "I'm the most respected girl in the whole school. The boys respect me so much, they hardly look at me."

"Come back down here!" Mr. Ellis shouted. "I don't want you wasting your time with a lot of boys: Look at the fun we have right here at home with our projects."

"You don't understand!" I said. "You don't understand at all. I wish your job was selling shoes and you only had one or two children"—*voice rises to a wail*, the script directed—"and neither of them was *me*!"

I wondered if I'd overdone it when I got to the end. Mr. Ellis just smiled and nodded and said, "Okay," and read the next name on the list.

"Jill," he said, "would you come up here and read Anne's part? And, Alice, please read the mother's lines. Page seventy-eight, where the mother enters."

I felt stones in my stomach. *No!* I didn't want to play the mother, especially Jill's mother! I tried to close her out as Jill came up to the front of the room and took Pamela's stool. Tried to ignore the scent of her haunting perfume. That would do Mr. Ellis in, if nothing else.

"Okay, begin," Mr. Ellis said.

Should I play this flatly so he couldn't possibly assign the part to me? I wondered. He had said to play all the parts as well as we could. . . .

I decided to do as he'd asked and took a maternal tone as I read my lines: "Aren't you going to eat any ice cream, dear?"

Jill shook her head and looked petulant. (*Choked*, the script read.) "I don't have much appetite," she said, and there was a trace of anger in her voice.

"Are you worried about the test?" I read.

"The test—and *everything*."

A little further on, when the character discovers that her father has heart trouble and no one told her, Jill put fire into the part. She was the teenager I wasn't.

"Okay," Mr. Ellis said. "Thank you both. Let's move on to the next person."

We waited while Liz read for the part of Martha. Mr. Ellis asked her to read for the mother, too, and Penny was asked to read for three parts—the mother, Lillian, and the housekeeper. Penny seemed to get in the spirit of all three, and everyone laughed, · even Mr. Ellis, when the housekeeper, grumbling over the father's motion study tips for her work in the kitchen, leaves the room muttering loudly, "Lincoln freed the slaves . . . all but one . . . all but one."

Most of us stayed to the end of the audition just to see what the competition was like. As Mrs. Cary stood up to stretch and Mr. Ellis stuck the clipboard in his briefcase, he said, "Check the list tomorrow, girls. Some of you may be called back to read again."

Out in the hall, Charlene said knowingly, "It's a good sign if you get a callback. If you don't, just forget it; you didn't get a part."

And then she added, "I've got to decide between *Cheaper by the Dozen* and a part with the Montgomery Players. They held auditions for *The Wizard of Oz* last week, and I tried out for Glinda. I guess it depends on what part I get here."

It must be great to be so sure of yourself, I thought.

"Well, I only want the part of Anne," said Jill. "I think I could add a lot to the role. She's too passive in the script."

Charlene nodded. "Directors are looking for someone who can take a role and put herself in it. I mean, *anyone* can read words on paper."

Karen had been waiting for Jill in the hall, and as they headed off, I heard Karen ask her, "Do you really think you should go out for this?"

"Why not?" Jill replied. "By afternoon, I'm feeling fine."

I had Sylvia's car—she gets a ride to work when I need it—but I'd promised to get home so she could go to a meeting. Liz was riding with Pam. You shouldn't drive when you're distracted, I know, and when I pulled in our driveway, I was scarcely aware of getting there. Thoughts were ricocheting around in my head like Ping-Pong balls, and I had the feeling I was going to do something impulsive.

Why *not* go in early tomorrow and tell Mr. Ellis that there was something he might want to know, that I didn't mean to be a gossip, but I was sure he wanted the play to be the best it possibly could be. . . .

My hands dropped from the steering wheel into my lap. If I were the drama coach, wouldn't I want to know? Wouldn't any director want to know whether one of the actors might be sick on opening night? If one of the actors was *pregnant*?

Then I thought of the impulsive way I had written up a Student Jury session last semester. Of all the spur-of-the-moment things I'd regretted later.

You don't have to decide this right now, I told myself. *You sure don't have to call him tonight.*

But I knew that tomorrow I would feel the same as I did right now: that Jill might get the part of Anne unless Mr. Ellis knew she was pregnant, and who else was going to tell him?

10
THE LIST

Things look different in the clear light of morning. It wasn't all that bright, actually, but as I lay there, imagining myself going to school early, tracking down Mr. Ellis and telling him Jill was pregnant, I knew I couldn't do it. Shouldn't.

If he *was* going to give Jill the part of Anne—and I would get it only because she was out of the picture—did I really want it by default? And how did I know I was even in the running? Six girls had tried out for Anne's part the first day, and there would be more coming that afternoon.

I didn't have any appetite for breakfast and ate only part of an orange. Was I more disgusted with my impulse to squeal on Jill or with my lack of confidence?

I felt alternately hot and cold as Dad drove me to school and let me off at the north entrance.

"Hope the rest of your day's a little better," he commented as I turned to open my door.

"It shows, huh?" I said.

"A little."

I went to the newspaper room to help Phil decide which photos from the sock hop we should print in *The Edge*.

"Definitely one with Daniel playing his drum," I said. "Ditto for one of the waitresses on roller skates."

When we'd marked the photos for Sam, Phil said, "Saw you got a callback."

I'd just gathered my books and had started to stand up. "What?" I said, dropping back onto my chair again.

"The list for the play. You're on callback. Didn't you check?"

"No! Who else was on it?"

"Uh . . . Penny. Jill, I think. I just walked over to see what everyone else was looking at and saw your name."

"It doesn't mean I'll get a part," I told him, trying to hide my excitement.

"No, but it means you've made an impression," he said. And then, "You know, if you're in the play, you've got to give up yearbook. You can't do the yearbook, the newspaper, and the play, too. That's too much. If you can't read proofs by deadline, you can't be listed on the yearbook staff."

I winced. "It would mean extra work for everyone else if I dropped it, right?"

"Yeah, but I think one of the reporters could fill in. In any case, if you get a part, go for it. You're only a senior once."

"Thanks, Phil," I said, but it unnerved me a little. If I wanted to work on a college paper, being on a high school newspaper *and* the yearbook staff would be a huge plus. But these were safe places for me; I'd already proved I could research, interview, write, edit. Acting was something new. Something entirely different. And scary. Decisions, decisions . . .

I hurried over to the dramatic arts room, where a little crowd had gathered, checking the list. All three of us—Pamela, Liz, and I—were on the callback list, but so were Jill and Charlene and Penny and a few others. And there were still girls waiting to try out.

Pamela came up behind me and gave my arm a squeeze. "Getting closer!" she said. "Fingers crossed!"

There was a smaller crowd at auditions that afternoon, but the atmosphere was even more tense. Jill and Charlene were sitting together this time by the windows, chattering like pros. Eight other girls were trying out, and Mr. Ellis and Mrs. Cary listened to each of them read before any of those on callback were asked to read again. Ellis had Jill read for the parts of both Anne and Miss Brill, and I read for both the mother and Anne.

It wasn't one of Anne's best scenes, and I was disappointed I couldn't do one with more emotion. It was a rather dull scene, actually, which made me feel Ellis didn't much care how I did it. He asked still another girl to read Anne's part twice, and I reluctantly gave her my place. Then he asked me to read again, but not for long.

When he called it a day and said he'd post the list on Friday after the boys' auditions, I hung back. Could he let me read just a little bit more? I wanted to ask. Couldn't I read some of the lines Anne had with Joe Scales, the cheerleader? A few with Larry, the boy she really likes?

But Charlene got to him first, and she and Mr. Ellis were having a serious conversation at the back of the room. I dawdled just a little to see if I should stick around.

"I haven't cast anyone yet," I heard him tell her, "but the school frowns on any one person getting major roles in two productions, so I want you to know that. You had a great part in *Fiddler*."

"But I was only a freshman when I played the part of Tzeitel!" she said. "If I'd known then that I couldn't have a major role in my senior year, I might have refused it."

"Come on, Char," he said. "I don't think so. That was a great part and you were the only one who fit the role that perfectly." He reached for his jacket and slipped one arm in the sleeve. "I haven't made up my mind about anyone yet."

I could tell he was eager to leave, and I figured I could only hurt my chances by begging to read more, so I left the room ahead of them, but my heart was down in my shoes.

Gwen met us after school, and we stopped at a chocolate shop for some Mexican hot chocolate, thick and spicy. The small table had barely enough room for eight elbows and four cups, but we managed. Ordinarily, I love Mexican chocolate, but it tasted bitter today.

I told them what I'd overheard from Ellis, that those who'd had major roles in another performance couldn't expect a big role in this one.

Liz looked at Pamela. "Would that apply to you? Because you were an understudy in *Guys and Dolls*?"

"Understudies don't count," Pamela said. "I already checked."

"Which guys are trying out? Does anyone know?" Gwen asked.

"I heard that Sam was interested," said Liz.

"Sam? Really? He didn't say anything about it to me," I said, but Sam does sort of go in for drama. I used to date him. I should know.

"How many guys' parts are there?" Gwen asked.

"Well, there are nine male roles, so this is a good way to meet guys," said Pamela.

"That's what Mom always tells me," Liz said. "If you want to meet a guy who shares your interests, get involved in things you love."

"Chocolate," I said, looking around the shop. "Don't see any chocolate-loving guys in here."

"Yeah, I hang out at libraries, but I can't say anyone looks at me with lustful eyes in the nonfiction section," said Gwen.

Strangely, I was missing my own mother right then. What wise thing might Mom have said to me about the play? What comforting words would she have for me if Mr. Ellis chose someone else and I lost the one big thing I wanted in my senior year? Would burying myself in Sylvia's arms be the same?

* * *

Patrick phoned me that night.

"How'd it go?" he asked.

"I got a callback, but Ellis had other girls reading too."

"Still, it means he's interested in you. When do the guys try out?"

"Tomorrow and Thursday. Why? Are you sorry you were never in the school play?"

"I would have had to give up eating and sleeping," he said, which was probably true, because Patrick went through four years of high school in three.

I started to ask if he was coming home for spring break, then remembered, with a pang, that "home" for him now was Wisconsin. So I reworded it: "Are you going home for spring break?"

"Yeah. I have to. Mom and Dad want some time with me before I leave for Spain."

"They're not the only ones," I said, then realized how whiny that must sound. So I added quickly, "But I'll have you for the prom."

"Right," he said. And then, "Don't plan for anything after. I'll take care of that."

"Okay," I told him, and liked the sound of it. Liked it very much.

Waiting. That was the worst. There were all sorts of rumors going around—one was that Ellis was choosing the cast based on height. The tallest ones would be the oldest children, and so on. Jill was taller than me. I even heard that Mrs. Cary suggested choosing the cast based on hair color.

I was restless and miserable Thursday evening. The cast list was going up the next day. What would I say, what would I do, if Jill got the part of Anne and I was given the part of her mother? I'd almost rather not be in the play at all.

The four of us—Gwen, Pamela, Liz, and I—went to school early on Friday. There was already a small crowd gathered around the doorway to the dramatic arts room. But the list wasn't posted yet.

I didn't think I could stand it. Jill was there in the crowd, leaning back against Justin, who was nuzzling the side of her face, arms wrapped around her midsection, hands on her belly. Charlene stood with her back to the door as though she was going to read off the names when they came through. Several people were looking out a window at the end of the hall, trying to determine if Mr. Ellis drove a Prius or a Honda and if his car was there yet.

"Remember," Charlene was saying in a voice loud enough for everyone to hear, "at least half of us could be understudies."

That was something I hadn't taken into account. What if I had to learn all the lines for a part, be dressed and everything—two nights a week for two different weekends—and never got to be onstage? Did understudies secretly hope that their leads broke a leg? Is that where the saying came from?

At 7:17, Mrs. Free from the office came down the hall smiling, holding two sheets of paper and a roll of tape.

"Excuse me," she said to the crowd. "If you'll just let me through, I've got some information for you."

We all made room and watched her red-painted nails press down on the first sheet of paper.

"Male roles," someone called out. "Hey, Broderick, you're the dad."

Cheers and backslapping among the guys.

The second sheet of paper went up, and Mrs. Free quickly moved back as students edged forward. I could see between the heads of the two girls in front of me.

Female roles, it read.

Mother: Elizabeth Price.

"Liz!" Gwen shouted.

Anne: Alice McKinley.

I stared, absolutely stunned.

"Omigod! Alice!" Pamela gasped.

Ernestine: Pamela Jones.

We screamed. The parts of Martha and Lillian were given to a junior in my gym class named Chassie and a sophomore, Angela, I didn't know. The part of Miss Brill went to Charlene, and the housekeeper was to be played by Penny.

Below the cast roster was the list of understudies. Jill was the understudy for me.

11
CARRYING ON

I was almost afraid to turn around. The right thing to do, probably, was to hug Jill and say, *Looks like we're a team!* but in all the excitement, I heard a girl's voice saying, "Well . . . shit!" And when I did turn around, Jill was gone.

I was too delighted and shocked to worry about it for long, and when Pamela grabbed Liz and cried, "Mo-ther!" we all broke into laughter.

"We'll be going to rehearsals together and everything!" Pamela said. "Did you ever . . . ?"

"No! I never dreamed it! I can't believe it!" I said.

It was funnier still when Brad Broderick looked around to find the rest of his family, and Pamela and I together yelled, "Daddy!" Everyone laughed, and he came over and hugged us both at the same time, then turned to Liz and said, "Well, Ma, looks like we created quite a clan!"

Sam Mayer got the role of Dr. Burton; Jay, an intense guy from my speech class last year, got the part of Frank Jr., whose dialogue with Pamela opens the play; Tim Moss, Pamela's ex, would play Fred, one of the sons; and a guy I didn't know, Ryan McGowan, from my physics class, won the part of Larry, my crush.

"Looks like *we're* going to get better acquainted," he said, smiling down at me as we studied the list again, checking out all the actors.

"First reading today!" I said, looking at the note at the bottom. *Read for characterization: Friday, February 18, 3:00 p.m.*

All morning people congratulated me on getting a part in the play. "Is that the part you wanted?" some of them asked. And "Were you disappointed you didn't get the part of the mother?" as though if the dad were the star, the mom was also.

"It's exactly the part I wanted," I told everyone, and drifted from class to class in a happy daze.

Mrs. Cary stopped me in the hall, smiling, and said, "I guess you won't be part of the set design crew, Alice. Congratulations!"

"Oh, I'm sorry, but . . . ," I began babbling.

"Of course you're not! You should be excited. It's wonderful!" she said.

I called Dad over the lunch period and told him the news.

"Terrific, Al!" he said. "You think you can handle this now, with all you've got on your plate?"

"Sure," I said, and didn't repeat Patrick's line about how he'd have had to give up eating and sleeping if *he* took on something like this. "I'm giving up yearbook to do this. I'll work it in."

The whole cast, including understudies, was supposed to show up at three o'clock, but Jill wasn't among us. Charlene Verona, though, was there with an announcement. She waited until we were all seated and then, before Mr. Ellis could even start the reading, she said, "I didn't want to leave without explaining, so I just came by to say that I got the second best part in *The Wizard of Oz* with the Montgomery Players, so I'm going to have to give up the part of Miss Brill. If it wasn't for that, I'd have loved to work with all you guys, but I know you'll do a fantastic job. So break a leg, everybody!"

Penny and I rolled our eyes at each other, and we each looked so funny, we almost laughed out loud.

Mr. Ellis smiled a little. "Good luck, Charlene," he said. "Thanks for letting me know." Then he looked at the understudy who had been sitting beside Charlene and said, "Well, Jenny, looks like you're Miss Brill."

Charlene smiled around the circle, picked up her backpack, and even waved to us as she went out the door. People ducked their heads to hide their laughter, and Mr. Ellis began reading stage directions.

Things still seemed unreal. When I went to my locker later, I thought, *When I was a freshman, I never would have believed I'd get one of the lead roles in the play.* I marveled at the coincidence that Pamela and Liz were in it too, even though it wasn't quite the way we had pictured it. Maybe, because we knew each other so well, the familiarity showed in our readings.

Liz had read her lines in the same comforting tone she used with her little brother when he was upset, and Pamela's voice was just right for Ernestine when she related some of the family's funniest memories, like the two noisy canaries—one that the father named "Shut Up" and the other, "You Heard Me."

But the biggest mystery of all: How did I get the part of Anne? Was I really that good at it? Jill had added some anger to the role—more than I had—and that was good, wasn't it? Original? Another girl had played it with more sadness, and that seemed real too. Anne seemed conflicted to me—love for her dad along with dismay and resentment, a subtle mix. Was it possible that this was what Ellis was looking for and that somehow I had pulled it off?

I called Patrick that night.

"Hey!" Patrick said.

"Hey!" I responded. "This is Anne."

There was a moment of silence, and then he yelled, "*Hey! You got it?*"

"Got it."

"Way to go!" Patrick said. "You *did* it!"

"And guess who's my understudy."

"Pamela?"

"No. Jill."

"Huh?" said Patrick. "I don't quite see that."

"I don't either, and neither, evidently, does Jill. She didn't show up at rehearsal. But Pamela got the part of the next-oldest sister, and Liz is the mother. Can you believe it? That all three of us are in the play?"

"You guys hit the jackpot," said Patrick. "Anyone else that I know?"

"Penny as Mrs. Fitzgerald, the housekeeper."

"The *housekeeper*? And what about the guys? Aren't you supposed to have a boyfriend in the play?"

"Yes. A guy in my physics class, Ryan somebody. Sam got a part. So did Tim."

"Uh, let's get back to Ryan. What's he like?"

I laughed. "Are you jealous?"

"Sort of. Is he hot or not?"

"Well . . . yeah. I'd say he is."

"Tall, dark, and handsome?"

"Tall and handsome, anyway. Sort of a brownish blond."

"Hmmm. Maybe I should come back for the play."

"Maybe you should," I said.

When we finally finished our conversation around ten, I reached for the schedule Mr. Ellis had passed around before rehearsal. Every single day except Saturdays and Sundays. Performances Friday and Saturday, April 8, 9, 15, and 16. I had to squeeze the rest of my life into what was left.

The home phone rang around ten fifteen as I was collecting

my papers and books and putting them in my backpack. Dad and Sylvia had already gone to bed, so I hurried out in the hall to pick it up. "Hello?"

At first I didn't think that anyone was there or that someone was playing around with the phone—the fumbling, the breathing, the background noise—but then a man's voice said, "Alice?"

"Yes?"

"It's Jack."

Which character was that? I wondered. It was a voice I knew but couldn't place. Then I realized it was Marilyn's husband.

"Yes?" I said eagerly.

"Just wanted to tell you about our new baby daughter," came his excited but weary voice.

"Oh, Jack! Wonderful! How's Marilyn?"

"More tired than I am, that's for sure, but she and Summer Hope are doing just fine."

Summer Hope. It was so right. So . . . Marilyn!

"What a beautiful name. What's the baby like?"

"Scrunchy-faced and scrawny, but already sucking her fist," he said. "We'll e-mail some photos when we all recover. It was a long labor, but Marilyn's doing fine. I've got a list of people to call, and you and your dad were on it. Just wanted you to know."

New life, I thought as I put down the phone. I guess that's what I was feeling right then. New everything.

When Jill didn't show up at rehearsal on Monday either, Mr. Ellis announced a new understudy for me, someone I didn't know. He gave no reason for Jill dropping out, but on Tuesday, when Jill and Karen condescended to eat with us at lunchtime, Jill explained in an offhand way:

"I'm just going to be too busy planning my wedding," she said.

"Wow! You're really going to do it?" said Liz.

Jill popped a cherry tomato into her mouth, closed her lips to crush it, then leaned back and folded her arms across her chest.

"Of *course* we're going to do it! If the Colliers won't agree to a church wedding, we'll just have a civil ceremony. And I don't think Justin's parents would care for that. They have to do everything up big."

"Have you told them? About the baby?" Pamela asked.

"Justin did last weekend. He said it would be better if I wasn't there, that his mom might say something she'd regret. She freaked out as it was. Kept screaming that she *knew* it, she *knew* I was going to pull something like this, and how did they know the baby was his?"

"She actually *said* that?" Gwen exclaimed.

"Yeah, before Justin's dad shut her up. He said why didn't they all just try to calm down and not make any big decisions for the next month." Jill stared out the window a moment before she picked up her club sandwich and took a bite. Tore at it, really, with her teeth, hardly letting it touch her tongue.

"He's at least trying to be reasonable," Liz said, in her usual soothing manner.

Jill gave a sarcastic laugh. "Yeah, like maybe I'll miscarry or something."

"I thought you said he wanted a grandchild," I reminded her.

"He does. I'm probably not being fair, but he's not wild about me either. It's the witch who runs that household, and he's probably under her spell."

I couldn't help myself. "Jill," I said, "how can you . . . I mean . . . manage with all that hostility? I'd be a wreck."

"Well, we're not moving in with them, that's for sure," she said. "Justin and I love each other, and we're not going to let them break us up. Justin says his dad will support us till he gets through college—he's not worried about that. But his mom will pull every trick in the book to make it hard for us. You can count on it."

We were sprawled on the floor by the window in the hall. The only reason I could figure that Jill and Karen were eating with us was because we had one of the few spaces left. No, I think there was a bigger reason: Jill wanted the largest audience she could get whenever she talked about her wedding. If she couldn't have a zillion bridesmaids, she wanted an envious crowd of enthralled girls listening to her every word, and that was us.

For a minute or so the only noise came from the cafeteria at the other end.

Then Pamela asked, "You're still planning a June wedding?"

"May or June."

"But . . . like . . . won't you be showing?" Pamela asked.

"Probably. A little. But I've already picked out my dress. It's gorgeous," Jill said, and her eyes were alive again. "Lace over satin, neck to hem. We'll make it work. Everyone knows a baby's coming anyway. Justin and I are even going over names:

Isabella Paige and Ethan Alexander." She gave a satisfied smile and took a bite of cookie.

"Do you ever expect to go to college?" I asked, and immediately wished I hadn't. Jill's expression went from day to night, and there was the slightest downturn at the corners of her mouth.

"Do you expect me to plan my whole life right now?" she asked. "Don't you think I have enough to deal with?"

"Sure," I said quickly. "That's me—always jumping ahead."

Amy Sheldon had just joined stage crew, someone told me. And I heard it firsthand from Amy the next morning.

"Alice!" she called when I was heading to second period. "I'm doing what you did last year!" When people turned to look at her, she waited till she'd caught up with me to tell me the rest. "I signed up for stage crew," she said, walking along beside me, several feet away.

"Yeah, I heard!" I told her. "That's great, Amy. I think it'll be fun for you."

"I'm on props," she said, and dug one hand in the side pocket of her bag, then pulled out a sheet of paper. "Here's what I have to get: a book—that one's easy; a manicure set; handkerchief—my dad uses handkerchiefs. Mom and I use Kleenex. A sofa pillow, a plant, and a sandwich. Only I'll wait till the last day to get the sandwich on account of it would be spoiled if I got it now. There's lots more stuff, but the other kids will get that. One boy has to find a dog."

I laughed. "Yeah, I wondered about that."

"It's a good thing a large lollipop was on someone else's list because if it was on mine, I'd probably eat it. They're bad for your teeth, though, because the sugar stays in your mouth for so long. I've had two cavities, but I don't get them anymore. Do you?"

"Not often," I said.

"We're both working on the same thing, only you'll be onstage and I'll be behind the curtain, but I'll be cheering for you. I won't make any noise, though. If you're on stage crew, you can't make any noise."

We turned the corner, and I stopped to get a drink of water at the fountain.

"And I have to dress in black. I don't like black, do you, Alice? Am I talking too much?"

"Sometimes you do rattle on, Amy," I said, grinning up at her.

She looked confused. "I don't rattle. Dishes and pans rattle."

I realized how difficult it must be for Amy when speech is inexact. Amy's world is so black-and-white, so either-or.

"You're right. And yes, sometimes you do jump—I mean, switch—from one subject to another without waiting for an answer. And sometimes I just use the wrong words. You'll have to stop me when I use the wrong words," I told her.

"I'll just give you a signal," said Amy. "Like, maybe I'll hold up my hand or something. Or maybe just a finger on one hand."

"Got it," I said. "I mean, I understand."

12
ROOMMATES

I had only been home fifteen minutes, and was eating the dinner Sylvia had left for me, when my cell phone rang. I swallowed a bite of lasagna and pushed away from the table, ambling into the living room in my socks to check the caller. It was Pamela, so I took it.

"What's up?" I said.

Her voice was almost a scream. "I'm *in*! Alice, I've got a scholarship to the Theater Arts College in Manhattan!" She *was* screaming.

"*What?*" I cried.

"The letter just came! Dad's at Meredith's, so you're the first one I've told! I went to New York and auditioned, and I'm *in*!"

"Pamela! My God!" I said. Why hadn't she told us she'd

applied for a scholarship? Why hadn't she told us she'd been in New York? I might have known that theater arts people had to appear in person, but . . . What was I, jealous? Shouldn't I be congratulating her? "It's wonderful! It's amazing! It's incredulous, Pamela! When did you audition?"

"Remember last December when I stayed home because of a sore throat? I was really in New York that day. Dad gave me the money."

"And you've kept it secret all this time?"

"I didn't want everyone feeling sorry for me if I failed, Alice. I mean . . . all that grief over my pregnancy, then the miscarriage . . . I was tired of people feeling pity for me. It's only a half-tuition scholarship, but . . ."

"Well, I don't feel sorry for you, Pamela, and I think it's great! Really! What did you do for your audition?"

"That ditzy Adelaide scene from *Guys and Dolls*. I guess I nailed it, Alice! Yay!"

All I could think of was that the University of Maryland had been her safety school, and down deep, I had imagined her being my roommate if I couldn't room with Gwen. Next selfish thought: "Does this mean you won't be working on the cruise ship with us this summer?"

"It means I absolutely will. Do you know what it *costs* to live in Manhattan, Alice? I'll need the money more than ever. Of course I'll be on that cruise ship."

And so I loved her again, but I wondered if I'd ever look at her the same. The girl whose grades were good but not remarkable, who had been careless enough to get pregnant, had somehow gotten her act together and was accepted into a theater arts school in New York City. . . . Maybe someday I would quit pigeonholing people—would realize how much they can change.

"I'm standing here listening to all of this and feeling so . . . *proud* of you, Pam!" I said. "Listen, call your mom. Let her in on it."

"I will. Right after I call Dad," she told me, and gave a little shriek again of pure joy.

It was hard to be as excited about the school play with Pamela destined for New York. I'd made a decision: If William & Mary would take me, I was going to go there. I could be adventurous too. But getting the part of Anne was still a big step for me— strange to be one of the cast, no longer part of the stage crew. I was so used to staying in the shadows, never venturing farther out in the wings where the audience might see us.

Now, after a week of reading the play together in the drama classroom, Mr. Ellis moved rehearsals into the auditorium and up on the stage, facing rows and rows of seats that morphed into darkness at the back of the cavernous hall. I was part of the curtains and lights now, not just the paint and the props.

When the actors weren't needed in a particular scene, we sat in the seats below. Ryan sat down beside me while Pamela and Jay were rehearsing onstage.

"The only time I can take a break is when you do," he said. "I'm never onstage if you're not."

"Ah! Power!" I whispered back, smiling at him.

His knees almost touched the seat in front of him and his jeans stretched tightly over his thighs. The body of an athlete, I thought, or maybe a dancer. I didn't know much about him except that he was playing the part of Larry, my boyfriend.

"I was surprised Ellis dug out this old play," Ryan went on. "My cousin said they did this nine years ago."

"Why did you try out if you don't like it?" I asked.

"Experience," Ryan said. "Don't you know that everything we do in senior year counts as 'experience'?"

Mr. Ellis, in the front row, looked around to see who was whispering, and we immediately faced forward, totally focused on Pamela and Jay.

Becoming a part of my stage family made me feel even closer to my own. The dialogue between Anne and her brothers made me think more about Lester and something he'd said in our last phone conversation, about how so many of the girls he used to know had moved away.

I called him that evening.

"How are things?" I said.

"Need you ask?" he answered. "Andy's here, the weather's lousy, we're out of cheese, and the Super Bowl's over."

"Want some company?"

"You could come by Friday night, if you want. We had some guys in last week, but I'm the designated sitter for Mr. Watts this Friday."

"Sure, I'll come," I said.

"Bring food," said Les.

As soon as I ended the call, I punched in Kay's number and asked if she would be needing any rescuing Friday night.

"I need it twenty-four/seven," Kay said. "If I don't have something planned every night of the week, my parents invite me over. I asked them the other day if they didn't agree this was a hopeless cause, and Mom just said that as long as James was in the States, it was our obligation to entertain him. And then I really made my dad angry, because I said, 'But is it necessary to involve me?' And he said, 'Since you are determined to do the least possible to help, yes, it is necessary for you to come along.' It's so miserable. James and I hardly even talk to each other. I don't think he can stand me."

"How would you like an excuse not to go to their place this Friday?" I said. "Could you get some girlfriends together and come with me to Lester's apartment? He's got to stay home that evening and needs cheering up."

"Great! I'll do it!" Kay said. "I'll say my boss's son is giving a party. They don't like to interfere in my work."

Asking Kay Yen to bring some of her friends to Lester's apartment Friday night was one of my more inspired ideas. The two other girls were about Kay's age—early twenties—fairly attractive, one Asian, one Caucasian, friendly and full of life.

"I've got food, but I figured friends were welcome too," I said, brushing past him with a grocery bag in my arms.

"Hi, Les," Kay said. "Nice to see you again. This is Lee and Judith."

"Well, come in! Come in!" Les said, holding the door open wide, obviously taken by surprise. I wondered if he even remembered he'd invited me.

"We were going to get together for dinner, and Alice said you were home alone, so we thought, 'Why not have dinner there?'" Kay explained, following me to the kitchen.

"Yeah, dirty up your kitchen instead of ours," I joked.

"Be my guests!" said Les, still puzzled but looking pleased. "I'll even put on shoes for the occasion." He went into his bedroom while we set out some stuff. Nothing fancy. Kay had bought a cheesecake from the supermarket, and I brought a jar of spaghetti sauce and pasta. The others purchased green beans almondine and garlic bread. A feast.

We put on water to boil for the spaghetti, and Les emerged from his bedroom. He had put on a clean shirt over his tee and combed his hair a little.

"Too bad Paul isn't here. He'd love this," he said.

"So we'll do it again," said Kay.

"You have a roommate?" Judith asked.

"Yeah, two of them, both out for the evening. I'm on duty," Les said. As we set the table, he told them about the arrangement with Mr. Watts, and they laughed during dinner at his account of how Andy got in on the deal. Lee found a soft-rock station, Les opened some beer, and as the evening progressed, it seemed as though we'd all known each other for a long time.

Judith entertained us with stories of her and Kay's canoeing adventures on the Potomac, especially the time they managed to collide with a kayaker, who threatened to sue.

"Can you believe it?" Judith said, imitating the man in the kayak, waving his paddle in the air and demanding to see their IDs.

We were still laughing when we heard the door click. I hoped it was Paul, that he could join the party. But a moment later Andy appeared in the kitchen doorway, her red-framed glasses fogging up slightly as she surveyed us there at the table.

"Hi," she said, and I was about to introduce her to the others when she turned and walked back down the hall to her room. We heard voices, and even though Andy's is low, we could tell that the other voice was male. And then she shut her door.

"She tutors," Les said in explanation.

A TV set came on in Andy's room, and the volume was turned down. A man's laughter. The women exchanged smiles.

"What subjects?" Kay asked.

"English, history . . . ," Les said, and then, catching their drift, "physiology, maybe? Hey, she's allowed to have friends, you know." We laughed and talked of other things.

13

SOUND OF THE WHISTLE

After work the next day, Kay and I went to visit Marilyn. Actually, we volunteered to go over and make a big pot of chicken and corn soup, and Jack said the kitchen was ours to do with as we liked. I brought along Sylvia's recipe for blueberry muffins and all the ingredients I'd need.

But first we wanted to see the baby.

Marilyn was sitting on the couch in an old pair of baggy jeans and a sweater, folding laundry, the baby snoozing in the narrow dip between her knees. All I could see when I came in was a wisp of fine golden hair over a pink scalp and two tiny fists clenched tightly.

"Oh, Marilyn!" I said, pushing some towels out of the way and sitting carefully down beside her.

Marilyn beamed as she studied her baby. "Isn't she the sweetest thing you ever saw?" she whispered, gently edging her fingers under the baby's back and neck, lifting her from her lap and handing her over to me.

The small body was so light! How could a baby weigh so little? The pink lips barely opened as the head tipped back a bit. But when I cradled her in my arms, she gave a soft sigh and the yellow flannel shirt she was wearing rose and fell again ever so slightly as she breathed.

Jack and Kay were hovering over the back of the sofa behind us. He chuckled as a tiny bubble of spit formed at the baby's mouth.

"She's adorable!" said Kay. "Oh, I want one of those!"

"Get a husband first," said Marilyn. "A *good* one, like Jack. They don't come any better."

I watched the baby's mouth twitch, the lips forming an O, almost a smacking motion, and she stirred slightly.

"She'll be getting hungry pretty soon," Marilyn told us. "Every three hours, she lets us know she's alive."

I stroked the side of Summer's face with one finger, marveling at the fine hair of her eyebrows, the dark lashes, the chrysanthemum-colored lips. "Grow up like your mama," I told her.

"Next?" said Kay, coming around the sofa to sit beside me, and I gently placed the little sleeping beauty in her lap.

Jack went off to run errands, and while Marilyn nursed her baby, Kay and I took over the kitchen. We'd brought a fruit salad that

Sylvia had made, and Kay set to work on the chicken soup, her grandmother's recipe from China.

The Robertses' house was small, but it had a large old-fashioned kitchen. It was a welcoming place, with a rocking chair in one corner on a braided rug, where the cat was sitting now. There were plants at every window and a big round table in the middle of the floor.

We soon had the windows steamed up, and as Kay followed the soup instructions, I concentrated on greasing the muffin tins and paid extra attention to the lines on Sylvia's recipe card that she had underlined in red: *Stir only until moistened. Batter will be lumpy. DO NOT OVERMIX.*

Once we had the soup simmering and the muffins in the oven, we allowed ourselves to talk to each other, and Marilyn, hearing the chatter, came out to the kitchen to make us some tea.

"Summer's sleeping," she said. "Now we can visit."

I couldn't keep my eyes off Marilyn. She was still a little thick at the waist, but even so . . . !

"You can go through having a baby, and two weeks later you're walking around like this?" I marveled.

"What do you mean, two weeks later?" Marilyn said. "I was walking around the very next day."

"Amazing!" I told her. "I figured you'd be all sore and bent over and—"

"Alice, it's a normal bodily function, having a baby," she said. "I take a nap each day. But the more I move around, the stronger I feel." She looked about the kitchen and inhaled.

"Mmmm. Everything smells so good. You guys are the best!"

We sat at the round table, drinking our tea, letting the steam moisten our faces, waiting for the muffins to finish baking so we could taste them.

"So how are things going with your parents?" Marilyn asked Kay.

"Nobody's budged," said Kay. "They invite James over for dinner twice a week and expect me to be there at least once. James sits there with a stoic look on his face, and more than once I've caught him checking his watch. I think his consulting job is over in April, so this can't last forever. I escaped last night's dinner at least, thanks to Alice—rounded up some girl-friends and took dinner to Les."

"Lucky Les," said Marilyn. "What's the latest with that new roommate of his?"

We told her how Andy's "student" turned out to be a boyfriend.

"And they didn't come out of her room all evening," Kay said.

Marilyn laughed. "Well, at least she has friends."

"Anyway," Kay continued, "Andy's on duty next Friday night, so Judith and I are going to take Les and Paul to a club. We promised them a canoe trip when the weather gets warmer."

"Les always lucks out, doesn't he?" Marilyn said.

"Not always," I said, but didn't say more. Jack was the lucky one here.

The rehearsal schedule for March was unrelenting. No holidays, no time off. Some were late rehearsals, which meant we worked through the dinner hour, ate alone when we got home.

On Friday there was an assembly right before lunch.

"Now what?" said Gwen, as she and I filed in with a couple of friends from physics. I knew what it was about but had to pretend I didn't.

"I think it's supposed to advertise all the spring activities," one of the girls said.

"Just so it's not another lecture on drunk driving or STDs," someone else said.

Principal Beck came to the microphone first and gave a two-minute history of all the awards and honors our school had won in the past, then talked about what a bang-up year this one was turning out to be.

When he mentioned the orchestra concert in May, three violinists in their white shirts and black bow ties emerged from behind the curtain and, playing a schmaltzy tune, crossed the stage and exited the other side. When he mentioned the coming band concert at the end of this month, a trumpet player, oboe player, bassoon player, and drummer came marching across the stage from the other direction, playing a polka.

The basketball team dribbled a ball across the stage when Mr. Beck gave a shout-out to the high school finals that weekend. The girls' soccer team followed, then the cheerleaders, and finally the madrigals, singing a short piece to promote the choir concert in April.

Gwen, a seat away, leaned forward and gave me a puzzled expression, like, *Where's any mention of the play?*—and I just shrugged and gave her a woeful look.

Then, as Mr. Beck walked off the stage, Brad Broderick entered, dressed in an old-fashioned three-piece suit, obviously padded around the middle. His dark sideburns had been grayed, he wore his round-rimmed spectacles halfway down his nose, and there were lines drawn on his forehead and around his mouth.

Without a word, Brad stood in the center of the stage. He pulled a stopwatch out of his vest pocket and held it out in front of him. Then, lifting a whistle to his mouth with his other hand, he blew a loud blast and pressed the button on the stopwatch.

Instantly, I leaped to my feet and yelled, "Coming!" and the girls in my row shrank back, staring at me wide-eyed. But all over the auditorium, the scattered Gilbreth children were climbing over legs in their rows, all heading for the stage, all yelling, "Coming, Dad!" and "Wait for me!" and "Just a minute!" as our classmates began to get the picture and broke into laughter.

Using the side steps of the stage, up we went, dropping our books in a heap and quickly forming a row in front of the footlights, from oldest to youngest, as our father clicked the stopwatch once more.

"Fourteen seconds!" Brad boomed, looking us over in disgust.

"That's pretty good!" said Jay cheerfully, playing the part of Frank Jr.

Brad glared at him.

Tim, as Fred, said, "Only eight seconds off the record."

"Where's your mother?" Brad asked.

"Upstairs with the babies," I told him.

Turning toward the audience, Brad said gruffly, "I had so many children because I thought anything your mother and I teamed up on was certain to be a success. Now I'm not so sure." He wheeled about abruptly. "Let me see your fingernails."

And as Brad moved down the line, all of us wincing, drawing our hands back or quickly buffing our nails against our clothes, the school principal returned to the microphone and said, "And you won't want to miss this year's spring production, *Cheaper by the Dozen*, to see what happens when two efficiency experts raise a family of twelve children and there's an uprising brewing over—you guessed it—romance . . . freedom . . . silk stockings and other unmentionables! Bring your family! Bring your friends! April eighth and ninth, fifteenth and sixteenth." And then all of us onstage shouted together, *"Cheaper by the Dozen!"*

And the assembly was over.

It was so much fun. Liz and Gwen and Jill and Karen were waiting for me out in the hall, and we all collapsed in laughter. Even Liz hadn't known it was coming, not being in that particular scene.

"You almost gave me a heart attack!" said Gwen. "I thought you were having a fit or something."

"It wasn't till we saw the other actors jumping up that we realized it was staged," said Karen.

"Yeah, Alice will do anything for attention," said Jill, but she said it jokingly, and for maybe the first time, I sensed that perhaps she was relieved she hadn't gotten the part of Anne after all.

"Even scared the wits out of me," Ryan McGowan said as we were leaving the physics lab last period. It was hard for me not to call him "Larry." "Pamela was in our row, and when she jumped up, I thought she was choking or something."

I laughed. "Mr. Ellis wanted us to keep it secret from everyone, even the rest of the cast. Have you done theater before?"

"Back in Illinois," he said. "My dad was transferred here last year. I had bit parts in community theater. How about you?"

"My first time, unless you count my sixth-grade production." He smiled a little. "What part did you play?"

"A bramble bush with branches thick," I said, and he chuckled.

"Well, I'll bet you were a darned good bramble bush."

"Not really," I told him. "I tripped up the star of the show, who happened to be Pamela, by the way, and she was furious. I was so jealous of her."

"The tragedies of life," Ryan said. "I'm thinking of majoring in theater. I've been getting some coaching."

"Really?"

"I'll see how it goes at college. Either theater or a fine arts degree. Publishing, maybe. You?"

"I want to be a school counselor."

He glanced down at me. "Yeah?"

"Yes." And when he didn't respond, I added, "I've been accepted at Maryland. I'm waiting to see if two other schools come through, William & Mary in particular."

"I've applied to Columbia and the University of Iowa. Also, a little college in Minnesota where my mom went, just to make her happy," Ryan said. "But I want to do my grad work at the University of Iowa, if I make it that far. It's the best writing program there is, if I go into that."

We reached the corner and I had to turn. "See you at practice," I said.

"I'm heading for the doughnut sale," he told me. "Can I get you something?"

"Yeah. One glazed. Thanks," I said.

Seemed strange, somehow, that I was sounding more and more like my life was on track and that it was other people's lives that were question marks. As Dad was fond of saying, though, "Life is what happens when you're planning something else." In fact, every new person you meet introduces a question mark. And Ryan was no exception.

14
NEWS

March Madness was going on, and I hardly got to watch any of the games. By the time rehearsals were over, I still had homework to do and didn't have much evening left, even for watching TV.

On Sunday, though, with Maryland poised for a slot in the Elite Eight if they beat Virginia Tech, I called Les to see if he and Paul were going to watch it and ask if I could come over to join them. It's always more fun to watch a college game with a Maryland student or, in Lester's case, two former grad students, him and Paul.

"Sure," he said. "Couple buddies are coming over, and Kay's dropping by. Join the crowd!"

Hmmm, I thought. Was it just possible that Les and Kay

were hitting it off? Was there remotely, conceivably, incredibly a chance that under the guise of rescuing each other from Andy and James, respectively, an attraction between them was blossoming under our very noses?

I had some errands to run first, and when I finally got to Lester's apartment, the place was rocking. The game had started, Maryland had the ball, and there were guys I didn't know on every available chair and couch cushion. Paul was lifting a couple beers out of a cooler and passing them around. Kay said that Judith would be coming too, but right now she was sitting cross-legged on the floor in front of the couch, between Lester's knees. I tried not to smile. I had managed to hook up Dad and Sylvia, hadn't I? Was I a matchmaker or what?

When I went to the door later to let Judith in, I noticed that Andy's door was shut. I took Judith's chips to the kitchen to get a bowl, and when Paul came out for more ice, I asked, "Nobody invited Andy to join in?"

"We did! We did! But she's doing a tutoring session," he told me.

I shrugged.

It was during the third quarter, when I was taking some bottles to the trash, that I saw one guy leaving Andy's room and another coming in from outside. They passed without speaking. Andy was waiting in her doorway in a knit top and silky leisure pants, purple dangly earrings at her ears.

"Hi," I said.

"How you doing?" she answered, ushering the new guy into her room and closing the door behind them.

Les came out to the kitchen to get more dip.

"How many boyfriends does she have?" I asked, nodding toward Andy's room.

"Haven't asked," said Les.

Maryland lost and was out of the play-offs, but it was a close game and the team played well. I love basketball because it's so easy to follow: If the ball goes through the basket and there's no whistle, the team scores. You don't have to know the rest of the rules.

But the play was taking my full concentration these days, especially now that the costume committee was beginning to outfit the cast. I hated what I had to wear for the first act, but Mrs. Cary thought it was just right, so I wore it—a black pleated skirt that came just below the knee, a long green sweater that fell halfway down my thighs, and a black belt a few inches below the waistline. Worse yet were the black cotton stockings that made my legs look fat.

Pamela and Chassie, as Martha, the third-oldest sister, got to wear white sailor tops with navy blue kerchiefs around their necks; and Angela, as Lillian, the youngest, got to wear a pinafore, white knee-length stockings, and Mary Jane shoes. But in the final act I would be wearing a thin, filmy sleeveless dress with silk hose. They made my legs shine, but it was still a beautiful costume, and I guess the audience was supposed to see how much I'd managed to improve between the first and third acts of the play.

The rehearsals were wearing me down, though, and by the last weekend in March, when Karen called and said a bunch of girls were going to Clyde's restaurant for dinner Saturday night, I said I'd go. I was so amazed to be invited that I was going mostly out of curiosity. Liz and Pamela were going too, but Gwen was singing in a concert at her church.

Pamela drove this time—her dad had finally let her use his car—and she said if I'd quit gasping every time she reached a stop sign, she'd drive more often.

"It's just that you never brake till the last minute," Liz told her. "Your passengers think you're going to sail on through."

"But I *do* stop, don't I?" said Pamela. "Do I have to sing an overture before I stop?"

"I'd settle for just taking your foot off the gas pedal," I said.

We drove to Clyde's at Tower Oaks in Rockville—a great place for crab cakes, a sort of safari-themed restaurant with animal trophies and canoes on the walls. Lots of couples go there before proms, but we like to go as a group because half of us order a plate dinner and the others order appetizers. Then we share, and we can stay as long as we like.

Jill had reserved a large table, and some of the girls were already there when we arrived. One of them was talking about receiving an acceptance from Towson State.

"It's so great to know that at least *some*body wants me," the girl was saying, and the discussion turned to how many colleges—four? five? six?—you should have applied for to be on the safe side.

"And what about Pamela here!" I said. "Isn't she amazing?"

We clinked our glasses in tribute, and Pamela made a funny face.

"She auditioned as Adelaide from *Guys and Dolls*," I said, in case anyone hadn't heard. "Just goes to show that even an understudy has possibilities."

I realized too late that Jill may have thought I was taking a dig at her for backing out. But Jill was biding her time, I guess, because she listened with a sort of condescending air, and then she said she had an announcement: "We're getting married April twenty-third."

We stared. "Whaaaaaat?" we said, almost in unison.

Jill basked in the limelight and smiled coyly around the table, her elegantly manicured fingers splayed out in front of her. Without a ring, however. "The Colliers gave in. Justin told them we were marrying as soon as school was out, and it would be either in a church or before a justice of the peace—it was up to them. When they realized that we were serious and, probably more to the point, that I hadn't miscarried yet—I'm in my second trimester now—Justin's mom caved and said they'd pay for the wedding. But, of course, there are conditions. . . ."

"Wow, Jill! Right in the middle of the semester?" said Liz.

"It'll be spring break. Mrs. Collier doesn't want me walking down the aisle obviously pregnant, and there's to be no civil ceremony for their son. Like I said, whatever they do, they do *big*."

"This is unbelievable," I said. "I never thought they'd give in."

"That's what Mom said," Jill went on. "She had the invitations engraved and in the mail before the Colliers could change their minds. And I wish we could invite you all, but the witch is in charge of the guest list."

"Where's it going to be?" asked Pamela.

"The Episcopal church near Chevy Chase Circle. That was one of the conditions. They'll pay for most of the wedding if we agree to the conditions."

"What are the others?" asked Liz.

Our drinks arrived and Jill leaned back, waiting for our server to leave before she continued. Then she began counting them off on her fingers: "Number one: We marry in April. Number two: We marry in their church. Number three: Justin finishes college no matter how many children I 'manage to produce.' His mother actually wrote that down. She crossed it out after and inserted 'you have' instead of 'Jill manages to produce,' but she left it in so I'd know she suspects I planned to get pregnant."

"Well . . . it *was* a plan . . . I mean, both of you planned it," I said.

"Damn right," said Jill. "And I don't care if she *does* know it. Number four: that we pay for the honeymoon ourselves. Ditto, the ring. Numbers five, six, and seven: Justin works summers for his dad's company until he's through college, we have to live in this area till he graduates, and we don't deny the Colliers access to their grandchildren."

Jill took a deep breath, held it, then let it out.

"Wow. She forgot to add the pound of flesh. She didn't put that in," somebody said. "And you don't have to name your first daughter after her?"

"Yeah, I know. They more or less own us till Justin's through college, but at least they didn't insist we live with them. They're paying for everything except the ring, our honeymoon, and our apartment, and Justin says we can pay the rent out of his trust fund. But Mom could never afford the kind of wedding the Colliers want for Justin."

The appetizers came and we began dividing them up—a bit of crab cake on each saucer, a wedge of fried onion. . . . Jill held up the chicken satay on a stick: "This is one of the appetizers we've chosen along with the shrimp," she said. "The dinner menu, of course, is completely Mrs. Collier's, but she did run it by Mom first."

"How do they get along—Mrs. Collier and your mom?" Liz asked.

"It's all surface, you know? Mom was terrified to meet her, actually—she'd heard so much about her from me. All bad. Mr. and Mrs. Collier came over on a Sunday afternoon—the usual courtesy call—and said that a spring wedding would be so much more appropriate than a summer one, didn't Mom agree? And asked how long we'd lived in the Washington area, meaning: Where are your 'people' from? Since then, everything's being arranged by a middleman—woman, I should say. Mr. Collier's secretary relays messages to Mom and she replies to the secretary.

Every day Mom gets a memo on something else that's been decided for us."

"And . . . you don't mind?" another friend asked.

"Of course I do. But I'm going to keep my mouth shut as long as they don't try to break us up. I've just been really, really tired lately. If they want to do all the planning, so be it. It'll be an even fancier wedding than I could ever afford, and I'm just going to pretend the Colliers aren't there. The parents, that is."

The dinners arrived and we divided those up too, and afterward Jill passed around photos of what the wedding cake would look like, the place settings and favors and flowers. I guess when you put everything in the hands of a wedding planner and money is no object, you can put together a wedding in six weeks and make it look like you've been thinking about it for a year or more.

"When you *do* go on a honeymoon, where do you think it will be?" Pamela asked.

"Hawaii. We're going as soon as school's out. We have to decide between a honeymoon and a diamond, though, and I don't want to start out with something small, so we'll put the engagement ring off till later," Jill told us. Then she reached in her bag and pulled out a brochure of a resort hotel on Kauai, tucked in a cove with palm trees and flowers and blue waves beyond a white sandy beach.

Jill was right. She did look tired. Just as pretty, just as svelte as she always looked, but tired. Just thinking about her next four years with a baby while Justin was in college made me tired too.

15
INSOMNIA

The feathery green of spring.

The star magnolias had blossomed in the middle of March. Crocuses came up next, then daffodils, and the forsythia was a brilliant yellow against the new green of the lawns. Near the end of the month, cherry trees had burst into bloom, and on every tree in the neighborhood, little feathers of leaves appeared, trembling in the breeze.

But I felt like I was trembling too. I had to give the University of Maryland a reply by April 1 as to whether or not I was going to attend. And every day I waited to hear from William & Mary. I couldn't believe that everything was coming at me at once, with the first play performances beginning the following weekend.

I wanted so much to be able to call Pamela and say, *Guess*

what? To tell her that I, too, was striking out in a new direction. And then, on March 29, after a late rehearsal, I got home to find that Dad and Sylvia had gone to a movie. A pile of mail had been dumped on a chair, unsorted, and there, near the bottom, was an envelope from William & Mary. My heart began to race. I pulled it out from among the stack.

But it was not a large manila envelope. It was a white business-size envelope, and I felt my throat constricting even before I opened it, my eyes filling with tears. I sat down on the bottom step of the stairs and balanced it between the palms of my hands. Then, furiously, I ripped it open and read the first two lines—*Dear Alice McKinley: We are sorry that we will be unable to admit you to our college this coming fall. We know that . . .*

I ran upstairs like a crazy person, sobbing loudly, and threw myself on my bed. Why? What was it about me that they didn't like? Wasn't I a B+ student? Didn't I have a lot of extracurricular stuff on my application? Hadn't Mrs. Bailey written an excellent recommendation? I loved the place; why didn't they love me back? And why did Dad and Sylvia go off to a movie when if ever I needed somebody's shoulder, it was now? Even though I knew that wasn't fair, that Dad and Sylvia hadn't even looked at the mail, I needed someone to listen to me, comfort me, and because there was no one there, I impulsively called Patrick.

Even as I punched in his number, I knew I was in no condition to carry on a conversation. At the same moment I was afraid he might answer, he picked up. "Hey, Alice!" he said.

"P-P-P-Patrick!" I sobbed.

"Alice? *Alice?*" His voice was instantly tense, concerned. "Alice, what *is* it? Where are you?"

"Oh, P-Patrick," I wept. "They d-didn't . . ." I couldn't stand the childish sound of my voice, the stammering. I could feel my cheeks blaze, and I suddenly pressed END and dropped the phone on my rug, doubling over in anguish.

Almost instantly the phone began to ring, and I stared at it there on the rug. Stared at it through the flood of tears dripping off my lashes. There was something steadying about the insistence of its ring, and I realized that if I had been childish calling him in the first place, I was even more childish not to answer now. So I picked it up and tried to get hold of myself.

"Patrick?" I mewed.

"Alice, don't hang up. Are you listening?" he said. "Don't hang up, no matter what. Where are you?"

I spoke so softly, I could hardly hear myself. "I'm home."

"Okay. Just take a couple breaths or something. I'm listening. I'm not going away."

"I'm s-so sorry," I said. "I knew I shouldn't have c-called. Are you busy right now?"

"I was watching TV with the guys. I'm out in the hall now, sitting on the floor, and nobody's around. What's the matter?"

When I remembered what the matter was, the tears came again. "William & Mary rejected m-me."

"Oh, man. I'm sorry, Alice. I really am."

"But—but that—that makes me even sadder," I wept. "Because I know y-you wanted me to g-go there."

"It's what *you* want, Alice! Why should I—?"

"It's true, Patrick," I said, wiping my nose on my arm. "You're going to Spain and Gwen's in a pre-med program and Pamela's going to New York and everybody's going places and doing things . . . and . . . and . . ." I was sobbing again. "Why do you even b-bother with me? Why do you like me at all? There are all kinds of girls who know m-more than I do and travel all over and speak Russian and Japanese, and I—I—All I know is here, P-Patrick! The only places I've l-lived are Chicago and Maryland. All . . . I really know . . . is . . . m-m-me!"

Patrick was quiet for so long I thought he'd hung up on me except that I didn't get a dial tone. And then I heard his voice, firm and steady.

"Alice, before we moved to Maryland when I was in sixth grade, I'd already lived in four different countries—"

"I *know*!" I wept, my voice high and tight. "That's what I'm talking about!"

Patrick continued: "There wasn't any one place to call home. And when we moved to Maryland and Mom said we'd be there for a while, it was the first place I started to make friends . . . I mean, friends I knew I'd see for more than a year or so. And yet, even there in Maryland, my dad traveled so much and was home so little that it never seemed like a real home, not the home that other kids had, and certainly not your home, the way you feel about it, the way you and your dad and Lester made it home. And *that's* what I love about you. Among other things," he added quickly.

"You love me because I stay home?"

"I love you because you *love* home. It doesn't mean you're never going to get out. It doesn't mean you're not curious about other people and places. You *are*! You care about people who are different from you—Amy Sheldon, for example. Lori and Leslie. That Sudanese guy you told me about. You want to know what it feels like to be them. You don't have to live somewhere else or go to William & Mary to do that. You open your mind to the world, Alice. That's what makes you you."

"Oh, Patrick. I wish you were here," I said, still crying, but managing it now. "I'm just so keyed up over everything and rehearsals run late and I'm behind on my homework and I've got to let Maryland know I'm coming and—"

"And it will all work out. Trust me. It will."

"I trust you," I said.

Patrick's phone call helped more than he knew, and I soldiered on, grateful for Dad and Sylvia's reassurance that Maryland was a fine school, which of course I knew. For the next week, I focused entirely on the play and got caught up in the excitement of our final round of rehearsals. *Too* caught up, because I started having trouble sleeping. I'd lie awake till two or three in the morning, then the alarm would go off at six thirty, and I'd feel half dead.

When I woke on Wednesday, though—just two days before

our first performance—there was no alarm sounding on my nightstand. The sun was already shining full on my bedspread. I rose up on one elbow and stared at the clock. Nine fifteen! I leaped out of bed, then saw the note stuck on the back of my door.

Alice, you've been exhausted, and we don't want you sick for opening night of the play. I've called the school and told them I'm letting you sleep in. They understand. Sylvia

Omigod! I thought. *I don't want anyone to think I can't handle this!* I showered, but I let my hair go, pulled on my jeans and a knit top. Sylvia had left two blueberry muffins on the table along with her car keys, but by the time I got to school, I'd missed the first two periods.

"Somebody was up late last night," Gwen said diplomatically when she saw me at lunch. Saw my hair.

"I'm not sleeping well," I told her. "I haven't been falling asleep till around three, and I'm exhausted when I try to get up. Sylvia turned off my alarm and let me sleep in."

"Best thing she could have done," Gwen said.

"Does this ever happen to you?" I asked her.

"Once in a while. I go through spells. I find that if I take a warm bath, read a while, drink some milk, and let my mind wander over old movies or books or dreams after I lie down— never what I have to do the next day—I eventually fall asleep.

The secret is to make a list before you turn in of all you have to do the next day so you won't forget something. Then tell yourself that those things are off-limits once you get in bed. You'll deal with them tomorrow."

"Gwen," I said, "you're a walking Google. No matter what I ask, you have an answer."

Pamela put my hair in a French braid in gym, and I felt reasonably recovered when I walked into rehearsal at three. But Ryan took one look at me and said, "You look tired. You getting as little sleep as the rest of us?"

"Even less," I said. "But this morning they let me sleep in. I didn't get to school till around ten."

Every rehearsal this final week was a dress rehearsal, and Penny waylaid us when we got to the dressing rooms and had a thin little paste-on mustache she wanted Ryan to wear for his part as Larry. "C'mon, just for a joke," she laughed, grabbing his arm. "See what Ellis thinks."

He was still fending her off when I went in the girls' dressing room and took off my shirt. It was stuffy in the room—the one window didn't open, and the lights over the long makeup table were hot. We took turns sitting on the worn stools in our underwear and bras, brushing color on our cheeks, darkening our eyebrows, going heavy on the eyeliner and mascara. Occasionally, we could make out bits of conversation from the guys' dressing room on the other side of the wall, and we'd grin.

Once in a while, when one of them raised his voice, we figured they wanted us to hear, and at some point I heard one of the guys say loudly, "Hey, dudes! Did you know there's a hole in the wall and I can see the girls half naked?"

We looked at each other and giggled.

I turned to Liz and said, just as loudly, "Well, if they haven't seen it by now, it's time they did."

Liz's eyes opened wide, and the other girls stifled their laughter.

"Who said that?" we heard one guy ask, both surprise and excitement in his voice. "Could you tell who that was?"

"Maybe Penny," said someone else.

"Didn't sound like her," another guy mused. "Sounded like Alice."

"*Alice* said that?"

We shook our heads, still grinning, and went on doing our faces.

Strange, the satisfaction I got out of that. Alice, playing the thoughtful, older, dutiful daughter, could be a little risqué now and then. Sometimes I surprise even myself.

I overslept on Thursday morning too. I was simply too wound up after late rehearsal, and when I got to the breakfast table, Dad was waiting for me with a note he was writing the office to excuse my missing the first two periods again.

"Dad, this is the second time it's happened. They won't let me keep skipping classes!" I protested, frantically trying to get my shoes on.

"Al, sit down," he said. "You're not leaving this house till you've had some toast and juice. I'm telling the school that the overload has given you temporary insomnia and that you will make up any work you've missed after the play is over."

"It makes it sound like I can't handle stress. The other actors show up."

"How do you know you're the only one coming in late? This will blow over, trust me. But when you get as tired as you've been, your resistance is down, and that's when you can easily pick up a bug that will knock you flat. You've worked too hard on this play to get sick for the performances."

That was the only part that stuck with me, that I might miss a performance, so I sat down and ate the slice of toast he had buttered.

"It's so scary," I said, reaching for the marmalade. "I've never done anything on a stage before. Not like this."

"Of course you have. You've been practicing on that stage for two months."

"Not in front of a zillion people. What if I forget my lines?"

"That's what prompters are for."

"What if I get so nervous that I throw up?"

"That's what custodians are for, Alice. Will you please finish your toast and let me drive you to school?" he said.

There was no dress rehearsal Thursday night. We were told to go home, have a normal dinner with our families, and get a good night's sleep. Nobody argued.

Dad and Sylvia were delighted that we could all have dinner

together, and I could tell they were keeping the conversation light. They seemed to move about the kitchen in slow motion and to prolong the meal just to keep me at the table, getting nourished.

"I won't need you at the store for the next two weeks, Al," Dad said. "I want you to take these two Saturdays off and sleep in."

"Dad, are you sure?" I asked. "Easter's coming. All that Easter Sunday music!"

"Churches bought that ages ago," Dad said. "Besides, I've hired two temps to help out."

"Wow! *Two* temps to replace me? I must be a real work-horse!" I said.

Dad grinned. "You'll do."

I didn't want to wait to see if Patrick would call that night, so I called him around nine, but he didn't answer. I wondered if I should try again and leave a message. What if he didn't call back? Would I worry and not sleep again? I spent the next hour getting more and more uptight. If his cell phone was ringing and he checked it, he could tell it was from me. Why wasn't he answering?

I called him again at ten fifteen, and this time he picked up.

"Alice? You okay?" he asked.

"No, but just hearing your voice helps," I told him. "It's the night before the play and we're supposed to be relaxing, but I've had insomnia and I've got the jitters and two mornings I've gone to school late and—"

"Hey, hey," he said, to slow me down.

"What are you doing, Patrick? I'll bet I've interrupted a great conversation, or you're at the Medici with friends, or—"

"Actually," said Patrick, and I could tell he was moving around as he talked, "I just saw a movie at Ida Noyes and came back to my dorm to get a jacket. I'm meeting some guys at a club over on Fifty-ninth."

"Oh, I don't want to hold you up. Go on and we'll talk tomorrow . . . or . . . sometime," I said.

"The club doesn't close till one, and the guys won't miss me for a while. So . . . talk. About anything at all."

"I just wanted to hear your voice. I called before and you didn't answer."

"I had my cell phone turned off during the movie. Okay . . . now I'm sitting down on the couch in our tiny living room—the couch you slept on when you were here—and I'm looking at an empty Pepsi can on the bookcase and somebody's sneakers on the floor, and my roommate's plant is dead, so almost *anything* you say will be more interesting than this," Patrick said, and that made me laugh.

"Tomorrow's the big night," I told him, "and I've never been onstage before in front of a lot of people—lights and everything—except for our little skit at assembly. I've done okay at rehearsals, but what if everything falls apart once it's for real?"

"Why would it? You won't be able to see past the first couple of rows. Pretend they're all from Pergatoria or something—"

"From *where*?"

"Never heard of Pergatoria? Yep, they're all from there, and none of them can speak English."

I was grinning now. "So it will be completely unimportant—the play?"

"Completely."

"And how we perform is totally irrelevant?"

"Totally."

"So it makes no difference if I show up or not?"

"Uh . . . not exactly," said Patrick.

"Oh, Patrick, just talking with you makes me feel better. I really wish you were here."

"I wish I could be in the front row cheering for you," he said. "But then, I wished you were here with me last night."

"What happened last night?"

"Nothing," he said. "That's why I wished you were here. It was great weather in Chicago. I was at the library till late, and on the way back I walked by Botany Pond. And I thought of you."

I felt warm all over. A rush of warmth in my chest, a throbbing warmth between my legs, thinking of Patrick's hands, his fingers . . .

"Patrick . . . ," I said, and was almost embarrassed, it sounded so much like the *Patrick* I had said back then.

Neither of us said anything for several seconds. Then, Patrick's voice, husky, "Two more months till the prom. . . ."

16
OPENING NIGHT

It helped that everyone else in the cast seemed as jumpy and excited and nervous as I was on Friday. Even more so. Angela confessed she really had been sick and lost her breakfast shortly after she got to school that morning. I found myself comforting her.

"Break a leg," people kept saying to us in the halls.

The short guy who played Jackie had a breakout of acne, not quite what you'd expect on the youngest son in the play. But when we got ready for the performance that evening, Mrs. Cary covered his face liberally with makeup and gave him rosy red cheeks. Unless you were in the first three rows of the audience, you wouldn't have noticed.

Some of the ushers were stage crew members, selected to give out programs at the door, and Amy was one of them. I passed her briefly in the hall, and she looked rather elegant in black jeans and a black turtleneck with dangling silver earrings.

Because this wasn't a musical, there was no orchestra. But when the houselights dimmed, the chatter and laughter in the auditorium died down, then stopped abruptly as a recording began of "Love's Old Sweet Song."

There were not only butterflies in my stomach, there were horses galloping and gorillas in hiking boots. My heart pounded, even though I didn't make an appearance until page 12 in the script.

Ryan saw me hyperventilating back in the wings. He smiled and came over to give me a quick back rub, and that helped. His fingers lingered up around my neck and cheek. *Whoa!* I thought. Too much coming at me at once. I was both relieved and sorry when he moved away.

I couldn't see the stage from where I was standing, but I saw Pamela and Jay move toward the front of the curtain where the spotlight would find them. And finally, when I heard Pamela's voice, as Ernestine, saying, "Can you hear the music, Frank?" I knew that the performance had begun.

I had an easier entrance than some, because I came on with the rest of the Gilbreth clan when Brad blew the whistle and we all lined up to have our fingernails inspected. By the time I *did* get some lines, I was eager for my part, more than ready to show how Anne was changing from a dutiful daughter to a more adventurous girl, ready for a boyfriend.

Mr. Ellis had told us to expect it, but I was still surprised at how the audience reaction helped us along. When "Dad" announces that he has bought two Victrolas—one for the boys' bathroom and one for the girls'—the subject of dance music comes up. And the father admits that the Victrolas are not for music, but for language lessons, French and German.

"Just play them, and finally they'll make an impression," he pleaded.

And when I cried, "Not every morning in the bathroom!" the audience broke into laughter. We'd never laughed at that line before.

One of my favorite parts comes halfway through the first act. The family is having a council meeting, and the father has been outvoted on whether or not the kids can have a dog. Outraged, he says, "I suppose next you want ponies, roadsters, trips to Hawaii—*silk stockings!*" And at that, I stand up, go to a table at one side, open a drawer, and take out a small package.

"I'm not hiding a thing," I say determinedly. "I want the entire family to see." And I unwrap a short, flimsy piece of underwear, a teddy, like the top of an old-fashioned lacy slip while the bottom part was lacy panties. "I'm going to wear them," I say, at which point Brad Broderick goes bananas. On top of that, I announce I also bought silk stockings.

This time I was amazed that the audience clapped after I disappeared. I didn't know if they were clapping for me as an actress or for the script—that I'd finally told my father off. But either way, it was a heady moment. When I reached the platform behind the curtain where the stairs ended, my heart was racing with excitement, and Ryan, down below in the wings, gave me a thumbs-up. I smiled back and let out my breath to show him I was glad it was over, and he winked.

I got through Act II without a hitch, and it ends with my character in tears after her father vetoes going to a dance with the boy she really likes, Larry.

The play was short enough that there was no intermission, but I didn't have to go on right away in Act III, so I found a box to sit on where I could still hear my cue. I knew that Dad and Sylvia were out in the audience somewhere, but I didn't try to find them when I was onstage. I wondered how Dad felt about the play—wondered how deeply it hit home. We got along pretty well together, but I remember times it seemed he said "no" for no good reason. About letting me dye my hair green, for example. It was only for a day or so, not forever. It wasn't like I'd asked for a full-body tattoo. I remember how angry he was that I did it anyway. I knew too that I hurt him when I had arguments with Sylvia, but he was really good about keeping out of it and letting us work things out.

"Alice," Pamela whispered, "we're on—next scene."

I jumped up, afraid I'd missed my cue, but then I heard Brad Broderick say, "I . . . I just don't much feel like . . ."

I entered and stood just inside the door.

Later in the play, Anne redeems herself in her father's eyes by passing a test with flying colors; the dad relents about her having a boyfriend; Ryan, as Larry, takes me to the prom; and the dad leaves for a speaking trip overseas while the family has a council meeting in his absence. Carrying on . . . Curtain.

The ushers came down the aisles bringing small cellophane-wrapped bouquets of flowers, which were distributed to some of the main players. Mine were from Dad and Sylvia, and I finally spotted them about halfway back in the auditorium, smiling at me and still clapping.

"One down, three to go," Tim sang out as we milled about backstage, friends gathering outside the dressing rooms, beaming parents hugging their offspring, all of us talking excitedly about the lines almost missed.

Penny was hugging everybody, including Ryan, who had just hugged me. But I saw Sylvia waiting in the hallway, and I squeezed through the crowd to get to her and Dad.

He pulled me over and gave me a bear hug. "So proud of you!" he said. "That was marvelous, honey."

"We could hear every word," Sylvia said, joining our hug. "Mr. Ellis must have really emphasized diction."

"Did he ever!"

"That little speech of yours from the stairs . . . I even felt myself tearing up. Well done, Alice. I really enjoyed it," Sylvia said.

"Alice!" Sam called. "We're going to the Silver Diner. Want to come?"

"As soon as I change into jeans," I called back. And to Dad, "Someone will drive me home."

He gave me a final hug. "Go on, honey. It's all downhill from here."

17
GETTING CLOSER

Saturday morning, I slept like the dead. I was in the process of waking up about one in the afternoon when my cell phone rang. Sleep was too delicious, so I didn't pick up at first, but then I realized it might be an unscheduled rehearsal. I swung my legs over the side of the bed and reached for my bag.

" 'ello," I said hoarsely.

"Omigod, you *were* still sleeping," said Lester.

"I'm awake," I said, but the frog in my throat gave me away.

"Sorry, Al. I knew you had today off work but figured you'd be awake by now. How'd the play go?"

"Fine," I croaked, and tried to clear my throat. "No big boo-boos. The audience clapped like they meant it."

"Well, I'll be there tonight," he said. "Listen. Has . . . Kay told you anything?"

Aha! I thought, and now I was really awake. *Here it comes!* Les and Kay were going out. I mean, really.

"No," I said curiously. "What's happening?"

"Well, that's what I'm trying to figure out," said Les. "We were supposed to go out last night, and she stood me up."

My eyes were wide open now. "She . . . didn't show or what?"

"I went to pick her up, and she wasn't there."

"Have you called her?"

"Yeah. She doesn't answer. I used Dad's direct line at the store when I called just now, so that I wouldn't get Kay on the phone in case she's teed off about something, but I don't know what that would be."

"Have you tried calling her parents?"

"Are you insane? No, I asked Dad who was working today, and he said that Kay was there and a couple clerks."

"So we know she's all right," I said. "Well, there's probably a good reason she wasn't home, and my guess is she'll call you sometime today when she gets a chance."

"That's sort of what I figured. Listen, I'm washing windows for Mr. Watts this afternoon, so I'll be here . . . if you find out anything."

"Sure."

"And . . . about tonight . . . have fun. I'll be out there applauding like mad," Les said. "If you deserve it, that is."

I went back to bed to finish waking up slowly, the way I like, but after three or four minutes I realized I was as awake as I was going to get, so I took my shower.

Two o'clock already. I had to be at school by six thirty. I had slept through most of the day.

Ryan called next and said that some of the cast was going bowling after tonight's performance, did I want to go? Of course, I told him. And I felt that old excitement you feel when a guy is interested in you.

I decided I was probably having more fun right now than I'd ever had before, and there were already a lot of great things to remember about my senior year. A few things to regret, of course, but being Anne in the play helped cancel out some of those.

Pamela and I peeked out about fifteen minutes before curtain time, and there seemed to be about as many people as there had been the night before.

"I see Les and Kay," I said excitedly, watching them sliding in the seventh row and getting two seats near the center. Both were smiling. Good sign.

Dad was right that having had one successful performance, I wasn't as nervous this time. Just as excited, though, maybe even more, because I knew how much the audience had liked certain scenes—Anne on the stairs, for one—and I was eager to do them again.

Ryan forgot one of his lines, though. It was the scene where we're having an argument. He suspects I'm seeing other guys and doesn't realize I'm worried about my father and responsibilities at home.

"You don't have to pretend with me," he says as we're face-to-face there on the stage.

"I'm not pretending," I say earnestly, taking his hands. "I wouldn't pretend with you. I don't think people should pretend with people."

I don't know whether Ryan forgot his next line or just forgot to say it. He was supposed to say, "I don't either," which is Bill's cue—one of Anne's brothers—to say, seeing us holding hands, "So you're at it again."

But Ryan was just looking at me. I gave his hands two quick squeezes. He blinked, looked panicky for a minute, then Bill came in with, "So you're at it again!" and we quickly dropped hands.

"He certainly has a wonderful sense of timing," Ryan said, and the play went on without anyone knowing he'd missed a line.

Les and Kay came backstage when the play was over, and Kay handed me a single rose.

"Hey! A budding actress!" she said, and gave me a hug, laughing at all my eyeliner and blush. "Wow, Alice! Look at you! *So* twenties! You were great."

Les looked happy, and I decided that whatever had happened the night before was explained and forgiven.

"Did you like it, Les?" I asked.

"Yeah, especially that Joe Scales guy."

"The cheerleader? You liked *him*?" I asked.

"Sure. You should have gone out with him, Al," Lester said, grinning, and imitated the cheer that Joe Scales teaches my younger brothers in the play. "Hoo, rah, ray, and a tiger!" We laughed, and then he said, "You were good, Al. Loved those black stockings."

"Oh, weren't they hideous!" I said.

"We're off to meet some friends," Les explained. "I'll drop by tomorrow, Al. Sylvia invited me to brunch."

"See ya," I said, and turned to look for Pamela and the others.

The whole cast went bowling afterward. I guess I was surprised how many people went bowling at eleven o'clock at night, but we had to wait for a couple of alleys, and then we got two side by side.

Ryan was an excellent bowler, and he knew it. Just the way he paused after letting go of the ball, the angle of his body, the tilt of his head, the position of his arm showed a guy who expected a spare, if not a strike, and he usually got one.

When I asked how he got to be so good, he said, "Hey, I was born in Bowling Green, what do you expect?"

I found myself studying his body, and I wondered if that was the way guys studied girls. I wasn't exactly undressing him with my eyes, but I did imagine the way his thighs must look in swim trunks, the V shape of his upper body. I think he caught me watching him once and paused just a nanosecond, watching me back, and I felt my face flush.

What was happening here? I wondered. My guy goes off to college, so I'm suddenly attracted to my "leading man"? Was this the Hollywood syndrome or something? Was I not to be trusted? Still . . . Where was *Patrick* tonight? How did I know what *he* was doing?

Penny was the real cutup. Because she's petite, you might expect her to be "one with the ball," since she's closer to the ground, and I guess she was, in a way. The ball was too heavy for her, and the first time she let it go, she sat down with that surprised look on her face that cracked us up.

The guys were teasing her, of course, but Ryan seemed more interested in showing me how to position my hand when I released the ball and had to wait till I quit laughing at Penny so he could demonstrate.

He drove me home afterward, dropping Penny off first, then Pamela. Liz was riding with someone else. When we got to my house, I reached to open the car door, but Ryan turned the engine off and gave me a little more than friendly hug—a sort of prolonged friendship hug—which is difficult to do in bucket seats.

"What are you going to do over spring break?" he asked.

"Recuperate," I told him, and he released his grip a little. We both sank back a few inches. "Catch up on sleep. I feel I could sleep for a week."

"Well, when you do wake up, maybe we could get together," he said.

"Maybe we could. If I ever catch up with homework. And I've got an article to write for *The Edge*." I knew I was making excuses as fast as I could think of them. Why? Hadn't Patrick said to enjoy my senior year? Hadn't I been having the time of my life? As he'd told me, we both knew how we felt about each other. "But I know I'll have some free time," I added. "Yeah, let's get together and do something."

He kissed me then. It wasn't a long, slow kiss or a quick peck on the cheek. If there was ever an in-between kiss, that was it—one hand cupping the back of my head, a soft kiss on the lips, both of us leaning over the center console.

Then he was smiling at me. "Okay," he said. "See you Monday."

"Thanks for the ride," I said, and got out of the car, my face warm, my head spinning.

Once inside the house, I waited for his car to pull away, then leaned against the wall and waited for my pulse to slow down. Oh, man! *Now* what?

18
HOLDING BACK

Sylvia made crêpes for brunch on Sunday. Crêpes with pow-
dered sugar and strawberry sauce. When I got up around
noon, I pulled on a pair of sweatpants and a long-sleeved jer-
sey, tied my hair back with a scrunchie, splashed water on my
face, and came to the table to find Les already eating a mound
of scrambled eggs with cheese on his plate.

"Awwwrrrk! What is it?" Les cried when he saw me, but I
only stuck my face up close to his.

"Here's what a female looks like without makeup," I said.
"Be grateful I brushed my teeth."

"Lester thought you were great last night. He told me so,"
Sylvia said.

"How did Kay like it?" I asked.

"Loved it," said Les. "Kay said she'd always wanted to be in a play or sing in a musical, but her parents wouldn't allow it. Too frivolous. Anything she did had to be 'academically oriented,' as she put it."

"Seems like a very controlling atmosphere to grow up in," said Sylvia, resting her elbows on the table and tucking her hands in the opposite sleeves of her kimono.

"And they're still at it. She called me yesterday and said that there was some big hassle at the last minute Friday night, and she apologized for standing me up."

"I'd think her parents would take the hint by now," said Dad.

"Oh, they get the hint, all right. They just don't seem to feel it makes any difference. They feel she *owes* them this, to marry into a respectable Chinese family that they've known for a long time. Her mother told her that after all they've done for her—bringing her to this country so she could get a good education—she's being disrespectful to her father by not marrying into the family of their friends."

"Wow," said Sylvia. "That's a lot of baggage to have to carry around."

"You know it," said Les.

"Any more news on the job search?" Dad asked him.

"Not much. I'm holding on to the one I've got until I find something better. I'd like something here in the area, but I'm beginning to send my résumés farther and farther out."

"Just make it something you love," said Dad.

"Meanwhile, what's happening back at your apartment?" Sylvia asked.

"With Andy?" Les shook his head. "That's what *we'd* like to know. For a woman who takes most of her meals in her room, she certainly has a lot of visitors. Mostly male, though not always."

"Maybe she's feeding them, and that's where all the food goes," I said, happy to probe around in the mystery.

"And Otto Watts likes her?" asked Dad.

"Seems to. No complaints there."

"Does she pay her share of the utilities?"

"Yep. First of the month. Cash. People come, people go. . . . Some stay a long time, some a little. Except for the man on Friday nights who turns on the TV, it's generally pretty quiet in there. Low voices."

"So there really is more than one boyfriend?" I asked.

"I can't tell. Maybe guys need more tutoring in English and history than women do. Or maybe she's just . . . uh . . . unusually attractive to men."

I couldn't help laughing. "What are you going to do? Evict her for corrupting the morals of a minor?"

"Too late for that," he said. "No, I guess we're just going to sit tight and see what happens. See where Paul and I get jobs, that's the main thing."

I should have spent the whole afternoon catching up on homework, but I took a couple hours off to go to the mall with Gwen and Liz and Pamela. We'd received invitations to a surprise baby shower for Jill on the eighteenth.

"Isn't this a bit early for a baby shower?" Sylvia had asked me when I'd opened the envelope. "I mean, even before the wedding? Is this done?"

"I don't know, but Karen's doing it," I'd said. "She figures that so few friends from school have been invited to the wedding, thanks to Mrs. Collier, that she'll give some kind of party they can attend now."

"Well, I didn't want to sound mean. It's just that sometimes a pregnancy doesn't go well, there isn't a baby, and then there are all those baby things sitting around to remind you. . . ."

I'd never thought of that. But this was a chance to be magnanimous, so we all decided to go along with it.

"When I get married, Sylvia, please don't shut out my friends," I'd said dramatically.

"I promise, but try to have your baby after, not before," she'd replied.

As we drove to Bloomingdale's at White Flint Mall, Liz said, "It's more fun buying baby gifts than towels. Besides, Jill and Justin are getting a bunch of hand-me-downs from Mrs. Collier, Karen said."

"That's what I heard. Things from their attic and odd pieces of furniture from their summer place at Hilton Head," Pamela told us. "Jill's not real happy about starting out with secondhand stuff. She thinks Justin's dad talked to the trustee at the bank, because she was all set to go furniture shopping, but then the bank told Justin the trust would cover only apartment rental, not furniture," said Pamela.

"Ouch. No shopping spree for Jill," I said. "That must have hurt."

We were being incredibly catty about someone we were about to spend more money on than we cared to.

"Do you realize that our main social activity for the next ten years will be showers?" Gwen said, turning into the parking lot off Nicholson Lane. She was driving the car she'd bought from her brother, and we were all impressed that she was the very first girl in our crowd to have her own car. "I've been to showers for three cousins and one aunt all within the last eight months," she said. "And I've been a bridesmaid at three of those weddings."

I found myself counting too. So far I'd been to a bridal shower for Crystal, one of Lester's old girlfriends. I'd been to Marilyn's wedding and a shower for her baby. I was a bridesmaid at both Carol's and Sylvia's weddings. . . . "Wow!" I said "We need to set aside a special account just for showers, I guess. They really start adding up. Jill is going to expect something exquisite, you know that."

"Why do you think we're going to Bloomingdale's?" said Pamela.

As we got out of the car, Gwen said, "I suggest we all go in together and get one gift from all four of us. Then, if she doesn't like it . . ."

". . . she can't pick on any one of us," I finished.

"No. Then she'll simply return it and buy a fantastic negligee for her wedding night," said Pamela, and we laughed.

It was easier knowing that all four of us would make a decision together and that the strain wouldn't be quite so heavy on our wallets.

Walking into the baby section at Bloomingdale's was like entering an imaginary land. There was a different stuffed animal beside each sign—BABY BOY, BABY GIRL, INFANTS, TODDLERS. . . . Some counters were arranged by color, others by article of clothing, and we milled about with young mothers and grandmothers, some with toddlers in tow and an occasional husband.

"This is more fun than looking at shoes," said Liz.

"Not quite, but close," said Gwen.

I held up a ruffled print top and matching leggings by Juicy Couture. "Did we ever wear anything this cute when we were babies?" I asked.

Gwen checked the price tag. "At seventy-eight dollars, no."

I dropped the outfit as though it burned me. "There's hardly anything to it!" I protested. "A yard of material at most."

"The smaller the package, the higher the price. First rule of retailing," Gwen said.

We proceeded toward the boutique section, where an elephant rocking chair had caught our attention. "Something like this, maybe, from all of us?" Liz said. She checked the tag and shook her head. "A hundred twenty, plus tax. Too steep for me."

"Let's decide what each of us planned to spend," said Gwen. "Twenty-five dollars is tops for me."

I was too embarrassed to say I was thinking more like fifteen. Liz and Pamela offered twenty. That made the ruffled top and matching leggings about right for our price range, but it seemed a rather puny gift coming from four girls. We kept looking.

"Look!" said Gwen, holding up a pair of UGG infant booties. We oohed and aahed until we checked that price too. Fifty bucks.

"I can buy a pair of stiletto heels for less than that," said Pamela.

Liz found a package of infant sneaker socks for twenty-eight dollars.

"Maybe we should buy a diaper bag and fill it with small items," she suggested, and we all were in favor of that. We checked out a Rebecca Minkoff baby bag and gasped at the price: three hundred ninety-five.

"I've got a better idea," said Gwen. "Why don't we buy the largest but least expensive thing they have here, ask for a gift box, then go to Old Navy and buy some more stuff to add to it. I was shopping with my aunt last month and we got a pair of baby fisherman sandals for eight dollars. A newborn pajama set for ten."

We considered that a moment.

"Yeah, but if she tries to exchange them, they'll tell her that most of the stuff wasn't from Bloomingdale's," said Liz.

Pamela had wandered off and was looking at a little pair of cotton jeans for seventy-nine dollars.

"You're not serious?" I asked.

She didn't answer, just pointed to the size tag: 3 MONTHS. I looked at her quizzically.

"That's how old my baby would have been . . . if I hadn't miscarried," she said.

That was about right, I figured. Three months. What is a baby doing at three months? Are babies rolling over yet? Laughing out loud? Sleeping through the night or not? What would *Pamela* be doing if she had a three-month-old baby? Nursing? She certainly wouldn't be thinking of working on a cruise ship come summer.

Two aisles up, a woman carrying a baby in a baby sling was comparing two packages of knit shirts. Her husband, who might have been slightly younger than she, stood with hands in his pockets, a diaper bag over his shoulder. Neither was smiling, though that said nothing about who they were or what they were feeling. Not everyone smiles when they're shopping.

But Pamela had seen the couple too, and as she put the little blue jeans back on the shelf she said, "That would have been Tim right now, and he'd hate me."

"Why do you say that?" asked Liz. "I don't think Justin hates Jill because she's pregnant."

"They'd been planning to marry," Pamela said. "Tim and I hadn't. And even if we had, who wants to start married life pregnant? Puking in the mornings? Jill probably won't end up hating Justin either, but I bet she'll hate living in an apartment with his parents' cast-off furniture. You know"—she looked around at us—"for the first time in my life, I sort of feel sorry for Jill."

I couldn't go that far. "Let's just hope they bring up a happy kid," I said. "So . . . what are we going to buy?"

We ended up purchasing a Ralph Lauren reversible blanket for twenty-five dollars, a Spunky dog for twenty, a white Ralph Lauren beanie hat and booties for twenty, and the infant socks that looked like sneakers for twenty-eight. It all came to ninety-three plus tax, more than we'd wanted to spend, but it all fit in a Bloomingdale's box and didn't look too bad for a present.

Patrick called me that night to see how things had gone. I told him everything . . . except that Ryan had kissed me. And that we were going out over spring break. I told myself that it had just been an affectionate kiss—that we were feeling close because we were in the play together, that it was our senior year—you can't help but feel a certain closeness, but it didn't necessarily mean anything.

"So how are you going to celebrate when it's all over?" he asked.

"I don't know," I said. "The first night we went to the Silver Diner, and the next night we went bowling. We'll probably do the same—a good way to get rid of tension. I don't think you need to worry that we're going skinny-dipping or anything."

"Here in Chicago they celebrate by jumping in Lake Michigan," Patrick said.

"What? In April? In the nude?"

Patrick chuckled. "Okay. I made that up. I'm not part of theater, so I don't know what they do. Something crazy, probably. You sleeping any better?"

"No, but I will by this weekend. I'd be okay if I didn't have to get up early for school."

"Well, I'll be thinking of you Friday and Saturday nights. Wondering what you're doing, who you're with. . . ."

"You already know most of the cast, Patrick."

"That's true. I know they'll take a lot of pictures for *The Edge*. Save a set for me."

"I will," I told him.

After I signed off, I sat on my bed, my arms locked around my knees, and stared at the wall. What does it mean when you hold something back? What does it say about a relationship? After all those wonderful things Patrick had said to me just over a week ago when I called him, crying, why would I even be *thinking* of going out with someone else over spring break?

Because we weren't engaged, that's why. Because we were expected to go out with other people till we could be together full-time. Would Patrick have told me if he'd driven a girl home and kissed her? If he had a car, that is? Would I be understanding if he did? Would I realize this was a temporary situation? How on earth did you ever know for sure?

19
MAIL

It was a surreal week. We had rehearsals again Monday through Wednesday, and I had trouble sleeping again; missed two more mornings of school because of it. But I went to the rest of my classes and did the best I could, light-headed for lack of sleep, excited, nervous about Ryan, thinking about Patrick. . . .

In physics Ryan told me he'd been accepted at the University of Iowa, that this might push him in the direction of becoming a writer.

"You've heard from them already? That's great," I told him. "I'm surprised you never got involved with the newspaper here. I mean, if you like writing so much."

"Small potatoes," he said. "And I've only been here a year. Where are you going to go?"

"Probably the University of Maryland," I told him, not wanting to admit it was a done deal, "though I'm still waiting to hear from UNC. I like the idea of being able to come home whenever I want."

"Yeah?" said Ryan. "Well, if you're going to major in counseling, I suppose you could go almost anywhere."

"Uh . . . not really," I said, but the screen lit up at the front of the room and we settled back to watch a video on quantum gravity, our minds on anything but.

More and more people were hearing from colleges—Liz got accepted at Goucher, her second choice—but even that took a backseat to the buzz about Jill and Justin's wedding. It was all Jill talked about when we saw her at lunchtime. It was less than two weeks away, and there was so much to do, she kept saying. The Colliers had worked out an agreement with the church that they could have the wedding the day before Easter if they left all the flowers for the Easter-morning services and had vacated the building by three.

Penny said what none of us dared say: "I'd think you'd want the wedding at the *start* of spring break, so you could have a week to yourselves."

"Not enough time to get ready," Jill said woefully. "Mrs. Collier is moving this along at the speed of sound as it is, and she needs every extra day she can get. We'll be spending the weekend at the Hay-Adams, though—forty-eight hours of pure luxury."

I'd been noticing the little "fault lines" that had appeared on Justin's forehead the last few months—all the bickering and tension with his folks, I guess. I thought *I* had problems making the leap from high school to college, but what if I had to throw in marriage and a baby too? If anyone should be at the breaking point, I'd think it would be Justin.

Some of us had received invitations and some had not. We couldn't quite see the reasons for the selection. Karen, of course, as one of the bridesmaids, got an invitation. Penny did not. Gwen got an invitation, Pamela did not. *I* got an invitation, Liz did not. All Gwen and I could figure was that Gwen, as class valedictorian and med-student-to-be, would be a prestigious addition to the guest list, and that I, as features editor for *The Edge*, might do a write-up of the wedding. Fat chance.

"Did I tell you that Justin and I have an apartment now?" Jill was saying. "We move in over spring break."

"Where?" we wanted to know. "What's it like?"

Jill toyed with a coil of her hair that had recently got new highlights—glorious strands of gold and brown. "Sixteenth Street in D.C.," she said. "I wanted one overlooking Rock Creek Park, but Justin said we couldn't afford it. This has to come out of his education trust fund. It pays for room and board while he's in college, and the trustee will stretch the meaning to include a basic apartment off campus, and I do mean 'basic.' Ha! I'll bet if Justin was marrying into one of those families in Capitol Hill real estate, the Colliers would spring for a gorgeous apartment we could show to all our friends."

"You can still show it to us!" I said.

She gave me one of her condescending looks, as though I didn't count, and continued: "First they said Justin had to buy the diamond ring himself if I wanted an engagement ring. Well, we'd already decided on that. I certainly didn't want to wear one of his mother's cast-off diamonds. Then they said we had to pay for our own honeymoon. I guess that's okay too, because if Mrs. Collier paid for it, she'd have Justin going to Paris and me to Siberia. But to make him pay for so much other stuff while he's in school . . . I mean, she'll do everything she can to break us up, I'll bet, even after we're married."

"It just might be . . . that they're doing everything they can to help you two become independent," said Gwen, and I was glad Gwen said it, not me.

Jill ignored her. "They didn't even mention baby expenses, but that's okay. Mom says she'll buy the car seat and stroller. The one good thing about our new apartment is it's on the top floor, so we won't have to listen to footsteps overhead. It's a one-bedroom with a den, but we'll do the den over for the baby. The living room faces the courtyard, so we're directly across from another apartment, and there are no balconies, but there's a little playground not too far away, so I can take the baby there." Jill seemed on a talking jag she couldn't stop. "Mom says fall's a good time to have a baby because the weekends are unusually good, and of course Justin will be studying a lot, but—"

"I can come over on weekends and keep you company," Karen said.

"Oh, we'll be fine," Jill said hurriedly. "And I love, love, *love* my dress!"

On Thursday, just as he did last week, Mr. Ellis said there would be no rehearsal—that all of us should have a relaxing evening with our families before the weekend performances. Gwen let Liz and me off at the corner, and we walked the half block to Elizabeth's house in the sweet April air.

"I think Ryan's hot for you," Liz said as we sauntered along, elbows bumping occasionally. There was a delicious scent of blossoms, and I realized how little time we'd had just to stroll like this.

"Oh, really?" I said, and we exchanged smiles.

"Yeah?" she said, studying me closely. Then, "Yeah?" a little louder. "And you . . . ?"

I continued facing forward "Oh, it's just a . . . fling."

"A lot can happen in a fling," said Liz. "How do you *feel* about him?"

"I don't honestly know," I said. "He's . . . hot, like you say. He's interested in me. We've actually kissed—"

Liz came to a complete stop. "*My God*, Alice!"

"Oh, it was sort of a cross between friendship and . . . "

"Passion?" she asked.

"Something like that. Not that much. He wants us to go out over spring break."

"Are you?"

"Yeah. I suppose. Patrick wouldn't want me to just sit around."

"Hmmm," said Liz. "Well, I guess you're never going to know if Patrick's 'the one' unless you experience other guys."

"*Experience?* Uh . . . as in all forty-nine flavors?"

"I don't know about that. Come on in. We've got some passion fruit sorbet. Just what you need."

It seemed perfectly wonderful to hang out like this, as though all the hurry and worry of senior year was behind us. Felt like it did back in eighth grade when we hung out on each other's porches after school.

There was mail in the box, which meant Mrs. Price was out somewhere with Nathan. Holding the envelopes in one hand, key in the other, Liz let us in.

Inside, she dumped her backpack on the sofa beside the mail. And then she gasped and grabbed for an envelope that had landed on the floor.

"Alice!" she cried. "It's from Bennington!"

"Omigod!" I said. "Open it! Open it!"

"They rejected me," said Liz, staring at the white business envelope in her hand.

It was déjà vu, but I managed to say, "Liz, you haven't even looked."

There were already tears in her eyes. "Everyone *says*! If it's an acceptance, it comes in a large envelope with a whole bunch of forms to . . ." The tears were spilling onto her hand.

She gave the envelope to me. "You read it. Just tell me."

We pushed the books and mail off the couch and sat down together. I opened the envelope, and Liz closed her eyes. I scanned the letter. "You've been wait-listed," I told her, trying to put some hope in my voice. "That's not a no."

"Wait-listed!" Liz wailed, her eyes filling up again. "That's even worse! That means I go on not knowing. And even if I get in eventually, it means I'm second choice." She was crying again in earnest. "Alice, I had my sweatshirt all picked out and everything! I have a map of the campus and a map of the town and . . ."

I put my arm around her, but oh, I knew the feeling. "This isn't the only place you applied. And you've been accepted at Goucher."

"But I don't want to go anywhere else! I w-want to be a Bennington Girl!" she wept. "How can I go all summer not knowing where I'm going to college? How will I know if I should buy ski clothes for Vermont or sundresses for Georgia?"

"Did you apply to a college in Georgia?" I asked.

"No," she said, and cried some more. I almost wished I had taped this so I could play it back to her when she was sane.

"Liz," I told her, "this is the final weekend of the play, and you have a leading role. No matter what happens, an actress dries her tears and the show goes on. You're going to put on a magnificent performance because you know you must!" I was putting on a pretty good performance myself.

"The play!" Liz said, and her eyes got huge. She wiped one arm across her face. "My eyes are going to look swollen, aren't they?"

"Everything that happens to an actress is something she can

use onstage, remember? Laughing on the outside, crying on the inside? Think of the play, Liz, and we'll worry about Bennington later," I said.

Liz hugged me, still sniffling. "What would I do without you, Alice?"

After we each ate a dish of passion fruit sorbet, I went across the street to our house, part aching for Liz, part smiling at her "Bennington Girl."

We have a mail slot in our front door, and some days there are so many catalogs on the other side that I can hardly get the door open. This was one of those days. Crate & Barrel, JC Penney, J. Crew, Territory Ahead . . .

And then I saw the words "University of North Carolina" peeking out from under the Crate & Barrel catalog. What was this—National Letdown Day? But the envelope from UNC was large. Heavy.

Mechanically, I opened it. *Dear Miss McKinley: We are pleased to inform you . . .*

Too late. But I wouldn't have gone anyway. I was a Maryland Girl now.

20
IN THE DINER

I guess actors always keep the possibility of disaster in mind—a set falling over on someone or actually breaking a leg onstage. Nobody thought of the possibility that college rejections the day of a show could affect a cast. At school on Friday, a few other people had heard from colleges, and someone referred to the hall outside Mrs. Bailey's office as the "wailing wall." I was pretty much over my own disappointment about William & Mary—it was just a dull ache in my chest. And even though I'd confirmed with Maryland that I was going there, I could still say, *Oh, yeah, well, I was accepted at UNC too, but* . . . And it *was* nice to know I was saving Dad a heap of money.

Liz came to school subdued, and I let her talk about Bennington when she felt like it. It was her story to tell, if she wanted to. By the time we gathered for the evening performance, she wore a stoic, determined look on her face, a "bravely carrying on" sort of look that made Mr. Ellis say, "Mrs. Gilbreth, your husband dies at the end of the play, not the beginning," and somehow Liz took on the warm maternal glow we needed, *she* needed, to see the play through.

Then the unexpected happened. Maybe what did it was a number of people saying "Break a leg" before the play instead of *Watch out for the dog.*

I don't think any of us in the cast were particularly nervous. We'd had two good performances the weekend before, and we arrived at the dressing rooms to find that someone had steamed the wrinkles out of our costumes, so everything was fresh and ready to go. Gwen came with a bunch of friends. She was sitting with Daniel Bul Dau and Yolanda. I could see them in the second row. Phil Adler and some of the other people from the newspaper were behind them.

In the play two of the Gilbreth boys are coming down the stairs holding their dog—the dog their father didn't want—and the audience hears Mr. Gilbreth shouting, "Get him out of here!" from above.

Dan had just said, "Of all the dumb dogs," and Fred had replied, "What do you expect for five dollars?" when the dog wriggled loose and began running from one actor to another onstage, tail wagging, leaping up, and putting its front paws in people's laps.

It was total chaos. "Guinness, no!" people were hissing, but the two-year-old Lab upset an end table and scrunched up the rug. When Jackie, his true owner, who wasn't even supposed to be onstage, came running in to get him, the dog thought they were playing and barreled away to the delight of the audience, which screamed with laughter. What could we do but pretend it was all part of the play? When Jackie finally belly flopped on the dog and dragged him off the stage, I managed to say, "That dog! Where was he this time?"

And Bill answered, "Up on Dad's bed again. The basement window . . . across the coal bin . . . up the back stairs . . . Dad's bed!"

"Dad was right about the dog," I said, continuing on. "Now he'll think he's right about everything."

"Clothes, makeup, everything," Pamela said, and we were finally back into the script.

When the phone rang, right on cue—Joe Scales, the cheerleader, calling to ask my character out—the scene played without a hitch, and I loved that a low chuckle went through the audience as I said innocently into the phone, "Where have I been all your life? Mostly, I've been right here. . . ."

Afterward, everyone was talking and laughing about the dog, and if Liz was still depressed over Bennington, she didn't show it. Mr. Ellis said we'd played it well. "Good show, guys," he said. "But tomorrow night, hang on to that dog!"

Mrs. Cary came out of the girls' dressing room just then to report that a water pipe overhead was leaking and it would probably be morning before anyone could fix it. She suggested we take our costumes home in case the drip got worse during the night.

So, still wearing our makeup and third-act costumes, we stepped around the wet newspapers on the floor, collected the clothes we had worn in Acts I and II, and with Gwen and Yolanda helping, carried them out to the car.

When the waitress at the Silver Diner saw us coming this time, in costume, she began hastily clearing tables as fast as she could, and we swarmed in, taking up half the booths.

"It's on him," Sam said, pointing to Brad Broderick, who was still in his three-piece suit and who, with lines on his forehead, gray powder in his hair, and a padded potbelly, looked at least sixty-five.

"Me?" cried Brad, standing regally by the counter. "Why, children, I'm sailing for Europe tomorrow. I thought this was my send-off party."

Everyone in the diner turned to watch now, some of them smiling, others just looking puzzled. But Brad hadn't been cast as the star of the play for nothing. He looked around the diner and said, "But I think we've got time for one last check." He pulled his stopwatch out of his vest pocket, then his whistle, and gave a loud blast.

Now all the customers had stopped eating and were staring at us, and the manager came out of the kitchen, curious. All nine of us children scrambled out of the booths crying, "Coming" or "I'm here, Dad," and we lined up in front of the counter, holding out our hands for fingernail inspection.

The manager watched, grinning, as Brad went down the row,

making up his lines: "I've seen better" and "What have you been digging?" When he got to young Jack, he bopped him on the head with a menu and said, "Filthy! Utterly filthy! Shame on you!"

The customers were laughing, enjoying the show, even though they didn't know who we were or what the play was about.

When Brad got to me, though—he'd started at the younger end of the line—he said, "Oh, Anne, Anne. You always were my favorite daughter, and since I'm leaving forever, I think you ought to know a deep family secret."

I played along. "Oh, what, what?" I cried. "Tell me!"

"Anne . . . ," Brad said, holding me out in front of him, hands on my shoulders. I could tell he was still in the process of making this up. "Anne . . . I'm not your real father."

The cast was hooting and laughing, and customers had turned in their seats to give their full attention.

"Oh, Daddy," I cried. "What are you saying?"

"That I am your lecherous Uncle Harry in disguise," Brad said, and with that, he pulled me to him, tipped me over backward, and gave me a movie-star kiss while everyone cheered and applauded.

The guy playing Bill, one of the brothers, yanked the cap off his head and went around to the tables, holding it out for tips, but not long enough for anyone to put anything in it, and the whole diner was laughing and clapping.

I couldn't tell if Ryan was all that amused when I went back to our booth. He was smiling, anyway. But I knew I'd remember this night forever.

* * *

Dad and Sylvia came to the final performance just to see it again. I think all of us in the cast had a catch in our throats when we said our lines for the last time. We wanted this performance to be our best, and so we probably overacted some of the scenes. When Penny recited the line, "Lincoln freed the slaves . . . all but one . . . all but one," friends in the audience cheered wildly, simply because Penny was so popular herself.

When the curtain fell at last, then opened as we all joined hands and stepped forward for our bow, a lot of us had tears in our eyes. A couple of the guys, even. Elizabeth and Chassie were smiling even as tears ran down their cheeks, and when we looked at them and laughed, they laughed with us.

Dad and Sylvia were still clapping along with the rest of the audience—a rhythmical clapping now, as though nobody wanted the evening to end—and ushers made their way down the aisles with bouquets of flowers, more flowers than usual because it was the last night. I could see a huge bouquet of red roses bobbing down the center aisle, but I couldn't see who was carrying it till Amy's head came into view. She came right up to the footlights and handed them to me.

Surprised, I bent to receive them, a little embarrassed. Most of the other bouquets were wrapped in cellophane, held together at the base with a rubber band, but these were exquisite, and I gave Dad a fond but surprised smile as I accepted them.

The curtain closed again, and everyone was hugging everyone else. Liz and Pamela gathered around me, however, and asked, "Who sent those, Alice? Who are they from?"

"My dad, I think," I said, and found the little card attached to one stem. I turned it around to read it. There was just one word: *Patrick.*

Mr. and Mrs. Ellis invited us all to their house for the cast party, and Mrs. Ellis herself wore a 1920s beaded dress. It was an exceptionally warm night, and some of us had opted for dresses instead of jeans. Sylvia had taken Patrick's flowers home with her, and she and Dad had brought both cars so that I could drive Liz and Pamela to the party.

The Ellises' house was even more Victorian than Mr. Watts's. It looked like something out of a Charles Addams cartoon, with little nooks and crannies at every turn, lace curtains, flocked wallpaper, overstuffed velvet furniture, old photos covering the walls, and pillows you could get lost in.

Mrs. Cary had changed her dress for the occasion, and she and her husband came looking like Daisy and Jay Gatsby themselves. On one side of the parlor, Mrs. Ellis had an open trunk filled with old costumes—tall silk hats, capes, corsets, vests. . . .

"Alice, this is for you!" Pamela cried, holding out a luscious black lace teddy, and of course everyone urged me to try it on, which I didn't. But I did pull on a pair of ruffled knee-length bloomers under my dress, the ruffles gathered at both knees. And when someone handed me a fitted corset, circa 1910, I put that on too over my dress, and Liz and Pamela were screaming with laughter as they stood behind me, tightening the laces to see how much tighter they could go before I passed out. Sam even took a picture for *The Edge*.

What surprised us all was watching the stage crew get in the act. When Mrs. Ellis put on a CD of the Charleston, a couple girls and one of the guys from the crew did an impromptu dance for us. We kept finding things in the trunk and putting them on their heads—strings of pearls, a boa—and it seemed the more we dumped on them, the faster they danced.

Amy Sheldon was there in her black pants and a black tee. Mostly she watched from one of the straight-backed chairs, laughing at the antics of the dancers, happy to be part of the celebration. I sat on a hassock at her feet as we ate the little meatballs and tiny hot dogs Mrs. Ellis had made for us, and I asked Amy if she was having fun.

"It's a silly party, isn't it?" she said. "I think you have your clothes on wrong. Your dress should be on the outside."

I laughed. "You're right. I wouldn't wear a corset like this in a million years, but tonight it's just for fun."

"It makes people laugh," said Amy, trying to analyze it.

"Exactly."

She smiled then. "I'm going to be on stage crew next year too. I already got invited," she told me.

When the party broke up a little after midnight and I drove Liz and Pamela home, we went over all the details of the party—who did what, said what, wore what. . . . And just before Pamela got out, she said, "Ryan asked me who sent the roses, Alice."

"Yeah?"

"I told him they were from your brother."

"My *brother*? Why?"

"Dunno," she said as she opened the door. "Just to make things more interesting, I guess."

21

TALKING WITH PATRICK

Spring vacation couldn't have come at a better time. Sylvia said that I slept until two thirty the following afternoon. That wasn't entirely true, because I woke around noon and debated getting up—then thought better of it and went back to sleep again.

When I finally stumbled into the bathroom, I felt as though I had molted into a new person, refreshed and alert. If spring hadn't always been my favorite season (I like fall), it was for today.

Dad and Sylvia didn't ask anything of me. There was a slice of quiche waiting for me in the fridge, some fruit salad, some ham. Dad was watching an NBA play-off game, Sylvia was altering a skirt, and the house had a blissful, contented sound—the low hum of the sewing machine, the sports commentator's monologue. It all just made me happy and totally absorbed in the deep red of the roses on our coffee table. I was thinking about the best time to call Patrick to thank him when the phone rang.

It was Ryan.

"Hi," he said.

"Oh, hi!" I said, wishing I could have talked to Patrick first.

"Tried calling you on your cell phone, but you didn't answer," he told me.

"It's in my bag upstairs and I didn't hear it," I explained.

"Just get up?"

I laughed. "About a half hour ago. How long did you sleep?"

"I've been up since eleven. Told Dad I'd wash the cars this afternoon, get the pollen off."

"It'll only get worse in May," I said.

"I know, but it'll give me something to do. I was wondering if you wanted to go out tonight. Take in a movie, maybe. . . ."

This was too much too soon. I wanted some downtime. I wanted to talk with Patrick, try on some summer clothes. . . .

"I sort of promised to hang with my family tonight, Ryan," I said, searching for an excuse. "They've hardly seen me at all the last several months." What was the matter with me? I couldn't say I wasn't interested, because I was.

"Understood," he said. "Tomorrow?"

"Oh, I'm sorry, I'm going to a shower for Jill tomorrow."

"She the one getting married?"

"Appears that way."

"Sort of weird, isn't it? Spring vacation and all," Ryan said.

"Well, there's a history to it," I told him. "What about Wednesday?"

"Okay. Wednesday afternoon or evening?"

"You decide. Whatever you want to do," I said.

"Till Wednesday, then," he said. "I'll let you know."

My heart was racing when we ended the call. I felt a certain excitement I hadn't felt for a long time—the growing certainty that a guy likes you and you maybe like him. The beginning of the flirtation dance, back and forth, where you're edging into unknown territory, and each question, each answer, is a clue.

I finished my breakfast, looked over the comics without really concentrating on them, then went straight up to my room and called Patrick. It was a while before he answered. I was afraid I'd have to leave a message, but then he picked up.

"Hi, it's me," I said. "You weren't sleeping, were you?"

"Sleeping? No. I'm here at the tennis court waiting to play," he said. "It's a gorgeous day in Chicago."

"Here, too," I told him. "Patrick, those roses are beautiful. I was bowled over."

"Glad you like them," he said. "I'd rather have been there, but I had to work for my prof yesterday. And I'd barely see the play before I'd have had to fly back again. This will be the first time I've had in a week to get some exercise. How'd the play go?"

I started to tell him about the dog getting loose onstage, but Patrick was saying something to someone else.

"I'm up next, Alice," he said. "I'll call you later, okay? You going to be in this evening?"

"Yeah, I'll be home," I said.

"We'll talk then," he said, and we signed off.

I sat on the edge of my bed, staring at my toes. The nails needed trimming, but I didn't make a move to go get the manicure set. What did I want from Patrick? I asked myself. His blessing? Permission? His telling me it was okay to go out with Ryan during spring break? Even after spring break, maybe? Did Patrick ask me if he could go out? He might even be playing tennis with a girl—how did I know? Why hadn't I told Ryan I'd go out with him tonight?

The truth was, I wasn't sure how I felt about Ryan. But another truth may have been that I was trying to think up reasons *not* to like him. What did it say about a relationship if I said no to other guys because I wanted to convince myself that Patrick was "the one"? Or why couldn't it be that Patrick really *was* special and I was protecting the relationship? Isn't that what people did when they were married? Committed themselves to the marriage as well as to the person? But who was talking marriage? We weren't even engaged. And Patrick was going to Spain in a couple of months.

I stood up and went to get a basin to soak my feet so my toenails would soften. That's me—always jumping ahead. Planning my life weeks, months, years ahead instead of savoring each minute of every day.

When Molly Brennan called later and said she was having a hen party cookout in her backyard Tuesday evening, I almost leaped into the phone saying yes.

"I'm inviting you and Gwen and Pamela and Liz and a few others," she said. "And guess who else will be there?" I tried to think, but before I could answer, she said, "Faith."

I squealed. "Oh, I'd love to see her. She's not—"

"Back with Ron? Nope. She's moved on—*way* on."

"Okay. What can I bring?"

"How about crackers and dip?" said Molly. "Hey, if I play this right, everyone wanting to bring something, I won't have to cook a thing."

Les took us to a steak house for dinner that night, so I obliged him and ordered a T-bone.

"Heard from any colleges yet?" he asked me after he'd ordered the drinks.

"UNC and George Mason said yes. William & Mary turned me down. I'm going to Maryland," I said.

He didn't say anything for a moment, just watched me. "Well, three out of four ain't bad, kiddo."

I gave him a fake pout. "I wanted *everyone* to love me."

"You'll be going to a good school, Al, and we're proud of you," Dad said.

"I just want to know *why*," I told him. "It's like when you break up with someone. You need to know why. You need closure."

Les reached for the pepper mill and ground away. "I broke up with a lot of girls and never said why, mostly because I didn't quite know myself. Just wanted to move on, I guess."

I hate that phrase, *move on*. Like no matter what happened or what you did, you just "move on," and that's supposed to make everything all right.

"I feel like writing the admissions office back and asking, 'Was it something I said? Something I wrote? My SAT scores? Not social enough?' *What?*" I told him.

"Just let it go, Al. There's a lot more to life than school."

"Yeah? So how is your life going? How's Kay?" I asked.

"How should I know? You probably see more of her than I do," he answered.

"Les, I haven't been to work for two weeks."

"Well, Paul and I had invited her and Judith to hear a new band in Georgetown last night, and only Judith showed. She said that Kay called her at the last minute and said she couldn't make it, she'd explain later. Something to do with her parents. Judith thinks she's starting to cave."

"No!" I said. "That would be horrible!"

"It's her life. And we had a pretty good time with Judith, though I cut out early."

"And Andy? What's happening there?" asked Sylvia.

"Same traffic, up and down those side stairs. Somebody every night. Often two."

"Les, is this something you should look into?" Dad asked after the waiter placed our orders in front of us and left. "She's using Mr. Watts's house, after all."

And I said what the others didn't: "You think she's a *hooker*?"

"Oh, Les!" Sylvia said.

"I've already been looking into it, doing a little checking at the U," Les told us. "Andy calls herself a grad student, but that was a couple of years ago. She claims she's tutoring, so I've got to be careful here. . . ."

"Just don't you and Paul get yourselves arrested if the police raid the place," Dad said.

After Les had gone that night and Sylvia and Dad were going to bed, I propped myself up on pillows in my room and called Patrick. I told him about how the dog got loose onstage and how Brad had kissed me in that funny act we put on in the Silver Diner, and I loved hearing Patrick's deep chuckle at the other end.

"You found out you had talents you never knew you had," he said.

"Kissing, you mean?"

"I mean the whole thing. Acting, being onstage . . ."

"Yeah, I guess I did. But I'm not thinking of making a career of it," I told him. "How did the tennis game go?"

"Got creamed. We were playing doubles, though, and I'd have to say that my partner wasn't quite up to it."

"Who was your partner?"

"Fran. We were playing Adam and John. You met them when you were here last summer."

My stomach did a flip-flop.

"Last week Adam was my partner and we won, so I don't think my own game was off. But, as I said, the weather was glorious."

I decided this was an incident I didn't have to file in my worry bank. Patrick's spring break hadn't coincided with mine, and he'd spent his with his parents in Wisconsin. Now he was back in school, and he needed all the relaxation he could get.

"What do you have planned for your spring vacation?" he asked me.

"R and R," I said. "I have a couple papers due and an article to write for *The Edge*. Tomorrow night there's a surprise shower for Jill, Tuesday night I'm going over to Molly's with a bunch of girls, and Wednesday I'm hanging out with Ryan. He was Larry in the play."

"Oh? Going anywhere in particular?" Patrick asked.

Is that all he's going to say? I wondered. *No surprise? No jealousy?*

"I don't know yet," I said flatly. "We just said we'd get together. Maybe he's invited some other people, I don't know."

"Maybe," said Patrick. And now I could tell by the tone of his voice that he was smiling again. "Or maybe he just wants you all to himself."

"We'll probably just talk about the play," I said. "Don't worry. He's going to the University of Iowa next year. He'll be even farther away than you are."

"Correction," said Patrick. "I'll be in Spain."

"Yeah, that's right," I said. I *wanted* to say, *So whose fault is that?* but I didn't. I told him I'd been accepted at UNC and George Mason but had confirmed with Maryland I'd be going there.

"Well, it's a relief to have that decided and out of the way," Patrick said.

"I suppose," I said. "All these decisions I've had to make this year, Patrick—whether to try out for the play, whether to try out for Ivy Day Poet, what colleges to apply for . . . they must seem so small compared to all the things you've done in your life. You've had a lot of great moments, but one of the biggest moments for me was receiving that bouquet of roses onstage." I felt as though I was going to cry again.

But Patrick said, "Then I'm glad your biggest moment was from me."

How could I go out with Ryan after that?

22
CATCHING UP

The surprising thing about Jill's baby shower was that she really was surprised. I could tell partly from her reaction and partly because she hadn't fixed herself up especially—just came to Karen's in a wrinkled shirt without mascara, thinking she was going somewhere with her mom. I almost thought she was angry at first, like she'd been set up to humiliate herself, but then I think she was genuinely moved that so many girls had shown up. Maybe even Jill, homecoming queen, had insecurities too, I decided, watching the number of times she tried to pin her hair back, hair that could have used a washing.

Her mom was there, looking lovelier than Jill, actually—a former model, I'd heard. As each gift was opened, it was placed inside the crib Karen had borrowed for the occasion.

"Did you ever see so much white and yellow?" Jill said, laughing as she opened a little romper set. "Nobody dares buy pink or blue till after they find out the sex of the baby. I want a little girl. I know just how I'll dress her."

"Just wish for a healthy baby, Jill," her mother said. "Little boys are nice too."

"Hmmm. Big boys are better," Jill said, and we laughed.

I noticed how frequently there was a snide remark about the person who wasn't there. When the doorbell rang a half hour into the party, one of the girls arriving late, Jill murmured, "Please don't let that be you-know-who." When the tiny cakes were passed around, Jill said, "I'm going to have two, even though the witch would frown at me."

I guess she liked the gift from Gwen and Pam and Liz and me. "Oh, Ralph Lauren," she said, more about the labels than the little booties and cap. I saw her peek beneath the tissue paper for a gift receipt, and when she found it, she smiled and said, "Thanks, guys! Cute!" and passed the box along to her mom.

Something was missing here, I wasn't sure what. I kept hoping the door would open and Justin would appear with a guitar, if he played a guitar. That he'd sit down and sing a song to her and the baby. That Jill would caress her tummy, even, and say, *It's okay, little man*, or something.

But the evening ended with people carrying cups and saucers to the kitchen, and Jill saying we were all invited to see their apartment after they'd fixed it up, and then we were in Gwen's car again, going home.

For the first minute or two, no one said anything. We were each struggling for something positive or kind or generous to say, but somehow words were hard to come by.

It was Pamela who finally spoke. "It would be nice if all mistakes were reversible, wouldn't it?" When no one dared take it further, she said, "If you marry the wrong person, you can get a divorce; if you believe in abortion, you can get un-pregnant; but the one thing you can never change is the father of your baby."

I was about to protest that Jill and Justin had wanted to marry, that they'd wanted—I hope—the baby for its own sake, that Justin was not a bad guy. Then I realized that Pamela wasn't, perhaps, talking about them at all.

"Well, you lucked out, Pamela," Gwen said, speaking for all of us. "You didn't have to make any of those decisions."

"That's what senior year is all about, isn't it?" said Liz. "One decision after another. Do you remember when we were little, and all we had to do was get out of bed in the morning and our moms had our clothes all laid out for us? They arranged our playdates. Drove us wherever we needed to go."

"I don't know," said Gwen. "I sort of like driving my own car, buying my own clothes, and I certainly want to arrange my own playdates."

There was something to laugh about at last, and we said we'd see each other the next day at Molly's.

I couldn't take my eyes off Faith. The last time I'd seen her, she was thin as a broom and was having some of her teeth replaced after her abusive boyfriend slammed her face down on the hood of a car.

Now she had gained about ten pounds and looked so much better—more curvy, more friendly, more . . . happy. Her hair was especially shiny, and even her skin looked better. Amazing what being healthy will do for your looks, I thought. I noticed she was wearing a lacy chemise, cut low enough to show her cleavage, now that she had breasts again.

"You. Just. Look. Fabulous!" I told her. "Really, really!"

"You know what?" she said as we hugged. "I *feel* pretty fabulous."

I thought of the guy she was going out with after she booted Ron. A nice guy. "Are you and Chris . . . ?"

"No. He went to Virginia Tech, and I'm getting my associate degree from Montgomery College in June. We still e-mail each other from time to time, but I'm going with a navy guy now. He'll be out of the service soon, and then we'll see what happens."

"Well, you're beautiful," said Pamela. "And you deserve the best."

So did Molly, come to think of it, and from all appearances, she was healthy too. She and Faith had seen the play the last night, but there was such a crowd at the stage door that they hadn't stuck around.

"The loose dog scene was a scream!" Molly said. "You guys played it so well, we weren't sure whether it was in the script or not. I'll bet Ellis was sweating bullets backstage."

"We were sweating bullets *onstage*," I said. "It was unrehearsed, believe me!" And of course she and Faith and Pamela and I had to reminisce about the plays and musicals that had gone on before: *Fiddler on the Roof*, *Father of the Bride*, *Guys and Dolls*.

"And guess what?" Pamela told them when we stopped for breath. "I got accepted at a theater arts school in New York."

We cheered all over again, stamped our feet, and Faith pounded on the patio table. "Pamela! Yay!" she cried.

I felt a twinge of jealousy again—would we ever stop celebrating Pamela?—but refused to dwell on it. I concentrated instead on what Patrick had said—about how you can be curious and intellectual and all the rest right where you are at the moment. You didn't have to go to someplace big.

I raised my glass of Sprite. "To *us*!" I said.

"To us!" the others chorused.

To all the bad things that could have happened that didn't, all the mistakes we almost made, but didn't. I marveled that Molly was sitting here cancer-free, that Faith had dropped Ron out of her life, that Pamela had miscarried, that . . . the list went on and on. What about the mistakes that were yet to come? I wondered. And I immediately thought of my date the next day with Ryan.

"What's this I hear about Jill getting married on Saturday? Is that for real?" Molly asked.

"It's for real."

"And is she pregnant? That's the story I got."

"It's no secret. They're expecting in September," Pamela told her.

"Is . . . is this a good thing . . . or what?" Faith asked uncertainly.

"Who knows?" Pamela said. "They planned it, and they've been going together longer than anyone else in high school. She's marrying a nice guy, anyway."

Who knows what's going to happen with any of us? I thought, looking around the group. If I had to make a guess about what any of us would be doing five years from now, I could be so far off. Who knew that Les would be going out with Kay? Who knew that Patrick would be spending a year in Spain? Who knew that Faith would be looking so great, completely leaving all that pain behind, or that I would have starred in the school play?

Wednesday morning, I started my next article for *The Edge*:

WHAT WE LEAVE BEHIND

You've felt it. So have I. I can't quite explain when it happens, but with college getting closer, I'm more conscious when it happens. Much as we've wanted to grow up, move on, move out, we're saying good-bye to something we thought we'd never miss: being kids.

I felt it a year ago when I was driving by a county fair and stopped to watch the kids on a merry-go-round, the calliope playing "The Sidewalks of New York" as the painted ponies rose and fell on their shiny poles.

I used to *love* that ride. I loved the summer my dad decided I was big enough to go on all by myself, but every time my horse got around to the gate, there he'd be, smiling, and I'd feel brave enough to let go with one hand and wave back. And though big people do ride the

merry-go-round sometimes, even teens, it will never be the same as it was then—
my dad waiting for me at the gate, smiling.

I remember promising myself, when I was nine, that I would never,
ever stop doing the two things I enjoyed most: reading the comics
and hanging upside down by my knees on the jungle gym. I've already
stopped hanging by my knees.

The beanbag chair in the corner of my room—the chair that's been
a refuge for me through all the hurts and disappointments of grade
school, and even some in high school—is getting too small for me.
The furry little monkey with the missing eye that has been a fixture on
my bed for as long as I can remember will not be going to college with me.

The shoes I once loved, my favorite books, reading the newspaper over
Sunday brunch with my parents—that'll all be left behind
when September comes; and along with the excitement of living on
my own, there's an emptiness deep inside me, and I wonder what
will take its place.

Saying hello to something new means saying good-bye to something old
and loved. Much as we seniors are looking forward to college or work,
to moving out and moving on, we have a little grieving to do, and it takes
us by surprise. We're leaving a part of ourselves behind. And it's okay
to feel sad along with happy, loss along with gain, regret along with
excitement. It's part of the process. Expected, in fact.

—Alice McKinley, features editor

23
EATING OYSTERS

When Ryan called around noon on Wednesday, he had the rest of the day mapped out, and I was glad I didn't have to make any decisions. I just wanted to drift, to float. I wanted someone to give me a nudge, and my body would move in whatever direction I was pointed.

"I'll pick you up about three and we'll play some miniature golf. Then we'll head for the marina on Main Avenue for dinner and maybe pick up some improv theater. How does that sound?"

"Very ambitious," I said. "What kind of theater?"

"You don't know improvisational theater?" he said. "Alice, you haven't lived till you've seen what a cast can do!"

"I guess I'm about to be born, then," I said. "Sounds fun. I'll be ready."

Actually, I did know what improvisational theater was, I just hadn't seen any professional performances. But Ryan seemed so gung ho about instructing me that I'd let him take the credit.

April in Maryland can be cold and rainy, and we'd probably get that yet. But the sun smiled down on our spring vacation and gave us a couple of beautiful days. I dressed in a good pair of jeans and a black tee, a yellow sweater, and went out to Ryan's car when I saw him drive up.

"How's your golf game?" he asked as I slid in the passenger seat.

"Even worse than my bowling," I told him.

"We'll have to do something about that," he said, and smiled as we started out. Then, "It doesn't bother you?"

"What?"

He shrugged. "Not being very good at either one?"

"No. Not particularly. Why?"

He turned down the music a little. "I don't know. It would bother me. I'd want to be fairly good at something or I wouldn't want to do it."

I gave him a quizzical look. "How could you ever try anything new if you had to be good at it first?"

"I mean, whatever I try, I keep at it till I'm . . . well . . . at least competent."

"You don't do anything just for fun? Just to be with a bunch of friends, having a good time?"

Ryan seemed to mull that over. "Not really, I guess. If I'm going to spend time at something, I want to be good at it."

Who was I dating here? I wondered. Another Patrick? Patrick—who was good at everything, it seemed?

"Well, I can't see that my life would change much if I got to be a good bowler or a good golf player, since I don't have time for either one," I told him. "But maybe we make time for the things that we like best."

"You're probably right," he said as he headed onto the beltway.

As it happened, I wasn't bad at miniature golf. Ryan beat me by four points, and when we played a second game, I beat him by two. It surprised us both.

"See? You're better than you thought," he said. "If you keep at it, you'd probably want to try real golf."

"It's not on the agenda," I said, laughing, as we turned in the clubs and walked back to the car.

"Why not?"

"I don't know. Doesn't appeal all that much."

"What sports do you like?"

"To watch or to play? I love watching basketball and football, but I'm sort of a loner when it comes to playing a sport. I like to run by myself in the early mornings. I like to swim when I get a chance. I like playing badminton with my girlfriends. I guess I'm not very competitive when it comes to sports."

We drove into D.C. and over to the marina along the Potomac. At one end, near the bridge, the road was lined with little shops selling fish, and farther on there were restaurants catering to the boating crowd.

We were early enough to get a table by the window, and it was fun watching the boats come in and out, unfurling their sails or making their way into their slots along the dock. Nice sitting there with Ryan, who looked especially handsome in an olive T-shirt that strained at his biceps.

"You ever sail?" he asked me.

"I've been on a sailboat—well, a boat with sails, anyway—but I didn't have to do anything," I said.

"You ought to try it. It's like nothing you've ever experienced before—just moving across the surface with the wind, the only sounds being the water rippling, the sails flapping now and then, the gulls calling. No one should reach his twenty-first birthday without learning to sail."

"There are a lot of people who don't live near water," I reminded him.

"Well, the ones who do, then," Ryan said. He scanned the menu. "What are you going to have? I recommend oysters on the half shell. Ever try them?"

"Nope."

"You should. How do you know you wouldn't like them if you've never tried them?"

"I didn't say I didn't like them. But other things interest me more," I said. And when the waiter came, I said, "I'd like the shrimp basket, please, and a glass of iced tea."

"Oysters on the half shell for the appetizer," said Ryan, pointing to the menu. "Then I'll take the crab Newburg with fries."

We didn't say much waiting for our dinner, just watched the people moving about on the dock outside the window. Some were hosing down their boats, and others were carrying ice chests aboard, ready for an evening's outing. They were all expensive-looking boats, with decks and cabins and helm seats—at least that's what Ryan called them. There was a dog on one of the decks, wagging its tail and excitedly running from one side of the boat to the other, eager for its master to get on board.

"Well, this is pleasant," Ryan said. "And we can take our time over dinner because I wasn't able to get tickets for the Capitol Steps. They don't have a performance tonight."

I was sort of glad, because Ryan had paid for miniature golf, and this dinner was going to be expensive. I didn't want the evening to cost him any more.

When the oysters arrived—glistening, semitransparent blobs in gray shells—Ryan immediately began giving instructions: "First," he said, picking up a bottle of hot sauce, "you give your oyster a quick shot of this or whatever you have handy. Then"—he glanced over to make sure I was watching—"you lift up the shell between thumb and forefinger . . . like so . . . then you tip your hand and slide the oyster and juice into your mouth without letting the shell touch your lips."

He showed me how to find the best place on the lip of the shell to pour from. "Once it's in your mouth, hold it there, savoring the fresh, briny taste, then mash the oyster a couple of times and swallow it down. You don't want to swallow it whole and you don't want to chew it to pieces—just enough to swallow it easily." He tipped back his head, slid the oyster in, chewed a couple of times, and swallowed.

I wondered what Miss Manners would say about insisting that your dinner guest try your food. I really didn't want a raw oyster. But I wanted to be a good sport, so I did as he told me, trying not to look at the oyster as I picked up one of the shells. I held it up to my lips, tilted my head back, tipped the shell, trying not to touch it with my teeth, and felt the slimy blob slide into my mouth and some of the liquid dribble down my chin.

Holding the oyster in my mouth, afraid to chew, I reached for my napkin and wiped my chin. And then, feeling as though I might gag, I chewed once and swallowed the thing, my mouth tasting like seaweed.

"Good, huh?" said Ryan. "But you forgot the hot sauce."

I reached for my iced tea and took a long drink, wishing I could swish it around in my mouth a couple of times and spit it out.

"Well," I said, "it's different. I suppose it's an acquired taste."

"You'll end up loving them," said Ryan. "Have another."

"No thanks," I told him. "They're all yours. I'm saving room for my shrimp."

I wanted to split the bill with Ryan, and offered, but he wouldn't let me.

"Tonight's on me," he said. "You can take the next one."

We ambled along the concrete walkway behind the line of restaurants, watching some of the boat owners, who actually lived on their boats, come home from work. Several men were in suits, carrying briefcases. They fumbled in their pockets for keys to the padlocks and opened the gates leading to their particular dock. A woman with a dry-cleaning bag thrown over one shoulder greeted a cat that waited for her on a deck chair.

"Are you going to miss the water when you go to Iowa?" I asked Ryan.

"Probably," he said. "We have some relatives in Maine, though. Chances are I'll go up there a lot over summers. I'll be busy in theater at Iowa, though. That and writing. Hope so, anyway. I want to keep my hand in theater in case writing doesn't work out and vice versa. What did you say you're going to major in?"

"Counseling," I told him. "It's part of the education curriculum."

"Why do you want to do that?" he asked.

"I think I'd enjoy it, and I might be good at it, I don't know. I think it would be satisfying work, if I am."

"For some people, maybe," said Ryan. "After getting a taste of the limelight, though, wouldn't you like to be more . . . well, visible?"

"Writing's rather invisible," I countered.

He chuckled. "Not if you get published. Get your picture on book jackets. Like I said, I'd like to see where I can . . . well . . . make a splash. I don't want to get stuck playing bit parts the rest of my life, but I don't want to end up just writing obituaries, either."

The breeze picked up, and I wished I hadn't left my sweater in the car. Ryan pulled me closer and covered my bare arm with one hand. It was warm. If this had been Patrick, I would have snuggled up against him. Maybe we would each have thrust one hand in the hip pocket of the other. I couldn't quite imagine doing that with Ryan.

We sat on a bench in a little plaza and watched the boats and the sky, talking about what Ryan would be doing over the summer— working at an uncle's hardware store when he wasn't up in Maine.

At one point, when the wind blew a lock of hair in my face, he reached over and tucked it behind one ear. "I think I liked your hair better the way you wore it in the third act," he said. "Back away from your face."

"I sort of like it the way it is now," I told him. "Long and loose."

He asked if I wanted to go somewhere and get some coffee and dessert, but I could feel the evening petering out, so I said I was still catching up on sleep and was getting a little tired.

"When can we get together again? Friday?" he asked as we drove along the parkway.

"Let me get back to you on that," I said. "The girlfriends have something planned that night, I think."

"Saturday?"

"That might work. I'll call you," I said.

He must have felt the way girls have felt for decades when a guy says "I'll call you" but has no intention of doing so. I could tell by his silence that he was already getting the picture.

If he was, then I was glad that somebody knew what was happening here, because I sure didn't. Ryan was good-looking— Penny had called him hot—he was smart, talented, motivated, and . . . ?

I don't know. Is there a term for when your chemistry just doesn't click? I guess I wasn't that into him because I could tell he wasn't that into me—into me as I am right now, anyway. The more I thought about it, the more controlling I realized he was. Not controlling in the way Ron had been with Faith, but he sure had a list of things he wanted to change about me—my bowling, my golf, my diet, my career, my hair. . . .

"Well," he said when he pulled up to my house, "I guess whether we go out again depends on you."

"Thanks so much, Ryan," I said. "It was a beautiful evening, wasn't it? And the dinner was delicious. If I see that Saturday night's open, I'll call, okay?"

"Yeah, I guess so. Good night," he said.

"Bye. Thanks again," I told him.

He pulled away from the curb the minute I closed the door, and for a moment I felt awful. Would it have been kinder to string him on for a little while? To at least have gone out one more time and paid for some of it myself? Let him know gradually that . . . ? That what? Had I even given him a fair chance, or had I been subconsciously making up my mind about him before we'd even gone out so I could stay true to Patrick? That was my biggest question.

Why is life so complicated? I wondered as I went slowly up the walk and into the house. I hoped that Dad was still up so I could talk to him. It was only nine thirty. But a note told me that he and Sylvia had gone to a concert at the Kennedy Center. I had to get used to the idea that once I went to college, there wouldn't be a Dad or a Sylvia in my dorm room, waiting for me to unload on them.

24
DEARLY BELOVED

Strangely enough, Penny called that evening because she'd heard from Liz that we'd applied for jobs on a cruise ship over the summer and wondered if she could get in on it too. Liz didn't know. I gave her the number to call, but explained that the cutoff date for applications had been March 1.

"Check with Gwen," I told her.

She sighed. "I'm always on the losing end."

"You *what*?" I asked incredulously.

"You and Patrick. You and Ryan. You and the cruise ship," she said plaintively.

I heard what she was saying, but the words didn't compute. "You're joking," I told her.

"No, I mean it, Alice." She sounded sincere. "I think the

whole time Patrick and I were going out, I knew it wasn't the same as his being with you. Oh, we had fun and a lot of laughs, but . . . It was hard to be serious with him, you know? Like, to find out how he really felt about me?"

"I can't quite believe that, Penny, but it's all in the past," I said.

"No, really."

"Well, you could have fooled me, then. You sure looked pretty close when I saw you together in the halls," I said, wondering why we were talking about this now, and over the phone no less.

"We were attracted to each other, Alice, but . . . even our kisses were playful. I always felt like, 'This is fun, but it's not the real thing.' Am I making any sense?"

"Maybe," I told her. "I guess the only two people who are banking on 'the real thing' right now are Jill and Justin." Why had I changed the subject? I wanted to hear more, more, more of how Patrick maybe liked me better all the while. But it was making me uncomfortable too.

"Yeah, seems that way," she said. "I know you and Gwen were invited to the wedding. We're all waiting to get an eyewitness account. When the minister asks if anyone knows of a reason those two should not be united in holy matrimony, I'll bet Justin's mother will have a speech all prepared."

We laughed a little.

"Anyway, thanks for the phone number," she said. "I'll call the cruise line and see if they'll still take an application. It would be more fun than babysitting my cousins, which is probably the only job I can get this summer."

"Good luck," I said. "And, Penny, just so you know, Ryan's available."

There were a few seconds of silence.

"I thought you were going out with him over spring break. That's what I heard."

"We did go out, but . . . like I said . . . he's available. Just so you know."

"Hmmm," said Penny. "I wonder if he's ever been to the U Street Music Hall."

"Ask him," I said. "I know he's got Saturday night open."

"Thanks, Alice," she said again. "Really."

"You're welcome," I answered. "Really."

Jill and Justin got married on April 23. It wasn't a sunny day, but it wasn't raining, either—one of those overcast April days when it looks as though it could rain but doesn't. Sort of like the wedding, where it might be happy for some people but not for others. Gwen and I had sent them a pretty ceramic picture frame and wore our very best dresses to the ceremony.

We sat together on the bride's side of the church. Like everyone else, we were watching for the entrance of the mothers. Jill's mom came in a purple dress, covered in lace, and Mrs. Collier, not to be outdone, wore a mauve creation that had "designer" written all over it. But they smiled at each other and took seats on their respective sides. Jill's mom, being divorced, was escorted by one of her brothers, and Mr. Collier had the stoic look of a man who knew that the next six hours were going to be devoted to shaking more hands and chitchatting more than he liked, but whatever was required or expected, he would do.

And Jill did make a beautiful bride. Her body was a little thickened around the waistline, and there was the beginning of a baby bump, but the gown was gorgeous.

"Wow!" Gwen whispered. "One look at her . . . and no wonder the groom and best man have their hands folded in front." I poked her with my elbow.

Jill looked a bit more anxious than I expected. She was smiling as she came down the aisle on her father's arm, but I saw her run her tongue over her lips a time or two as though her mouth were dry. When she reached the front of the sanctuary, her dad kissed her cheek and handed her over to Justin, who escorted her the next few steps toward the altar.

It was a traditional ceremony, not the kind that brides and grooms write themselves. No personal references to "overcoming obstacles" or "a ceremony of healing." Just "love, honor, and cherish" and "till death do us part." We were sitting close enough to the front of the church to look over and notice that when Justin took his vows—"I, Justin, take thee, Jill, to love, honor, and cherish . . ."—there were tears running down Mrs. Collier's cheek. But her lips never moved when the tears reached them. No hand came up to wipe them away. When the minister asked if anyone knew why Jill and Justin shouldn't marry, she sat like a sphinx and didn't move a muscle.

Then, after the magic words "I now pronounce you man and wife," Jill and Justin kissed. There was no clapping or cheering as there might be in some churches. I think all of us sensed that in this congregation, it wasn't appropriate. We were relieved when the organ peeled out the recessional and Jill and Justin, looking relieved themselves, went happily back up the aisle, followed by the parents of the bride and groom. I detected a thin line of mascara on both of Mrs. Collier's cheeks.

The bridal party retired to the minister's chambers for the official wedding photos after the church was cleared, and Gwen and I drove to the club where the reception would be held, sipping the champagne punch and sampling the shrimp, till Jill and Justin got there.

When they came in at last and formed a receiving line, we said all the right things to Jill and took the opportunity to hug Justin, laughing at the moisture on his forehead.

"Well, we did it," Jill murmured to us.

"We really pulled it off," said Justin.

We moved on down the line, telling Jill's mom it was a beautiful wedding, shaking hands with the father we'd never met, and on to the Colliers.

"So glad you could come," Mrs. Collier said, giving us her hand but scarcely looking at us or asking our names. Her makeup was repaired and her manners faultless. She turned to the next guests, her smile never wavering.

We sat together at the lavish dinner farther down the hall, behind a set of mahogany doors, and didn't know a single other guest. We were glad we had each other to talk to, because the rest of the people at our table were younger cousins of the groom who fidgeted in their seats, arranged lemon wedges in their mouths like tooth protectors, then grinned menacingly at each other and received glares and threats from their parents. We stuck it out through the introduction of the new Mr. and Mrs. Justin Collier, the toasts and the dancing, and as soon as we comfortably could, we said our good-byes and went out to Gwen's car.

"Well," I said, "what do you think?"

"I think she looked beautiful, I think Justin looked relieved, and I think Jill's mom is glad it's over. And I think Mrs. Collier is saying to herself, 'This is only the beginning,'" Gwen said.

"Really? You think she'll cause trouble?"

"I think Jill married into trouble. But you know, somewhere down the line, Mrs. Collier could end up crazy about her grandchild. Who knows?"

"No one," I said.

I helped Elizabeth hide Easter eggs on their lawn Easter morning after her family came home from Mass. Then I sat on the porch steps with her, and we laughed as Nathan, her little brother, found another egg, screaming at the top of his lungs.

"That's something else I miss," Liz murmured.

I looked over at her. "What?"

"Oh, just one of the things I used to love that has lost its pizzazz. Remember how exciting that used to be—knowing your mom or dad had gone out when you weren't looking and hidden all those eggs? What do you suppose we'll outgrow next?"

"Not guys, that's for sure," I said. "Speaking of which, what's the latest with you and Keeno?"

"Not much. But we're going to the prom. I asked him last night," she said.

"Yay," I said.

"But . . . everything's up in the air right now. We don't even know whether or not we have jobs this summer. I don't know which college I'm going to in the fall, and wherever it is, who knows whom I'll meet there?"

"Right," I said. *And Patrick will be in Spain,* I was thinking. *Who knows whom he'll meet there?*

25
LOOKING AHEAD

I was still sitting on Elizabeth's steps when I saw Lester drive up. I don't think he noticed me over at the Prices' house, because he got out, slammed the door, and walked soberly up the walk to our house.

"What's up with Les?" Liz asked me. "No maple creams in his eggs?"

"I haven't the faintest," I said. "Usually he can't wait to get to Sylvia's cooking. We invited him for Easter dinner. I'd better go see if I can help."

She didn't look very sympathetic. "Tell him Nathan will share his candy, if that's his problem," she said, and grinned.

I crossed the street and went inside. Les was leaning against the kitchen doorway. He'd obviously got a haircut recently, because the sideburns were neatly trimmed, the back tapered. He was also wearing a new shirt.

"Happy Easter, Les," I said, coming up behind him and giving him a hug. "What's up?"

He reached around and swatted at me, not even bothering to turn. "Got any candy?" he asked.

"No, but the little boy across the street might share some with you," I said, and moved where he could see me. "You look like someone the Easter bunny forgot."

"Well, it wasn't a bunny," he said, and when Sylvia paused as she sliced the ham, he said, "Kay hasn't answered my last two phone calls. Can't figure her out."

Dad looked up from the sink, a bowl of spinach leaves in his hands. "That's really strange, Les. She's been having some dental problems, but nothing serious that I know of."

"Was she at work yesterday?" Les asked. "Because I left a message there."

"No. She was at the dentist having a wisdom tooth extracted. I told her to take the rest of the day off," Dad said.

"That probably explains it, then," Les said.

"She's seemed in a good mood lately," Dad went on. "I think James is going back to China at the end of the month."

"That's good," said Les. "I just get annoyed when people aren't honest with me." He took off his jacket and moved to hang it up in the hall closet. The thin brown stripe in his shirt brought out the brown of his eyes, and I realized again how handsome he was. Not surprising he's had a long string of girlfriends. When he came back in the kitchen, he said, "Nothing serious between Kay and me—we've just gone out a few times. But it would be nice to know I didn't make some cultural gaffe or something."

"I don't know what that would be. She's not easily offended, as far as I can tell," Dad said.

"Well, if any hot babes happen to ask, I'm available," he said, and raised an eyebrow at me. "Any hot babe my own age, Al. Don't give Pamela any ideas." Pamela's had a crush on Les forever.

I went out to the buffet in the dining room for the good silverware, placing it around our china there on the table. It was Easter, and we were all together, and that was reason enough to celebrate.

We were halfway through the meal when the doorbell rang. Dad had gone back to the kitchen for the butter. "I'll get it, Sylvia," he called. "Stay put."

I heard the front door open and then Dad's voice saying, "Why, Kay! Come on in."

We stared at Les, then turned toward the doorway.

"Oh, my goodness!" I heard Kay exclaim as she entered the dining room. "You're still eating. And . . . it's Easter! I forgot! We don't celebrate Easter. I'm so sorry."

"It's okay. Please pull up a chair," Dad said.

But Kay looked uncomfortable as Les gave her a puzzled smile.

"I drove over to Lester's apartment, and Paul told me he'd be over here," Kay said. "I wanted to talk to him face-to-face and . . . Oh, this is so embarrassing."

"You . . . uh . . . want some privacy?" Dad asked.

"Come on, sit down," Les said genially, and reached around to pull an empty chair to the table.

She sat. "Les . . . well, you know, two weeks ago, when I didn't keep our date?"

"Yeah?"

"That really wasn't my fault. I hadn't planned it. Someone knocked on my door, and when I opened it, James was standing there. Alone. He looked really miserable and asked if he could talk to me for a few minutes, so I let him in. He was sort of . . . well, bowing and scraping, I guess you'd call it, and said he just wanted me to know that he was as embarrassed over this whole thing as I was, but that both sets of parents were making unreasonable demands of us and he was going back to China in a week.

"I told him I knew it wasn't his fault. Since we both had made excuses for not being at my parents' house for dinner that night, he said he didn't want my dad to drive by and see his rental car and know we were in the apartment alone. He asked if there was anywhere we could go to talk. So I suggested a sandwich shop, and we drove there. We just got talking, Les, and there was so much to say. His parents practically ordered him to come back with a wife. A wife-to-be, that is. Namely, me. He just wanted me to know that this wasn't his idea of marriage and would tell his parents so when he got back."

Lester had stopped chewing now, and we were all sitting there entranced. Kay let her jacket slip off her shoulders because sunlight was pouring through a side window now, warming the room and making her black hair positively shine. She turned to Lester.

"Les, we . . . I had no idea we had talked so long, and when I realized it was an hour and a half past the time I was to meet you, I was . . . I was just too embarrassed to call. I made up some story the next day about my dad. I shouldn't have, but I was too confused to explain. Well, James called me a few days later to say he was on standby for a flight to China, and maybe we could talk once more, just for friendship's sake, so . . . we met again at the sandwich shop."

I think we all guessed the end of the story.

"We've . . . been to the sandwich shop six times now, and tonight we're going on a for-real date."

We all started to smile. Even Lester.

"The thing is, we don't want anyone to know. We want to see how this goes completely on our own, without any pressure from our parents. If . . . if we 'click,' as you'd call it, then we'll decide all the rest. I'm *really, really* sorry I didn't tell you sooner, but . . . I wasn't sure of anything."

Les gave her a real smile now. "Hey, babe, no problem."

Kay giggled a little, but then grew serious. "James has declined my parents' dinner invitations, and my parents are furious with me. They say he'll go back to China and tell everyone what a disrespectful daughter I am, unfit to be his wife."

"You're not telling them anything?" I asked.

"Not yet. If this works out between James and me, it will

be on our own terms. We've been miserable enough on theirs. Now it's like we just met and know nothing about each other, so we're starting at the beginning. Mr. Stone Face, I tease him, and he calls me Miss Nose in the Air."

This was better than any romance book.

"Kay, I've got lemon pie for dessert," Sylvia said. "Won't you have some with us?"

"I'll just take a glass of water," she said. "We're going out for dinner tonight."

"I hope you have reservations," said Dad. "It's almost impossible to get in a restaurant on Easter without a reservation."

"A Chinese restaurant," Kay said, laughing. "You can always get a table at a Chinese restaurant on an American holiday."

I just sat there grinning at Kay. "Wow!" I said. "Who would have thought?"

"Not in a million years," said Kay. "But my *parents* are going to be the last to know."

We got our letters on May 2. Gwen, Liz, Yolanda, Pam, and I were tentatively hired for the cruise ship. Five two-week cruises on a new line, providing we passed our interview and the training session.

Everyone else at school was envious of us, including Penny, who hadn't got her application in on time. It was hard enough to find a summer job, not to mention one that began after graduation and ended before any of us had to start college.

Sometimes I'm blown away by how coincidental life is. If

Gwen's mom hadn't worked for the Justice Department, she wouldn't have been having lunch with a woman whose brother-in-law had just been hired to be the assistant cruise director for a new Chesapeake Bay line, and we wouldn't have summer jobs.

I was trying to explain this to Liz and Pamela as we ate our lunch outside under the oak tree at the side of the school. But Pamela can take just so much philosophical thought before she barfs.

"Alice," she said, "did you ever consider that in spite of all the twists and turns of fate, there is only one reason why you are here on this earth?"

"No," I said. "What?"

"Your parents had sex," she told me.

And who would have thought that the senior prom would be scheduled on my eighteenth birthday, May 14!

"Now, *that's* pretty incredible!" said Sylvia.

My gift from them would be any prom dress I wanted, with shoes to match, she said, and she went with me to try some on. She said as long as we stayed out of the designer collections, I could have whatever I wanted. I chose a gorgeous gown in a deep, brilliant yellow. The long, full skirt was covered with a layer of white chiffon that made the whole dress look sort of ethereal, cloudlike. It almost seemed to shimmer with every step I took.

But somehow I couldn't find the right shoes to dye. I already had a pair of neutral sling-back heels that I loved because the flesh color seemed to elongate my legs, and a pair of bright yellow shoes would give my legs a chopped-off look if I lifted my skirt. And where would I ever wear bright yellow shoes again? So I decided to wear what I had, and Sylvia bought me a cute little clutch purse instead.

Patrick called the Wednesday before the prom to give me his itinerary.

"I'm winding up some research for the professor—a graph to go in his book—and I should be finished by Friday," he said. "*Late* Friday, probably, but I'll have it done. I'll fly into National at eleven forty Saturday morning, and I'm staying with the Stedmeisters."

That was no surprise, because I'd heard Mark's parents offer their home to Patrick whenever he came back for a visit. Patrick was good company for them, having been one of Mark's best friends. He always did converse easily with adults—maybe because he was an only child.

"Mr. Stedmeister's picking me up at the airport and taking me to get my tux. I pretty much guessed at the measurements. You and I are going to have dinner before the dance with the gang. But I've made our own plans for what we do after. It's your birthday, you know." As though I'd forgotten.

I felt my heart speed up. Patrick may have had plans, but Dad also had rules. And the one big nonnegotiable rule of the evening was that I could not go to a hotel room after the prom was over. I tried to explain to him that people just got together and rented a room to have an all-night party, not an orgy, but Dad held firm.

"It's a lot safer than driving around with all the drunks on the road at three in the morning," I had said the week before, pulling out all the stops.

"Not necessarily," Dad had answered.

Patrick continued: "Just wanted to make sure you weren't counting on the after-prom party at the school."

"No, I wasn't. But my dad's just being a dad, Patrick, and there's a nonnegotiable rule: I can't go to a hotel room, even if there are twenty people there."

Patrick was quiet for several seconds, and I wondered if his plan for an intimate evening had just gone up in smoke. "Tell your dad that there's no hotel room in the picture and that you'll be perfectly safe with me," he said.

I wasn't sure I wanted to hear that, either, especially after what came next: "I have to fly back Sunday, Alice. I have a huge—and I mean *huge*—test on Monday."

I know that for some girls, prom night is when you're supposed to lose your V card—the atmosphere, the romance, the glamour, the gown. Something to make it special, to remember it by. And this was already special, being my eighteenth birthday, with a boyfriend who was leaving for Spain for a year.

But I had already decided that wasn't the way I wanted to have sex my first time—intercourse, I mean. That would seem so . . . so stereotypical. Everybody dressing up and expecting to get laid afterward. I wanted Patrick so much, it almost hurt to think about it, but I didn't want it to be a single night. I wanted us to be someplace really private with all the time in the world—before, during, and after.

It didn't look like that was going to happen anytime soon, though, and Patrick didn't live here anymore. He would be leaving for Spain the minute spring quarter ended at the University of Chicago. He would be in Spain a whole year—four quarters. Maybe this night was all I was going to get, I thought nervously. Maybe it was now or never.

But what if we tried to make love and it was terribly awkward? What if it really hurt, or he came too soon, or I bled and was too sore to try again? I'd heard accounts of other girls' "first times." I'd read articles. I knew the old joke about how Niagara Falls was a bride's "second biggest disappointment." Did I really want Patrick and me separating for a year with an awkward, hurried "first time" to remember?

Patrick had just asked a question and was waiting for an answer.

"What?" I said.

"What color is your dress?"

"Yellow," I said. "Daisy yellow."

"I can get you daisies, then?" he teased.

I smiled. "Even dandelions would do if they're from you."

"Till Saturday, then," he told me.

26
MAY 14

Sylvia did my hair and nails and even gave me a pedicure (still part of my birthday present, she kidded). I wondered if this was a setup where she'd ask me personal questions about what Patrick and I would do after the prom, seeing as how I was a prisoner of sorts, with one leg on a towel in her lap. She didn't, though.

But she did say, "It must be hard to have Patrick so far away."

"It is," I said. "And he'll be gone all summer."

"So will you."

"I know, but when I come back from my summer job, he still won't be here. He won't even be in Chicago. I wouldn't be able to see him if I visited Aunt Sally or Carol. He'll be half a world away."

Sylvia carefully buffed the heel of my foot with a pumice stone. "Thank goodness for e-mail and cell phones," she said. "Maybe he'll get an international phone card and call you now and then. Maybe you won't be quite as lonesome as you think."

I didn't tell her I wanted more than that. Didn't say that maybe I'd make enough on my cruise ship job to fly over and see him in Spain. Didn't say that maybe with the money Dad was saving by my not going to an out-of-state college, he could afford to send me to Spain and back a couple times a year. And it was that idea that made it bearable.

Austin and Gwen drove up with Patrick around six o'clock. I could feel my excitement building as I watched the passenger door open and Patrick stepped out. He seemed even taller than when I saw him at Christmas. He'd be eighteen in July. Wasn't a guy supposed to have attained his full height by eighteen?

I rushed to the door and opened it before he got to the porch, and then we were in each other's arms, lips together, and I think he even dropped the corsage box, but we didn't care.

When we finally stopped to breathe, we smiled at each other sheepishly, then kissed again, a short kiss this time—it was mostly a hug—and then Patrick picked up the box.

"Happy Birthday," he said, his eyes smiling down at me.

"I'm so glad you're here," I told him, pulling him inside the house.

Sylvia hugged him too, and he and Dad shook hands. I opened the corsage box. The flower must have been something from the orchid family, it was so delicately shaped. A very pale yellow, with sprigs of white baby's breath. Patrick fastened it to my wrist, and we posed for pictures in front of the stone fire-place in the family room.

"Come by for lunch tomorrow, Patrick, and we'll drive you to the airport," Dad said.

"That would be great," Patrick said. "I was planning to come by anyway."

I tucked my cell phone in one of Patrick's pockets so we could take pictures of our friends. I had Sylvia's wrap over one arm, but as we were about to leave, I asked, "Anything more I should bring, Patrick? A change of clothes or something?"

"No. What you're wearing is fine. But . . . well, sneakers, maybe, in case you want to get rid of those high heels."

I went back upstairs to get them, Sylvia fetched a bag, and after the obligatory "Be safe" from Dad, we went out to the car.

"Have a great time," Sylvia called as they watched us go.

We drove to Normandie Farm in Potomac, where we met the others, and everyone greeted Patrick with hugs and cheers.

It was an old establishment with huge fireplaces at each end of a great hall and geese roaming the grounds. No fire was needed on this evening, but the hall was half filled with prom couples. Pamela was already there at our table with Jay, the guy who had played Frank Jr. in the play. Throughout rehearsals, I'd wondered if something wasn't clicking between them, so I hadn't been at all surprised when she'd told us that he invited her to the dance the night of the cast party.

We all looked positively great. Gwen was in red, Pamela in white, and Liz in lavender. Along with my yellow, we looked like a summer bouquet. It wasn't long before our table of eight was buzzing with happy chatter, questions zinging back and forth, talk of game scores and vacation plans. All I could think of was how normal, how comfortable, how familiar it all was, having Patrick back again, and yet . . . how different, because we were all going off in different directions, like seeds from a dandelion—Patrick going farthest of all.

"Patrick, college must agree with you," Pamela told him. "When you get back from Spain, you'll probably be doing the rumba or something."

"That's Cuba, Pamela," said Austin.

"Well, the tango, then," said Pamela.

"That's South America!" said Liz, and we laughed.

There was so much to talk about. Both Austin and Keeno went to different schools from ours. Austin was in his second year at Howard University in the District, Keeno would be entering the naval academy in Annapolis, and Jay would be going to Montgomery College after graduation. I told them how long Patrick and I had known each other—as long as I'd known Liz and Pamela—and how we had all been in Mr. Hensley's seventh-grade World Studies class together, when we'd buried a time capsule and were supposed to come back when we were sixty to open it.

"Old 'Horse-Breath Hensley,' we called him," Pamela said.

"And could that man spit!" Patrick put in. "You almost needed an umbrella if you sat in the first row."

"But we liked that time capsule," I said. "Hensley won't be around when we open it, but I plan to be here."

"We'll all come," said Liz. "From wherever we are, we've got to be here. And that means you too, Patrick, even if you're in Samoa or someplace."

"How do you know the time capsule will still be there?" Austin asked. "That the *school* will still be there? I'll bet there's a town house development over the playground."

"Don't be so pessimistic," Gwen told him. "The school undoubtedly recorded it somewhere. What did the class put inside it?"

"All I remember is that we were each supposed to write a letter to our sixty-year-old selves," Liz told them.

"Won't *that* be a scream!" said Pamela.

We rode to the Hyatt, where each end of the ballroom had been decorated like an Arabian tent, with huge pillows and rugs and an artificial sky above. In between dance numbers, seductive belly-dance music came from the tents, along with wafts of incense from elaborate copper burners. We took turns posing in front of the tents and took pictures of each other.

During some of the numbers we walked around the halls, Patrick greeting old friends, and I felt as though I were showing off a movie star or something—Patrick in his black tux, the yellow boutonniere in his lapel; Patrick looking down at me, smiling; Patrick shaking hands with some of his former teachers, telling them where he was going to school now. But every time there was a slow number, we were in each other's arms again, gently rocking on the dance floor, my cheek against his chest.

"Well," he said, "Happy Birthday. I guess I can say I spent the evening with an older woman."

I laughed. "Only by two months."

"Yeah, I was probably building block fortresses before you even learned to crawl."

"Yeah? I'll bet I was potty trained before you," I said, and when a couple next to us overheard and turned to stare, we laughed out loud and Patrick whirled me away. I danced once with Austin and Keeno too, and even once with Sam, who looked especially nice in a gray tux with a wine-colored cummerbund and boutonniere. We danced like old friends, which, I guess, we were.

Ryan, I noticed, was there with Penny; Phil and another guy from the Gay/Straight Alliance had come together; and Lori and Leslie were still partners, both in white tuxes and looking smashing. When Lori saw me and cut in on Sam, I danced with her, and we laughed when the spotlight—which was focusing for a few seconds on one couple, then another—shone on us.

"You look great, Lori," I told her as she turned us so the glare wasn't in our eyes.

"You know what? This has been the happiest year of my life so far," she said. "Everything's going good."

"I can tell," I told her as she swung me around again. "It shows."

"You look pretty happy too," she said.

"For a girl whose guy is going to Spain for a year, I guess I am," I said. "Trying to focus on the here and now."

"It's all any of us have got," said Lori.

Patrick claimed me again as the lights went even lower and artificial stars overhead began to twinkle. Patrick's hand was firm on my bare back, and I leaned into him, my face against his neck, hand resting on his chest as he enclosed me in both his arms. I felt so safe, so secure, so loved.

We were barely moving to the music now, our bodies pressed against each other. One of his fingers caressed my back, my lips brushed his throat. *If only the here and now could last forever,* I thought. *If I could just stay wrapped in his arms like this . . .* When we kissed, I was conscious once more of the spotlight. I just closed my eyes and moved with him to the music, enjoying the warmth of his hands, the caress of his thumb on my back, the feel of his breath in my hair.

The spotlight stayed, and some of our friends were applauding. I realized they had stepped back to give us a small space on the floor as long as the spotlight was there, and then the moment was over—we were in shadow again. The crowd moved away, and we lingered over a long kiss.

About eleven Patrick said we were leaving, and he suggested I use the restroom first. Where would we be going that we wouldn't have a restroom handy? I wondered. And who was driving? But I did as he said, then picked up my wrap and sneakers at the coatroom. When I got back to the main entrance, where Patrick was waiting for me, he held open the door while I went outside. There in the hotel driveway was a black limo. When he saw us, the driver immediately hopped out and opened the door.

"Patrick!" I said breathlessly, staring up at him, but he just smiled and helped me get in. Then he slid in beside me.

It wasn't a large limo, but the seats were soft and spacious, with a small bouquet of fresh flowers at one side, along with a DVD player, chilled bottles of mango and lime juice, a jar of chocolate-covered raisins, and some macaroons. A sliding panel of dark glass separated us from the driver.

"The next few hours are for you," Patrick said, putting one arm around me. "Happy Birthday."

"What?" I said. "Where are we going?"

"We have the limo for three hours, so I thought we'd just go to all your favorite places. You know, drive around."

I stared at him in astonishment.

"Patrick, all my favorite places are within five miles of my house. We could do the whole tour in a half hour."

"Oh," said Patrick, looking dumbfounded.

Was it possible that Patrick Long, who could speak at least three languages and had traveled all over the world, hadn't thought out what to do with a limo in Maryland for the next three hours?

"Well . . ." he said at last, as the driver waited. "Hmmm."

I broke into laughter. "Patrick! Every minute we sit here is costing you money! Are you sure you want to do this? I mean, whatever it is we're doing?"

"There's got to be some place you'd like to go," he said. "I mean, dancing, dining . . ."

We'd already dined and danced. I knew that all my friends who had watched us leave were wondering what we were doing. I knew that Pamela's question to me would be, *You won't be seeing Patrick for a year, right? So . . . tell all. How far did you go?*

"Patrick," I said, "how far have we been together? Away from here, I mean."

"Chicago?" he said, thinking.

"Well, we can't get to Chicago and back in three hours. What about Ocean City? Remember that summer Lester brought you out there when Dad rented a house?"

"It's a three-hour drive just to get there," Patrick said. "The farthest we could get would be the Bay Bridge and back."

"Okay," I said, settling myself into the plush seat. "I want to drive to the Bay Bridge with you."

His face spread into a grin. "Really?" he said, laughing. "Okay, you got it." Leaning forward, he slid the dark glass to one side. "Bay Bridge and back," he said.

I suppose limo drivers are used to all sorts of directions. There was no answer that I could hear. Patrick slid the window closed again, and the limo rolled out of the circular drive, heading for the beltway.

27
VIEW FROM THE BRIDGE

I think we laughed all the way to the Bay Bridge. It was such a crazy idea, and we had to go over every detail of the evening—the tents and the incense; how great Gwen looked with her hair coiled on top of her head, a silver thread in the braids, how comfortable she and Austin seemed together; whether Keeno would make it through the academy; whether Liz would get to Vermont. . . .

After we'd passed the Annapolis exits, I wanted to roll down the windows and look for the bridge, but all I could see was night.

"It's dark!" I said.

"Duh!" said Patrick. "What did you expect?"

I guess I'd never been over the Bay Bridge at night that I could remember, but when at last we spotted those high towers holding up the long span, the lights illuminating the miles of cable, the limo slowed and we heard the intercom come on and the driver ask, "You want me to cross?"

"Yeah. Go across and find a place to turn around. Then we'll head back," Patrick told him, but he kept the sliding window open now so he and the driver could talk.

We rolled down the rear windows so we could stick our heads out both sides of the limo. Even though we couldn't see the water, we could sense the salty air. It was after midnight, and there were only a couple of cars at the tollbooth. Usually the traffic was going east on one span, west on the other. But on this weekend night, two lanes of one bridge and one lane of the other were all heading toward the ocean. The bridge we were crossing had lanes going both ways.

I grabbed Patrick's hand. "This is the farthest we've ever gone together, Patrick. I mean, in the same car. Both at the same time."

He smiled. "So, what do you want? A souvenir or something?"

"Yes, I wish we could."

I crawled over on Patrick's lap so we were both leaning out the same window, the wind blowing in our faces. Patrick said the bridge was almost four and a half miles long. We figured when we got to the very center that we were probably higher than we'd ever been before, since we'd never been on a plane together.

"So this is a first," I said.

Finally, when we reached the other side, the driver pulled into a restaurant parking lot to turn around.

"Patrick," I said, "when we get to the top going back, I want to get out and take our picture."

"You can't stop on the bridge," he said.

"What if you blew a tire or something? You'd have to be able to stop."

"Not for a picture, though."

"So what would they do? Arrest us? It would only take half a minute."

He laughed. "You're crazy."

"Please?"

He had a low conversation with the driver, but I could only hear his voice, not the driver's. Finally Patrick settled back beside me. "He says he's going to wait until there are no cars coming in the opposite lane, then he'll pull out and head back across. He'll slow down and stop just long enough for us to get out and will move on very slowly, but we'll have to take a picture in about five seconds and run to catch up. If we dawdle, we'll have to walk back and he'll wait for us at the other end, at which point they'll probably arrest us."

I didn't know if the man was kidding or not, but this was about the most exciting thing I'd ever done.

"Okay!" I said, and immediately took off my sling-backs and pulled on my sneakers.

There were few cars heading away from the ocean at twelve thirty on an early Saturday morning. When there were no cars at all coming as far as we could see, the driver pulled out and crossed over into the return lane.

"There aren't any sidewalks on the bridge," Patrick murmured, studying the span out the window. "If we had to walk back, we'd be right on the roadway. We *have* to ride back."

"Get my camera out, Patrick," I said.

When we reached the top of the span, the limo slowed and stopped. Patrick jumped out first, helped me out, closed the door, and we climbed over the low wall and moved to the cable railing, laughing wildly.

"Ready," Patrick said, holding my cell phone out in front of us. It flashed.

"Take another one," I begged, as the wind blew my hair in my face and I could see only a reflection of the moon on the water.

The limo was slowly moving away. Another flash.

"One more?" I cried. "Please!"

"Alice, we have to go!"

"Just one more?" I pleaded.

"You crazy person!" Patrick said, but he held out my cell phone once again, and the moment it flashed, we scrambled over the parapet again, my skirts billowing out above my knees, and went racing along the grid surface to the limo, which barely stopped as we climbed in and closed the door, shrieking like maniacs.

We were trying to see our pictures in the backseat, but the driver told us to fasten our seat belts, so we did, and it wasn't long before we started down the long incline where, we saw with pounding hearts, that a patrol car waited, an officer standing outside it.

There was no tollbooth at the bottom of the return span,

but the driver slowed anyway and obeyed when the officer motioned him over.

"Oh, man," said Patrick.

"You'll bail me out?" the driver said sardonically.

A car behind had caught up with us, the passengers rubbernecking as they passed to see what we had done. The officer walked over.

"You are aware that only emergency stopping is allowed on the bridge?" he asked. They must have had motion detectors or cameras along the span, I decided.

"Yes," the driver said, "but I wanted to make it special for the young couple here on their prom night. I wouldn't have tried if there had been cars behind us."

"Sorry. No dispensation for being the only car on the road or for prom nights," the officer said. "License, please?"

The driver presented his credentials.

Patrick spoke up. "I'm the one who asked him to stop. If there's a fine or anything, I'll pay it."

The officer didn't answer for a moment. Still checking the driver's ID, he said, "I'll get to you next."

He did. He moved to the back window and asked us to get out of the car. We obeyed. I was still wearing my sneakers and almost tripped over my dress till Patrick caught me.

"It's my fault!" I cried. "It was all my idea, and I just wanted a picture before Patrick goes to Spain, and it will be a year before—"

Patrick squeezed my arm and I shut up.

The officer turned on his flashlight and checked the backseat to be sure there was no one else inside. No beer bottles on the floor.

"ID?" he asked.

Patrick fished around in his pocket. "I left everything back at the Stedmeisters'," he murmured to me. And then, to the policeman, "This is all I brought with me," and handed the officer a credit card. "It's my dad's."

"Stay here, please," the officer said, and went back to his car. He slid in, and we could see him calling in the numbers on his radio. He waited. We waited.

"Patrick, I feel horrible! I got you into this," I said. "Do you think we'll go to jail on our prom night?"

"I'll ask if we can share a cell," Patrick said, but he wasn't smiling.

"There's going to be a heck of an extra charge for this," the driver complained.

"I know. It's okay," Patrick told him.

"Not if I lose my license," the driver said.

I was feeling worse by the minute. The old impulsive me again. I just don't think!

Finally the officer got out of his patrol car and walked over. He handed the credit card back to Patrick.

"Okay," he said. "Move on. But don't try this again. Not in this high-security age."

"Thank you," said Patrick. "We won't."

"Thank you so much!" I burbled. "We really didn't mean to cause any trouble. I just—"

"Get in the car, Alice," Patrick muttered, steering me through the open door.

The officer didn't answer. He waited till another car went by and walked back to his patrol car. Then we were moving forward, on the road again.

"No tickets? No fines?" the driver asked over the intercom. "You guys must have a guardian angel or something."

"Or something," said Patrick. "Maybe it's just this crazy lady I'm with."

"This has been the most amazing night!" I said. "I was sure he was going to arrest us. He didn't fine us or anything. Why?"

"All I can figure is that it was Dad's credit card I gave him. Dad said I could use his this weekend. Maybe it was diplomatic immunity or something."

"But I thought your dad retired from the State Department?"

"He did. But I'm sure his history is all in his records."

"Wow, Patrick!" I said.

"Roger that!" said the driver from up front, and we laughed as Patrick closed the little glass window again and the intercom clicked off.

We checked out the photos Patrick had taken and laughed at the camera angle of the first one. We were on a slant, and the left side of my face was missing, Patrick's eyes were wide and goofy. The second photo got us both in, my hair tossing in the wind, me smiling a little too broadly, Patrick striking a moody movie-star look. In the last photo I'm looking away from the camera at the receding limo and Patrick's chin was cut off.

"The second one's best, Patrick," I said. "*Look* at you!"

"Look at your hair." He laughed.

"We're like that couple at the prow of the *Titanic*."

"Except for your grin."

"That's a smile, Patrick."

"Whatever it is, I'll take it," he said.

The lights of the bridge had disappeared far behind us and the dark of the trees closed in. And then we were in each other's arms again.

The driver cut through D.C. on the way back, and we had almost every street to ourselves. He drove us by the Jefferson and Lincoln Memorials, all lit up. Past the reflecting pool, where tourists walked when cherry trees were in bloom, around the Washington Monument. It was like we were the only ones in Washington. Like all the lights were on just for us, celebrating my eighteenth birthday.

Finally we were on our way home again. Patrick asked the driver to take the scenic route—the slow lane along Beach Drive. We didn't see any of the rest. Patrick and I were entwined together on the backseat, caressing each other and kissing the parts we couldn't see.

"Patrick," I whispered, "when we're together again, I want it to be for a week, at least. I want seven days and seven nights. I can't stand wanting you so much and never having time for more than a taste."

His lips were buried against my neck. "If you only knew how much I've wanted you. . . ."

When the limo pulled up to my house, the driver turned off the engine and sat, unseen, in his seat up front while we gave our good-night kisses. At last, when we heard him open the door and get out, we knew we had reached the end of our magical evening.

"I love you," Patrick said.

"I love you," I whispered back.

28
BY THE HOUR?

Pamela invited us over the following night so we could relive the prom in slow motion, dissecting every incident, commenting on every dress, reflecting on every couple, every expression, each word. . . . Her dad and his fiancée were out for the evening, so we had the place to ourselves.

Liz and Pamela and Gwen, of course, wanted to know what happened after Patrick and I left the prom, and Pamela's ears were like antennas, practically vibrating, wanting to know all the passionate details.

"Well," I said, "Patrick and I went farther than we've ever gone before."

"You . . . ?" Liz said, eyes huge.

"Together," I added.

"Meaning?" said Pamela.

I told them about the limo ride to the Bay Bridge and how we stopped and got out and how a policeman was waiting at the other end. Everyone loved hearing about it, but Pamela was getting impatient.

"Meanwhile, back in the limo . . . ," she prompted.

"We were about as close as we could get," I said, skirting the question.

Liz studied me. "No waves crashing? No earth moving? No violins?"

I sighed. "Not in the way you're thinking."

"And don't expect it either," Gwen said. "It'll be a while before you get violins."

"What about you and Austin?" I asked.

"I don't know," she said. "Eight years is a long time for me to be in school, and who knows where he'll get a job? We're just enjoying what we have. But guess who I saw at the prom?"

We shook our heads.

"Legs," she said.

"Leo? The guy who—?" Liz began, and stopped.

The guy she'd had sex with way back when. The guy she finally broke up with when we were counselors together at camp. The guy who had been cheating on her all the while.

"Did you talk to him?" I asked.

"No. I'm not sure he even knew I was there. I was trying to see who invited him, but I couldn't. He and Austin are so . . . It's like they're from different planets. I'm dancing with Austin, wondering what I ever saw in Legs. Just the fact that he liked me, I guess. I figured that he must think I was really special if he wanted to have sex with me."

We all groaned at that, even the two of us who were still virgins.

Pamela told us how much fun she'd had with Jay, and Liz said she and Keeno were going out a few more times before we left for the cruise ship. But while they chattered on, I settled back against the cushions, remembering the way Patrick and I had said good-bye at the airport that morning. Mr. Stedmeister had driven him over to our place around noon so Patrick could have lunch with us and talk with Dad and Sylvia. Then Patrick and I got in Dad's car, and Dad drove to Reagan National, then around and around the traffic circle while I walked with Patrick as far as the security gate.

What do you say when you know you won't see someone for over a year? Call me? E-mail me? Think of me? Love me? All the above? All those promises. . . .

When we embraced for the last time, I felt as though if I held him tightly enough, he wouldn't leave. Like I was imprinting him on my body. But finally he gently pulled away, squeezed my arm, then picked up his bag and went through security.

We waved for as long as we could see each other, Patrick heading down the long hall. Then another passenger came between us, and he disappeared.

I hadn't wanted to talk on the way home. I'd looked around twice, thinking Patrick might possibly be running after our car.

That he might have forgotten something—left something in it and I could see him one more time. But then we were turning onto the George Washington Parkway, Dad had the radio playing, and I just closed my eyes, drawing in my breath, trying to detect Patrick's scent. But it was gone.

I was like a robot the following week, partly because there was so much to do before graduation and partly to keep from missing Patrick. I had a checklist of things I needed to complete for every class before finals, and I set myself on automatic. I put in eight hours at the Melody Inn on Saturday, catching up on the work I needed to do there, and Dad let me have his car afterward for a whole evening of errands if I'd take some insurance papers over to Lester while I was at it.

I picked up Sylvia's dry cleaning, stopped at the shoe repair shop, returned a book to Silver Spring Library, bought some stuff at the drugstore that I'd need on the cruise, and by the time I got to Lester's apartment around nine thirty, the evening had turned from cool to cold—typical, unreliable May weather.

He was waiting for me in the living room, watching an ESPN sports special that not even he seemed especially interested in.

"You're on call tonight?" I said, giving him the insurance papers and throwing my jacket on a chair. "What are you eating?" I asked, looking at what appeared to be brownie crumbs on a saucer.

"Well, make yourself at home, why don't you?" he said.

"I'm trying. I've been running errands all evening and I'm hungry."

He motioned toward the kitchen. "Rubbermaid container," he said.

I got a couple brownies, checked the milk to see if there was enough for me, and poured a small glass. Then I came out to sit beside him. "You going to miss me when I'm gone all summer?" I asked, savoring the first bite of chocolate.

"I'll save some on food," he said. "Though Andy will probably eat your share."

I'd noticed her door was closed when I came in.

"Still in business, huh?"

"It's a mystery. I'm doing all the checking I can, and things keep turning up. She evidently was a straight-A student when she was at the university. No evidence that she took part in any extracurricular stuff—no clubs or sororities—all nose to the grindstone. But she . . . and those students . . . just don't add up somehow. I've got a call in to a friend in the finance office. He says there was a memo going around a month or so ago about an Andrea somebody or other, but he couldn't remember what it said. He's checking."

"I almost wish I were staying home this summer. Alice, Girl Detective."

"Naw. You'll have a ball. Where does that cruise ship go, anyway?"

"Just around the bay. All the little towns and byways. Passengers explore some on rubber dinghies, and there are picnics and stuff. Sometimes we get to help at cookouts. I'm going to come back with a toned body like you wouldn't believe."

"You're right, I don't believe it."

"Les," I said, "if you were going to be separated from a girl you really, really liked—okay, loved—for a whole year, what would you do to make sure the . . . romance stayed alive?"

"Hmmm," said Les. "Well, first I'd make sure we both tattooed the other's name on our foreheads—"

"Les . . ."

"And we could each wear a tiny vial of the other's blood around our necks."

"Seriously . . ."

Lester turned the TV down so we could talk. "It's easier to say what you shouldn't do than what you should. You shouldn't make each other promise anything—that you won't see other people or fall in love with anyone else. You want Patrick to come back to you because he *wants* to, not because he said he would. And you don't fill your letters and phone calls with woeful tales of how much you miss him or whine about how boring your life is without him. He doesn't want to come back to that. Tell him about all the exciting things you're doing, places you're going, books you're reading, people you're meeting. He wants to come back to somebody interesting, not boring."

I was barely chewing my brownie. I'd done a lot of whining and wailing already about how much I'd miss him, and here he was, going to Spain!

"I don't know if 'Life on the Bay' can equal 'Life in Barcelona,'" I said.

"It will if you're on the lookout for adventure. Use the time he's away to really broaden yourself, try new things. You've already made a good start."

"I'm thinking about going to visit him in Spain, if I can save enough for the plane ticket."

"*There* you go!" said Les. "Now, that's positive thinking."

I divided the second brownie and gave him half. "Thanks, bro," I said. "You're a good listener." I took my glass out to the kitchen, then picked up my bag and said, "Dad says to sign the three places he's marked on that insurance policy. But *read* it first, he says. You can get it back to him next week."

"Will do," Les told me, and I went on outside and down the steps. The full moon made my shadow on the path to the street. It was only when I fumbled for my car keys that I realized I'd left my jacket back in the apartment. That was exactly the hoodie I needed for my summer job. I retraced my steps across the lawn and had just reached the evergreen at the bottom of the outdoor staircase when I heard footsteps coming down and a man's voice saying, "Be good, Andy, but not too good."

I paused.

Andy's voice: "Hey, Bob, aren't you forgetting something?"

"Oh, yeah," the guy named Bob said. "Sorry."

A couple more footsteps. Another pause. I wasn't about to go on up in the middle of this.

Andy's voice again: "This is only a fifty."

"Well . . . listen, I don't have any more on me."

"Come on, Bob. I gave you the full treatment. I did everything."

"Honest! Here. Check my wallet."

"We've been through this before."

"Aw, I'll get it to you, Andy. I'm just—"

"No, you won't. Don't call me again. No more jobs. That's final."

And then the guy saw me.

"Uh . . . company," he said over his shoulder, and came on down, passing me at the bottom of the steps.

Andy moved out a little farther on the second-floor landing so she could see me, and we stared at each other for a couple of seconds.

"Oh, Alice, hi," she said. And then, "Just a business transaction, sweetie. Students always claim poverty, you know."

I didn't like the patronizing tone in her voice. I didn't like being Alice the Innocent, lectured by Woman of the World. I headed back to the car and sat behind the wheel hyperventilating. At last I turned on the engine and headed home. I could pick up my jacket another day.

I'd intended to call Les when I got home and tell him what I heard on the stairs, but Pamela called and wanted me to check out some new prom photos on Facebook. And when I finally remembered to call Les, he didn't pick up. So I went to bed.

Around noon on Sunday, I reached him and said I wanted to stop by again—I'd left my jacket.

"How about right now?" he said. "I want to show you something."

I wondered what that could be as I drove back to Takoma Park. Show-and-tell, that's what, not that what I had to tell was all that conclusive. Andy could have loaned this friend some money and he was supposed to pay her back. She could have bought something for him, and he'd forgotten to pay her.

I pulled up in front of the big yellow house with the brown trim and climbed the side steps.

"Come on in!" Les yelled when I knocked, and I opened the door. He was coming down the hall in his stocking feet.

"I got up about fifteen minutes ago, and Paul's at the gym," he said. "Take a look at this."

Now what was Andy up to? I wondered as he opened the door to her room. Cautiously, I peeked inside. Then I stared. Except for the curtains and furniture, the room was empty. The dresser, the bookshelves, the desktop . . .

I looked all around before I spoke, as though Andy might be in the closet or something.

"*When?*" I asked.

"While I was asleep this morning, I guess. It's like the wind blew in and whisked her away. And just in time, because I got an e-mail from my friend at the U. He found the memo he was telling me about. Andrea Boyce has been a ghostwriter for more Maryland students than you could count. Her 'tutoring' consists of not just helping them write essays and term papers, she does the whole job, and charges accordingly. And she's good at it."

"So she's not a hooker?"

"Don't think so. Wasn't selling her body so much as her brain. My friend said they haven't been able to trace any of these students' essays to the Internet, but there were just little phrases that seemed to turn up often enough to let them know they were all being written by the same person. She's original."

"And this is a crime?"

"It's aiding and abetting cheating. Mostly it falls on the shoulders of the students who pass it off as their own work, but it's been worrisome enough that some professors have talked about grading almost entirely by test results, not essays, just to shut her down. It means that students who don't really know their subjects are passing their courses, and this reflects on the whole school."

"Did you tell her what you'd found?"

"Yeah, tried to. I knocked on her door around eleven last night and said, 'Andrea, we need to talk,' and she didn't answer. First time I'd called her Andrea—first time I *knew*—and that must have spooked her. This morning she was gone. No forwarding address."

Whoa! I couldn't believe it!

"You've been harboring a fugitive, Les!" I said excitedly. "Have you told Mr. Watts she's gone?"

"No. I've got to break it to him today. Thought I'd pick up some apricot strudel to take with me."

"And now you've got to rent her room all over again. Well, you have to admire her entrepreneurial spirit."

"Or not," said Les.

29
PRANK DAY

It was as though everything between prom and graduation had a good-bye tag on it—everything said, *This is your last . . .* The Ivy Day Ceremony (a guy from my history class was the poet and a girl from choir carried the ivy); the senior class gift to the school—(two more armchairs for our library); the arrival of our caps and gowns. . . .

If I thought I'd been busy with the play and homework and articles for *The Edge*, I'd had no idea what the last weeks of May would be like. Not only did I have to get through all my final exams while simultaneously doing all my packing for ten weeks of work on a cruise ship, but when I got back from that, I'd have only a few days before I left for the University of Maryland.

I was frantically going through my closet, my dresser drawers, my chest like a madwoman, tossing stuff into three different piles: "Keep," "Toss," and "Maybe." Every so often I'd have a change of heart and pull something out of the "Toss" pile and add it to the "Keep" pile or vice versa. It was the "Maybe" pile that grew higher by the minute, meaning I was only deferring the decisions until later.

"I hate to even suggest this," Sylvia said, looking in on me, "but since you'll be living only forty minutes away come fall, you'll be able to do a little of this on weekends once you start college."

"Don't even think it!" I wailed. "I need all the motivation I can get."

At school people were carrying their yearbooks around from class to class so friends could write sentimental, embarrassing, or crazy stuff in them no one else would understand. Luckily, I didn't have to show mine to Dad and Sylvia. Some of it they'd understand and approve: *To a talented girl who helped make* The Edge *what it is today: controversial. Phil.* And *To one of the best friends I ever had. You've got my shoulder to cry on whenever you need it if I can use yours. Hugs, Gwen.* From Pamela: *To Alice, the girl who can't wait to lose her V card. Pamela Jones.* Some people wrote the usual *HAGS* (Have a great summer) or *Yours till the chocolate chips.* I was taken aback when Sam wrote, *To the only girl I really loved.* But when I found out he wrote, *My love goes with you* in Jennifer Sadler's yearbook—another of his ex-girlfriends—and *A piece of my heart will be with you always* to the girl he was dating now, I decided that Sam was in love with love. I hope he goes into theater someday.

There were all these grad parties also—so many that there might be three or four scheduled on the same Saturday afternoon, a few more in the evening. I was picky about the ones I'd attend, and even then, I dropped in for maybe an hour at each one. I avoided the ones where people were most likely to be sloshed, went to the parties of my best friends, had a party of my own on a Sunday afternoon just so I could attend Gwen's that night. . . .

At one party Sam's cheeks were brighter than I'd ever seen them, and Liz and I were laughing at how red they got when he drank. "Hope he doesn't have another one," I said. "They'd pop." At Tim's the keg was disguised under a scarecrow costume. To reach the tap, you lifted the shirt, and that was a lot of fun.

I didn't go to Ryan's—it would just have been too awkward—but it still was a week of saying good-byes and forgiving faults and truly wishing everyone good luck.

At our school Senior Prank Day usually falls on a Thursday, the day before Senior Skip Day, when students take off en masse, many of them heading for the beach. Because the forecast for Friday was chilly and rainy, and I'd be on a cruise ship all summer, I decided to save my money and skip both school and the beach. Gwen, Pamela, and Liz planned to do the same. I wouldn't miss Prank Day, though. Usually a bunch of seniors put their heads together and come up with some big joke. But somehow, when we got to school on Thursday, a week before graduation, we knew this was going to be a day like no other.

Phil had got word of it first and had told us the jocks were in charge of Prank Day this year. He alerted the newspaper staff to take notes or photos for our last hurried edition of *The Edge*.

I was driving Dad's car, and as I approached the school, I could see the racing lights going around and around our school billboard like the lights on a marquee, and instead of our school's name, followed by the principal's, followed by the words *Spirit Week* or *Cheaper by the Dozen* or any of the other themes or productions we'd promoted, there was a huge full-color advertisement for Budweiser Light.

Drivers were already honking with amusement as they turned into the student parking lot, and I knew that Mr. Gephardt must have okayed this one, as it couldn't have been rigged up electrically without his consent.

What really made me laugh, though, was the big maple tree in the center of the circular drive, because it had been lavishly decorated during the night with bras and jockstraps, hanging from almost every branch.

So I entered the building knowing that almost anything could happen, and almost everything did. As the news traveled around that each athletic team had been assigned to pull one prank, we looked for signatures—a football was dangling from the billboard out front, and a bra on the maple tree had a softball in each cup, signed by members of the girls' softball team.

It was hard to settle down to anything like a normal school day, and at first, when we heard the microphone click on in homeroom for morning announcements, no one was paying attention. Then someone said, "Hey! Listen!" And suddenly everyone grew quiet.

There was something like a moan, followed by deep, heavy breathing and a husky male voice saying, "Oh, baby . . ."

Half the class was shrieking with laughter and the other half was saying, "Shhhh. Be quiet!"

We were all giggling, trying to figure out which guy and girl were doing the vocals. The breathless female voice said, "This . . . is your . . . morning . . . wakeup call, all you hot-blooded, hard-bodied dudes and chicks out there—(*oh, yes, baby, yes!*)—and [pant pant] we wanna give you . . . the news . . . of the . . . day." At this point we got a recording of bedsprings squeaking loudly and then the guy and girl moaning together, "Oh, yeeeeccssss!"

There was so much laughter, we could hardly hear what the daily announcements were. I guess most of the teachers were resigned to the fact that not a lot was going to be accomplished on Senior Prank Day because as the morning went on, some were already prepared with short documentary films to show in class or fun quizzes, played like a game show.

When we heard a commotion in the hall outside the conference room next to the office, we got there just in time to see a life-size blow-up doll in a black negligee being carried through the doorway on the hands of students, while our laughing but red-faced principal tried to explain to the budget committee why she had been lying on her side on the conference table. *See you around, big boy,* said a note tied to her toe, signed by the captain of the basketball team.

"This is wild!" Liz exclaimed when we found a couple of goldfish swimming in a bag of water submerged in the iced tea canister in the dining room, courtesy of the swim team.

"Who did the voices on the morning announcements?" everyone was asking, and it turned out to be one of the girls on the gymnastics team and a guy from tennis.

Things got even wilder that afternoon when the inflatable doll was found seated in a history teacher's chair when he entered and later in the chem lab. I think all the teachers had their eyes on the clock, waiting for the day to be over, but it didn't end the way everyone hoped.

It was still fun when someone looked out the window and saw that all the cars in the student parking lot had *For Sale* soaped on their windshields. But shortly after the last bell, we could hear a banging and rattling from the sophomore corridor, angry yells, and when I went to check, notebook in hand, I found that someone—many someones—had glued all the handles of the sophomore lockers in place. They wouldn't move up or down and the doors wouldn't open. Only a lucky few were able to get inside.

"I've got to get my bag, or I'll miss my bus!" one girl was yelling.

"My dad's waiting outside," said a guy. "Who the hell did this? I've got a dental appointment!"

Buses sat idling in front of the school, and the line of cars and buses grew longer, snaking out into the street and far down the block. Horns were honking. The day had gone so well—been so funny—and now . . . It was too late for the wrestling team to take back their mascot, a blue monkey with long arms, dangling from one of the lockers near the end of the row.

The only guy I knew on the wrestling team was Brian Brewster, so I went looking for him. We'd had a great story for our last issue of *The Edge*, and I hated to see it ruined.

"Brian!" I yelled when I saw him far down the hall, and I knew he'd heard because he half turned, then ducked into a restroom with two other guys.

I could hear them talking when I got up to the doorway.

"They *know*, man!" Brian was saying.

"You said one good yank," another voice protested. "Shit! I yanked one myself and the thing wouldn't budge. We've got Beck out there, Gephardt, the security guys. . . ."

I walked in and they stared. Two guys at the urinals quickly repositioned themselves until they could get their jeans zipped.

"You're right," I said. "The whole school's waiting."

Brian stared at me. "I tried it with epoxy on a basement cupboard at home," he explained. "Four good yanks and it opened. I don't know why these handles are so different."

"Whatever. Senior Prank Day is riding on this," I said. "Somebody needs to make a statement."

To his credit, Brian went out first, and the others followed.

Beck and Gephardt were furious, and so were a bunch of parents, car keys in hand.

"It wasn't supposed to be like this," Brian apologized. "We thought a good hard yank would do it. We really messed up."

"Yes, you really did!" one father yelled. "My son has a trombone in there and a lesson in ten minutes. Suppose you work on number 209. Chew it open if you have to, dammit."

Brian and another guy headed for that locker, but neither could get the handle to budge.

The maintenance supervisor came on the scene with a small can of acetone and a rag. He poured some on the rag and applied it to the door handle, trying to jiggle it up and down until at last the handle began to move. Finally the door opened. He handed the can and the rag to Brian. "Only a few hundred more to go," he said. "Come on down to the maintenance room and get some more acetone."

"None of you leaves until every locker is open," Mr. Beck told the wrestling team. "Then I want to see Brian in my office."

Why are there always a few, it seems, to ruin something for the many? It had been such a great day—probably the best Senior Prank Day in the history of the school. But epoxy had practically been poured down all the sophomore locker handles sometime that afternoon, Phil told me when he called that night, and it had taken until almost seven o'clock before they all had been unglued. Music lessons had been missed, jackets left behind, homework gone undone, car keys not retrieved. . . . Nobody was injured because of it, and nothing had been irreparably damaged—except, that is, the reputation of the wrestling team and the goodwill of the parents.

"So how do we write this up when we don't know the outcome?" I asked Phil. "Prank Day was going to make such a great story."

"Let's write two separate stories," he suggested. "We'll title the first story 'Best Senior Prank Day Ever'—you can write that one—and I'll do 'Except for This,' concentrating only on the wrestling team stunt."

Like all the other seniors, I took advantage of Senior Skip Day the next day, but I almost wished I'd gone to the beach, rain or not, because there was texting all day about Brian and the locker incident. One of the rumors was that he wouldn't get his diploma. And though Brian has never been one of my favorite people, he was still part of our "family"—and we didn't want to see that happen.

Some people, I know, self-destruct. They get just so far, so high, so popular, so famous that they eventually light the fuse that blows them up. Maybe Brian was one of those people. Maybe he would always test the limits. Go one step further than he knew he should. We'd thought the car accident he'd been in last year might change him, but it didn't look as though it had.

But Friday night I got the news. Phil called. "It's over," he said. "We can print an end to our story."

"What happened?"

"Brian and every member of the wrestling team showed up

this morning in Beck's office. They asked if they could work the whole day helping out in maintenance, whatever needed doing around the building, to help make up for the epoxy incident."

"None of those seniors skipped?" I asked, incredulous. "I'd heard the whole team was going to Ocean City for Memorial Day weekend."

"They were, but they didn't. They stuck together to help out their captain and didn't leave for the beach till a little while ago. Beck took them up on their offer, the maintenance supervisor put them to work, and six hunks working eight hours got a lot of stuff done, I heard. On Tuesday, after we all get back, the sophomores will find a letter of apology in their lockers from the wrestling team, and Brian's cleared for takeoff."

30
ANYTHING COULD HAPPEN

It was Dad who found the printout on the coffee table.

"Al?" he said. "What *is* this?"

It was four days until graduation, and I had just looked out the window to see if anyone was hiding in the bushes.

Dad read a paragraph out loud: "'No killing during school hours. No killing on school days within a block radius of school. To and from grad parties you *can* be killed, but not at your own. . . .'"

"Relax already," I said, laughing. "It's a game. The seniors are playing Assassins. We only use foam darts, and it's a blast."

I don't know who thought this up. Other schools have played it, I know, but 156 of our seniors signed up for it on Facebook, and Drew Tolman was appointed record keeper.

Over Memorial Day each of us had put five dollars in the pot, and Drew divided us up into thirteen teams of twelve each. He was the only one who knew who was on what team and what names were on each other's hit lists. Each of us bought our own NERF dart gun, and as soon as you "killed" someone, you had to text Drew with a cryptic message, like: *Jane Doe shot Charlie Smith @ 7:32 p.m.*

When Dad was convinced that nobody was going to get hurt and that everything took place out of school hours, he said he'd leave it to my own common sense. But we had our own rules:

No killing @ work—going to and from OK.

No killing @ church, synagogue, or any other religious-affiliated event.

No killing at school-related events, practices, or games. Going to and
    from is OK.

No killing inside someone's house unless invited in by a family member.

No shields. If you are hit anywhere once, you are dead.

DO NOT bring your gun inside school. This is not affiliated with school.

DO NOT shoot at point-blank range and hurt someone.

The rules went on and on. The thing was, you had to keep your hit list secret. Most of my friends had signed up, and none of us had any idea which person or team had our names on their list. You could offer someone a ride home, and the minute he got in your car, he could shoot you. Once you left the one-block radius outside of school, you were fair game.

If you wanted to freak yourself out, you remembered that

someone was always out to get you. It could be your closest friend. A neighbor or a person you hardly knew. The school population came from all over Silver Spring and Kensington. The only people on my list that I knew well were Pamela, Phil, and Sam, and I figured Pamela would be the easiest to shoot. But I couldn't give myself away.

Dad said I could use his car for the rest of the week so I could get to school early and park in the student lot. A block away, and I'd be a target for the assassins. Teachers had lived through this before, evidently, and put up with our furtively checking our cell phones to see if anyone else had been zapped. The team that scored the most hits got to divide the pot—sixty-five bucks for each of the twelve players.

We broke into laughter when we got to history and the teacher started class by pulling out a NERF gun and shooting a dart at the clock. Then he announced that we could spend the whole class time talking about current events. How did we feel about gun control, for example? Who should be allowed to buy assault rifles? How was it that anyone could buy a gun at gun shows? And for the next forty minutes, we forgot we were assassins and concentrated on something with a little more depth.

Gwen hadn't signed up for the game and thought we were out of our minds to spend so much time at it, with all we had to do. Jill and Justin hadn't signed up either. They walked the halls with their arms around each other, and I think Jill was a little annoyed that they weren't the chief topic of conversation any longer.

As soon as school was out on Tuesday, I got in the car. People were ducking behind walls, aiming at friends who were running toward their cars farther down the street. I went straight home, then sat in the car, scrutinizing the territory before I made a mad dash for the house.

That night Liz called and asked if she could come over for a minute. Immediately, I was suspicious.

"What for?" I asked.

"I want to show you something," she said.

"Uh . . . no," I answered. "Show me at school tomorrow."

"What's the matter with *you?*" she demanded.

"I know what you're up to," I said, laughing.

"You're not on my list! Honestly!" she protested.

"Yeah, that's what an assassin would say," I told her.

"It's a picture of the haircut I want for summer," she said. "I want your opinion."

"Tomorrow," I said. "It can wait."

"You're no fun," said Liz, and hung up.

Things were getting really wild at school. The longer it took an assassin to find me, the more nervous I got. I'd had to get to school even earlier Wednesday to find a space at all, but Pamela hadn't been so lucky. I was just pulling out of the student lot at the end of the day when I saw her running down the street toward her dad's car at the corner. Someone was chasing her.

I pulled alongside.

"Pamela!" I called. "Hurry! Get in!"

She gave a little shriek as the gunman fired but missed, and as he reloaded, she made a dash for my car and collapsed in the seat beside me, locking the door.

"Saved!" she screamed happily to the guy who rushed the car and tried to get in, then walked away. But when Pamela turned to thank me, she was looking at my NERF gun pointed at her leg.

"You dog!" she screamed, trying to grab it from me, but I got her, and we were both yelping with laughter, even though she claimed she was crippled forever.

"What are friends for?" I said, and pulled slowly into traffic.

When Gwen picked me up later to go to her house—I wanted to see the bag she'd bought for the cruise ship, the bag with the zillion pockets—I sat on the floor of the backseat and didn't get out till the car was in her garage. I even wondered if someone had bribed her so they could assassinate me at her place, but I'd been desperate to get out for a while.

"Wouldn't it be easier just to die and get it over with? Then we could talk about packing," she said.

"Hey, I got through the first two days. I like living danger-ously," I told her.

I shouldn't have stayed so long at Gwen's, though, because when I got home and looked at the stuff yet to sort, I was more conscious than ever of how little time I had left to pack. We'd be leaving for the Bay at noon.

I'd been listening to music while I decided what underwear to take and how much when Sylvia called from below. "Alice, Ryan's here to see you."

Ryan? I thought we were over. I thought he knew it. I stood there with a bra in one hand, pants in another. Was it possible he hadn't seen me at the prom with Patrick? And suddenly I realized that Ryan was playing Assassins too.

"Can he come up?" Sylvia called, waiting.

"Don't let him in!" I screeched, wondering where I'd left my NERF gun. But he wasn't on my hit list, so even if I shot him, he wasn't officially dead.

"What?" cried Sylvia.

I heard Ryan laughing. "Sorry about this," he said, and I realized he already *was* in. And then I heard rapid footsteps on the stairs. I screamed and ran into Dad and Sylvia's bedroom, their walk-in closet.

Dad and Sylvia were laughing too down on the landing as Ryan went slowly from room to room saying, "Might as well give up, Alice! I know you're here!" like a stalker in an old Hitchcock movie. My heart was pounding anyway.

When I heard him walking around in Lester's old room next door, I sprang for the bathroom and managed to lock the door just as his hand grabbed the knob.

"Too late!" I yelled. "So, so sorry!"

He was laughing then. "There's always tomorrow!" he said.

"Need any help up there, Al?" Dad called.

"I'm not coming out till he's gone and the front door's locked behind him," I said.

"I know when I'm licked," Ryan said. "And . . . by the way, Alice, you looked great at the prom."

"So did you," I told him, "but I'm still not coming out."

When he was gone at last and Sylvia assured me I was safe, I opened the door and collapsed on the pile of underwear on my bed, which I suppose Ryan had seen.

"How am I going to get through school tomorrow?" I said, still breathless. "I'm a marked woman!"

Sylvia sighed. "I'm so glad I don't teach high school," she said.

I'd only made one hit, and that was Pamela. I knew now that Ryan was gunning for me, but there would be others, too. I felt quite sure I wouldn't make it through the day without getting zapped, but I wanted at least one more notch in my belt before the game was over.

So on Thursday, I got up at five thirty, ate a piece of toast, and drove to Phil's house in Kensington. We'd been there once for a newspaper party, and I parked on a side street. Phil's house was on a cul-de-sac, only one way in and out.

It was six twenty-five, and I doubted he'd be leaving for school before seven. I dropped the car key in my jacket pocket, made sure my dart gun was loaded, then walked stealthily from tree to tree until Phil's house came into view.

I stopped and reconnoitered. There was a large lilac bush on one side of the front steps but not the other. To hide behind it, I would have to come in from the other direction. I would have to follow a neighbor's hedge to the backyard, then cut over into Phil's and come around from the other side. There was no garage and two cars were parked in the driveway, so I felt quite sure that this was the door Phil would use.

Checking to see if there was any activity in the neighbor's house, I entered their yard, hurried along their side of the hedge, head down, until I reached an open space in the backyard.

I ducked behind the toolshed in the neighbor's yard, behind the toolshed in Phil's, stood for a while behind the trunk of a large poplar at one side of the yard, then zipped around to the other side of the house, finally edging up to the lilac bush by the front steps, my heart beating wildly.

At any moment I expected a window to open and someone to call out. But nothing happened. A car went by on the street, and the driver didn't even look my way. Far off in the distance, a dog barked, then stopped. I waited, NERF gun in hand.

It's harder to hide behind a lilac bush than you might think. It's not thick, like a hedge, and the branches go every which way. The ground was wet from an overnight shower, and my shoes sank down a little in the bare earth.

What if I had miscalculated and Phil had gone to school early? It was Thursday, the day we usually distributed the newspaper, but this week it was coming out one day late to get in all the news. Still . . . What if he was cleaning out old files, getting ready for the new staff that would take over in the fall? It was hard to think of someone else putting out the newspaper, someone else being in on all the news and gossip, a new set of bylines showing up weekly.

I looked at my watch. I'd been standing there in the semi-mud for eleven minutes and it seemed like half an hour. I wondered if anyone was looking out a window overhead. A blue jay scolded me from a Japanese maple in the front yard. I was probably standing too close to its nest.

"Sorry. I'm not moving," I said under my breath.

Six fifty-eight. Phil had to come out soon if he had any hope of making first period, but then, probably half the seniors were sleeping in today. Tomorrow was graduation. We had it made.

Suddenly a voice behind me said, "Die, scum!" and I felt a little thump on my back. I wheeled around, and Phil was standing there grinning at me, his NERF gun in hand, a foam rubber dart on the ground beside me.

"Awwwwwk!" I screamed as I heard neighbors laughing from the porch next door, and Phil took out his cell phone: "Alice McKinley killed by Phil Adler at six fifty-nine a.m." he said aloud as his thumbs texted the message.

"I can't believe this!" I cried. "How did you know I was here? I was so careful."

"Neighborhood Watch Program," he joked. "Two different neighbors called and said there was a suspicious-looking girl lurking around my house, gun in hand. They relayed your every move."

"So I was on your hit list and you were on mine?"

"Looks that way," he said.

As it turned out, another team got the most hits, and each of those members got sixty-five dollars each, but I had more than my five bucks' worth of fun.

"Do you think we'll have this much fun in college?" Liz asked as we skipped one of our afternoon classes to wander around the school, saying good-bye to favorite teachers, our counselors, the security guys, even Mr. Beck and Mr. Gephardt. We were about to be has-beens, and we weren't too sure how we felt about it.

"We're going to try," I said.

And then . . . it was graduation. Each senior had been given four tickets, and I was astonished when my cousin Carol arrived at our house a few hours before we left for Constitution Hall.

"Carol!" I screamed. "Omigod! I had no idea! You came all the way from Chicago to see me graduate?"

"How could I possibly miss it?" She laughed, both of us knowing that even our closest, dearest family members had mixed feelings about sitting through a two- or three-hour ceremony. Then she told us that when her husband found out he had to be in Washington for a hotel conference, she called Dad and asked if there was any chance she could come to my graduation. "And a ticket miraculously appeared! So I get to sit with Les," she said.

I think Carol will go on looking glamorous well into her nineties. With Dad in his best suit and tie, Sylvia in a blue silk two-piece dress, Carol in a coral polka-dot top and black skirt, and my hunk of a brother in a brown shirt and yellow tie, I felt as though I were descended from royalty as I spotted my clan when I walked in during the processional, cap jauntily placed on one side of my head, the tassel flicking against my cheek.

All of us clapped like crazy when Gwen gave the valedictory. She thanked our parents for all they had done for us and said that graduation was a fork in the road in many ways, but we would be choosing the best parts of our parents to take along with us on life's journey, leaving the rest behind, as each generation must do. And it was this fork in the road, this choosing, these choices, that would, hopefully, make the world a better place.

And then, after the speeches and honors, the music and tributes, after all the names had been read and we'd received our diplomas, we tossed our caps wildly in the air.

Some had taped words on the top of their caps; some had special symbols to help their relatives spot them in the crowd. I don't think I believe in heaven, but I believe in eternal love. I had taped I MADE IT, MOM on the top of my cap, and I threw it as hard and as high as I possibly could, so that if Mom, wherever her spirit was, could see or sense it, she'd know I'd gotten this far. Then we marched back out into the June sunshine, holding whoever's cap we had managed to catch, and . . . it was over. We were leaving the nest.

Some of us would stick around our families all summer. Others would travel. Many would begin a summer job, and some, like Gwen and Liz and Pamela and me, would be combining work and travel. Ten weeks of dawn-to-dusk work on the Chesapeake Bay.

"Do we really want to do this?" Pamela murmured as we posed for pictures after the ceremony.

"Take pictures?" I asked.

"Clean people's toilets for ten weeks?" she said. "Wait on tables? Change linens? Get up at five every morning?"

"Well, don't we want to sit out on the deck and let the breeze blow our hair?" I answered.

"Don't we want to visit all the little towns and shops on the eastern shore?" said Gwen.

"Don't we want to meet *guys*?" said Liz.

"Smile, everybody. Say 'guys,'" said Les.

"Guys!" we all cried together, and summer, for us, had begun.

How it would end, I didn't know. As we were all so fond of saying, anything could happen.

ALICE
ON
BOARD

Phyllis Reynolds Naylor

FIND OUT HOW ALICE HANDLES
THE SUMMER BEFORE COLLEGE IN
ALICE ON BOARD.

THE *SEASCAPE* AND THE *SPELLBOUND*

The ship was beautiful.

Of course, since none of us had been on one before, almost any ship would do. But this one, three stories of white against the blue of a Baltimore sky, practically had our names on it. And since it would be our home for the next ten weeks, we stood mesmerized for a moment before we walked on down toward the gangway, duffel bags over our shoulders. The early June breeze tossed our hair and fluttered the flags on the boats that dotted the waterfront.

This might possibly be our last summer together, but no one said that aloud. We were so excited, we almost sizzled. Like if we put out a finger and touched each other, we'd spark. We needed this calm before college, this adventure at sea.

"Which deck do you suppose we'll be on?" asked Liz in her whites. She looked like a sailor already.

"Ha!" said Gwen, the only one of us whose feet remotely touched the ground. "Dream on. I don't think we'll even have portholes. We're probably down next to the engine room."

"What?" exclaimed Yolanda, coming to a dead stop.

"Relax," Gwen said, giving her arm a tug. "We're not paying customers, remember. Besides, the only thing you do in crew quarters is sleep. The rest of the time you're working or hanging out with the gang."

"With *guys*!" said Pamela, and that got Yolanda moving again.

It's a wonder we were still breathing. Five hours earlier, four of us had been marching down an aisle at Constitutional Hall for graduation. And when picture-taking was over afterward, we had stripped off our slinky dresses and heels and caps and gowns, pulled on our shorts and T-shirts, and piled into Yolanda's uncle's minivan, which had been pre-packed that morning for the mad dash to Baltimore Harbor. The deadline for sign-in was three o'clock. Yolanda had graduated the day before from a different school, so she was in charge of logistics.

It wasn't a new ship. *Completely refurbished*, our printout had read. But it was a new cruise line with two ships—The *Seascape* and the *Spellbound*, though the *Spellbound* wouldn't be ready till fall. The line sailed from Baltimore to Norfolk, with ports in between. The only reason all five of us were hired, we figured, was that we got our applications in early. That, and the fact that when we compared the pay to other small cruise lines along the

East Coast, this line offered absolutely the lowest of the low. But, hey! Ten weeks on a cruise ship—a pretty glamorous end to our high school years!

A guy in a white uniform was standing legs apart on the pier, twirling a pen in the fingers of his left hand. A clipboard rested on the folding chair beside him. The frames of his sunglasses curled around his head so that it was impossible to see either his eyes or eyebrows, but he smiled when he saw us coming.

"Heeeeey!" he called.

Pamela gave him a smart salute, clicking her heels together, and he laughed. "Pamela Jones reporting for duty, sir," she said as we neared the water. Flirting already.

"I'm just one of the deckhands," he told us, and checked off our names on his clipboard. öúvq his nameplate read. "Where you guys from?"

We told him.

"Silver Springs?"

"Singular. There was only one," Gwen corrected.

He scanned our luggage. "Alcohol? Drugs? Inflammables? Explosives?"

"No . . . no . . . no . . . and no," I told him.

"No smoking on board for crew. They tell you that?"

"Got it," said Liz, then glanced at Yolanda. We're never quite sure of anything with Yolanda.

"Okay. Take the port—that's left—side stairs down to crew quarters, then meet in the dining room for a late lunch. Follow the signs. You'll get a tour of the ship later."

We went up the gangplank, and even that was a thrill—looking down at the gray-green water in the space between ship and dock. Now I could *really* believe it was happening.

On the wall inside, past the mahogany cabinet with the ornate drawer knobs, was a large diagram of the ship, naming the major locations—pilothouse, purser's office, dining room, lounge—as well as each of the four decks: observation deck, at the very top; then Chesapeake deck; lounge deck below that, and main deck, where we were now. Crew quarters weren't even on the map.

A heavyset guy in a T-shirt and faded jeans, carrying a stack of chairs, called to us from a connecting hallway, "Crew? Take the stairs over here," and disappeared.

"How do you know what's port side if the ship's not moving?" I asked, confused already.

Nobody bothered to answer because we'd reached the metal stairway, and we hustled our bags on down.

Gwen was right; we had no porthole.

There were five bunk beds in the large cabin—large by shipboard standards, they told us. Ten berths in all, and other girls had already taken three of the lower berths. We claimed the remaining two bunk beds, top and bottom, and Gwen volunteered to sleep in the empty top bunk of an unknown companion.

"Ah! The graduates!" said a tall girl with freckles covering her face and arms and legs. She looked like a speckled egg—a pretty egg, actually. "I'm Emily." She nodded toward her companions. "Rachel and Shannon," she said, and we introduced ourselves.

"First cruise?" Rachel asked us. She was a small, elflike person, but strong for her size—the way she tossed her bags around—and was probably older than the rest of us, mid-twenties, maybe.

"We're green as they come," Liz answered.

"Same here," said Shannon. "I'm here because I'm a smoker."

We stared. "I thought there was a rule . . . ," Pamela began.

"There is. I know. I'm trying to kick the habit. Compulsory detox. I figure it will either cure me or kill me."

"Or drive the rest of us mad," said Rachel. And to us, "She's a dragon when she doesn't have a cig." She looked at Shannon. "Just don't let Quinton catch you if you backslide."

"Who's Quinton?" I asked.

"The Man. The Boss. You'll see him at lunch"—Emily checked her watch—"in about three minutes. I worked under him on another cruise line a couple of years back, so I know some of the people on this one."

"What's he like?" asked Gwen.

"Pretty nice. He's fair, anyway."

The last two girls arrived. The younger, Natalie, had almost white-blond hair, which she wore in a French braid halfway down her back, and then there was Lauren, with the body of an athlete—well-toned arms and legs. Only three of the girls had worked as stewards before—Rachel, Emily, and Lauren. And out of the ten of us, Lauren and Rachel seemed to know the most. Rachel, in fact, was a wellspring of information, the kind of stuff you never find in the rule books. Like Quinton's favorite drink when he was onshore—bourbon on the rocks—and how to keep your hair from frizzing up when you were at sea. She chattered all the while we put our stuff away, cramming our clothes in the three dressers provided.

So here we were—ten women in a single room with a couch, a TV, and a communal bathroom next door. The walls were bare except for notices about safety regulations, fire equipment, the dress code, and various prohibitions: no smoking aboard the ship; no food or alcohol in crew quarters; no pets of any kind; no cell phones when on duty; no men in the women's cabin and vice versa. . . .

Welcome aboard.

The first thing we did was eat—on crew schedule, as I'd come to learn—and we were starved. I guess they figured that "stews," as we were called, would pay more attention in training later if we were fed. There were thirty of us in the dining room, counting the chef and his assistant—ten female stewards, ten male stewards, and eight male deckhands. We sat down to platters of hamburgers, potato salad, fries, and every other fattening food you could think of.

"Don't worry," Rachel told us. "You'll work it off. That's a promise."

But we weren't doing calorie counts as much as we were working out the male-to-female ratio. All the ice cream we could eat, guaranteed not to settle on our thighs, and two guys to every girl? Was this the ideal summer job or what, lowest salary on the Chesapeake be damned!

The guys, who had come in first, were grouped at neighboring tables, and we could tell from their conversation that most of the deckhands were seasoned sailors, older than the rest, who had worked for other cruise lines in the past. They were undoubtedly paid a lot more than we were. A couple wore wedding bands.

"I just decided to ditch my theatrical career and devote the rest of my life to the sea," Pamela breathed, after a muscular guy in a blue T-shirt grinned our way.

"Yeah, and what will you do in the winter months when the ship's in dry dock?" Lauren asked her.

Pamela returned the guy's smile. "Three guesses," she said.

I tried to imagine what this dining room would be like in two days' time when passengers came on board. The large windows spanning both sides would be the same, of course, but I'd seen pictures on the cruise line's website of white-clothed tables with sparkling glassware and candles. It must have been a special photo shoot, because this ship hadn't sailed before—not as the *Seascape*, anyway. Still, I bet it would be grand.

Quinton came in just as the tub of peanut butter ice cream was going around for the second time. We'd met Dianne, his wife, when we'd picked up our name cards. She did double duty as purser and housemother, Rachel told us, but it was Quinton who called the shots.

He looked like a former basketball player—so tall that his head just cleared the doorways. Angular face, with deep lines on either side of his mouth—the sort of person who always played Abraham Lincoln in grade school on Presidents' Day. Dianne was as short as Quinton was tall, and it was hard not to think of her—with her curly hair and the bouncy way she carried herself—as his puppy.

"Welcome, everyone!" Quinton said. He had a deep, pleasant voice and the look of a team player, standing there with his shirtsleeves rolled up to the elbows. "Glad to have all the new men and women on board as well as you old salts who have worked with Dianne and me on other cruises."

He gave a thumbs-up to two more guys who'd just come in, still in their paint clothes.

"This will be a first for all of us, though, as the Chesapeake Bay *Seascape* takes her maiden voyage," Quinton continued, "the first, we hope, of a long and successful run on the bay. This fall her sister ship, the *Spellbound*, will be launched. Dianne and I are from Maine, but we've both worked and played on the Chesapeake and are familiar with all that the bay and the eastern shore have to offer. . . ."

There were lots of handouts—work schedules and tour itineraries, names of officers and crew. There were lists of nautical terms—*abaft, bridge, gangway, starboard*; another list of emergency procedures—*fire, man overboard, abandon ship*; and Quinton and Dianne took turns doing the rundown.

"There are no days off, no vacations," Dianne reminded

us, "though you'll get two or three hours of downtime in the afternoons and occasionally an evening out at one of our ports of call. You are going to be asked to work harder, perhaps, than you have ever worked before; you will have more rules regarding your appearance and behavior than you've ever had to follow. . . ."

I thought of all the requirements posted on the wall of women's quarters—*earrings no larger than the earlobe; clear polish on the nails; hair worn back away from the face, especially for servers at mealtime.*

"And for every minute you are in the public eye," Dianne continued, "you are required to be friendly and professional, even though, at times, you may be faced with the appalling conduct of a guest."

We gave each other rueful smiles.

Quinton did the closing remarks: "Remember that you are in a unique situation. You'll be living in close quarters, eating and sleeping on odd schedules, and working ridiculous hours at low wages." General laughter. "But you'll make some good friends here, have some fun, and will, I hope, look back on this summer with pride and say, 'I signed on for the maiden voyage of the *Seascape*.' And now let's get to work."

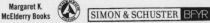

When you need a friend
who *really* understands . . .